To Aaron,

with hope that this will passes like a short nightmare, and that the utopian elements within us all will one day,

AMERICA 2034:
UTOPIA RISING

Jonathan Greenberg

America 2034: Utopia Rising
Third Edition

Progressive Source Publishing
www.progressivesource.com

ISBN Number: 978-0-9993419-8-8

Rights were obtained for the use of the song entitled
"The Four Directions"
The Four Directions Copyright 2018 by Andrea Culbertson
Sung by the band Utopia Rising

Chapter 1: State of the Union

```
Monday May 1, 2034
2:00 p.m. Mountain Time
Good Foods Corn Plantation
Siebert, Colorado
Trump's United Enterprises of America
```

Winston Smith pulled back his respirator mask and wiped the sweat from his forehead.

George Scudder, his old friend and the director he'd assigned to the ludicrous commercial for pesticide-drenched corn that he was being forced to produce, had called a short break. "Grab your respirators, get some oxygen and water," Scudder instructed the actors. "We're getting closer, but I'm still not feeling the love for the corn. Eat it like you mean it, team!"

The half-dozen actors were dressed in unusually clean versions of the standard grey coveralls worn by all slave farm laborers. They stepped away from the tall row of corn, guzzled water and rushed to huddle around a bank of oxygen tanks offering unpoisoned air.

Winston replaced his respirator and stretched his legs as he looked at the miles of corn rows stretching out around him, thinking about how much he hated his job.

In the 16 years since founding TV1.com, Winston's feeling about his work had gone from *I can't wait to get to the office* to *It's a paycheck* to *This sucks; I cannot possibly do this much longer.* On days like this, he thought, *What the fuck am I doing with my life?*

At this point, as his ex-wife always advised him, he needed to think of his two sons, how much he loved them, and how fortunate he was to make a comfortable living, unlike the 110 million American "debtors" who, unable to pay their bills, were stripped of their citizenship and doomed to work till they died in slave labor camps.

A second later, Winston heard George Scudder calling for him.

"We're in position and ready when you are, boss."

Winston joined the crew behind the camera. "Don't call me boss," he said, smiling at Scudder. "You know I hate that word. Just like I hate …"

The men exchanged knowing glances. All conversations, anywhere, were recorded. Any suggestion of dissent could result in arbitrary dismissal, or far worse. In their relatively idyllic youth, neither man would have dreamed they would one day be reduced to shilling pesticide-poisoned genetically modified corn for export to reluctant consumers in Asia and South America.

"Okay, folks," Scudder yelled as the crew and actors took their positions. He snapped a clapperboard with the words, *Happy Farmers / Good Food, Inc* and announced, "Roll Sound… Action!"

The healthy-looking men and women hired to play convict farmers picked and dropped ears of corn into shiny electric wagons that had been rented for the video. "I'm looking forward to eating a couple of these beauties for dinner," Jennifer, a young actress with flowing clean blond hair, said eagerly.

"I'm hungry right now," said Lester, a muscular, dark-skinned man. Winston recognized him from a blockbuster action film made before California seceded from the United States, taking Hollywood, and the movie industry, with it.

It seemed to Winston that it was a lifetime ago that Scudder was the most prolific producer/director for TV1.com, his fast-growing start-up company. TV1 created a system to find and organize video content for tens of millions of subscribers, and also produced news-breaking content of its own. For two years after Winston's founding of the company in 2018, Scudder had helped create media exposés that informed and inspired. In the months leading up to the 2020 Presidential election, Scudder joined Winston in creating an award-winning investigative series, "American Corporatocracy," which "peeled back the curtain of corruption of the Trump White House and the U.S. Congress by corporate donors."

The series joined dozens of other media exposés and investigations about the Trump Administration's corruption, which added to an already raging fire of public outrage. A string of criminal convictions of Trump accomplices and multiple congressional investigations into abuse of power and obstruction of justice resulted in his impeachment in the House of Representatives. But the two-thirds votes required for his removal fell short in the Republican-controlled Senate.

Trump countered his widespread unpopularity by escalating the Republican Party's voter suppression war against poor and non-white voters. Draconian voter ID laws and massive purges of registered voters flourished in almost every Republican-controlled state in the nation.

Despite this, one poll after another predicted that the most unpopular president in history would still lose the 2020 election by huge margins to a populist Democrat who had campaigned to end Trump's rampant corruption and return government to the people.

The events leading up to the most controversial election in history began early Monday morning, November 2, 2020, the day before most Americans headed to the polls. At dawn, bombs exploded at polling locations in 7 states. Nobody was hurt—and many, like Winston, suspected that Trump's agents had planted the bombs. But the morning news reports quoted White House officials calling the incidents a "9-11 style attack on American democracy."

A few hours after the bombings, Trump appeared in a live state of emergency newscast that overrode programming on every network. Trump addressed the nation from the secure Situation Room under the White House. The news showed the President sitting at the head of a table filled with generals in uniforms glistening with medals. Behind Trump's head was a slide show of buildings demolished by the bombs. Trump spoke with a somber, vengeful tone:

"My fellow Americans: our country is under attack! This morning, radical terrorists ignited bombs in 7 polling places across our great nation. The F.B.I. has informed me that the far left Antifa organization sent an email taking credit for the crimes, with a warning that far worse attacks will greet Americans voting in Republican leaning districts on Election Day. The violent army of the far left are attempting to scare off voters who want to reelect me to keep making America great. Instead they want to get millions of illegal immigrants and felons to fraudulently vote to elect radical Democrats, who will then round up your guns and install a Communist dictatorship. I join every red-blooded American when I say: Over my dead body! We will not surrender our sacred democracy to terrorists! Ne-vah!"

"I am hereby declaring a national state of emergency, blacking out all non-government communications and ordering the

Attorney General to mobilize all national security agencies to take federal control of registration and vote counting at every polling place in the nation. But we will not wait around like sitting ducks for the next attack. As I speak, thousands of Antifa terrorists and their enablers are being rounded up and arrested."

"As part of this national emergency decree, I have signed an executive order nullifying all mail-in ballots. Every bonafide American voter will be required to appear in person on Election Day. Citizens must bring their official ID to their regular polling place. I assure you, as long as I am president, it will be safe to vote in the United States of America. God bless you, and God bless the greatest country on earth."

Election Day 2020 found Winston exhausted after working an all-nighter at the TV1.com office near Boulder, Colorado. Trump's state of emergency decree following the bomb attacks had shut down all internet, TV and phone communications nationwide. This stopped the freelancers working for TV1.com in other American cities from sending in their coverage, but it did not prevent Winston's local reporters from gathering news about the historic roundup of political dissidents, or his editors from receiving citizen videos that people brought to their office. The videos showed teams of heavily-armed masked men in black uniforms raiding homes and arresting suspected dissidents. Those who tried to run were shot dead.

Dozens of concerned bystanders who had taken videos of the merciless crackdown streamed into TV1.com's offices through the day and into the night. Some drove hundreds of miles so that the scandalous footage they had saved onto SD cards could be webcast over the TV1.com network.

Winston and his editors worked all night to process the content and prepare newscasts. They also received two videos from top Antifa leaders denying that they had anything to do with the bomb blasts. Winston and his teams uploaded the video content to an internal server so that TV1 could provide firsthand news of the crackdown the moment the government allowed internet service to be restored.

At first, Winston and his staffers were sure that the media shutdown would be lifted for Election Day. But they were wrong. The only broadcasts permitted that day were from the government-controlled emergency channels, repeating President Trump's speech while informing voters nationwide that the polls were open and safe.

Finally, in the late afternoon, Winston headed out to vote. Like more than 150 million other Americans, he refused to allow the explosions to stop him from voting in the most important election of a lifetime.

When Winston reached the nearby Boulder elementary school that had been his polling place since moving to Colorado from California five years earlier, security was heavier than he had ever seen it. Local voting officials checked his identification against a voting roster, but before handing him a verified Voter ID card, he was hustled to a second line, where his ID was checked by a federal agent against a database of names of millions of suspected illegal immigrants, as well as millions of others with pending immigration cases.

He noticed a Latina woman near him arguing with a registration agent. "What do you mean I cannot vote today!" she yelled. "I have voted here for 20 years. My grandparents voted in Colorado before you were born!"

The federal official held firm. "Rosa Sanchez," he read from a laptop in front of him. "Says here you entered the country two years ago and don't even have a green card. You know it's a felony to vote illegally punishable…"

"You're not serious, are you," she shouted. "Do you know how many Rosa Sanchez's there are in Colorado? Are you telling me that you are removing the right to vote from every American with a Spanish name? Is that what you're doing?"

Winston considered trying to record what happened, but within seconds the woman was being forced out of the tent by two police officers.

Winston voted with a distressing awareness that what he had witnessed was being repeated in tens of thousands of polling places across the country. Returning home, he and his wife stuffed their vape pen with marijuana to reduce the stress of watching the results of a stolen election.

By midnight, when Trump's state of emergency communications blackout was lifted, national news networks reported that President Trump had won reelection in a stunning upset. Trump held every state he had taken in 2016 as well as six more states. Republicans had also won every contested Senate race in the country and enough seats to take control of the House of Representatives, defying all polls and historic voting patterns.

The election coverage concluded with President Trump's gleeful victory speech. He said: "My fellow Americans: we are victorious, with the largest landslide in history. Today we stopped more than five million illegal immigrants as they tried, as they have done before, to vote and steal this election for the Democrats.

"But tonight, we have reason to celebrate, to look forward, not backward, to an even greater future. To those who want to fight about the past, to those who want to resist and violently protest law and order, I have this message: We have zero tolerance for the subversion of our democracy. A new day has arrived, in which God's bounty—and his justice—rains upon our great nation and on every red blooded true American, like never before. Good night, and God Bless America!"

The next day, millions of Americans began mobilizing for a historic march on Washington and a nationwide strike to shut down the government at the end of the week unless a new election with paper ballots counted by the states and monitored by the United Nations was held.

That Friday morning, Trump issued his second state of emergency. Appearing in another emergency broadcast, he said, "To protect public safety from the communist mobs planning riots across our great nation today, I hereby declare martial law nationwide. Today it is illegal to open businesses or gather in public places. This is an advisory, and a warning. Stay indoors today and obey the law if you value your life. Our army, national guard and police will take whatever steps necessary--whatever steps--to maintain order!

Americans defied Trump by turning out en masse to protest. More than 2 million people converged on Washington from all directions for the largest protest ever.

Protesters in the capital and in cities across the country were met by platoons of heavily armed soldiers and riot police. After they refused orders to turn back, soldiers opened fire on the crowds, killing dozens and injuring hundreds while sending a message that tyranny was now the law of the land.

Protesters fled in all directions. They were corralled and arrested by teams of waiting police and national guardsmen who handcuffed and arrested them. They were then loaded onto waiting buses, which ferried them to massive makeshift federal internment camps that had been set up in fairgrounds and fields surrounding every major city.

That day, nearly 10 million Americans were detained as felons under Trump's martial law decree. Those able to pay a $20,000 fine to a new private prison company secretly owned by Trump were released, with a felony conviction record that banned them from ever voting again.

Half of them were unable to pay the fine. They were designated "debtor felons," to spend the rest of their lives in what was to become the world's largest network of slave labor camps.

Trump lifted martial law that Sunday. But on Monday morning, as Winston drove into the office park that housed TV1, he realized that a new day had indeed dawned following Trump's reelection. He noticed dark-windowed SUV's parked in front of the building. Armed security forces in black uniforms stood by the entrance with a dozen other men in suits.

During the next five hours, under armed guard, Winston and his employees gave the technicians representing the government access to all their work stations and cloud-based accounts. The officials seized all video cards and drives, while wiping computers clean of all news videos that TV1.com had ever acquired or created.

Before they left, at 1 p.m., Winston was required to sign a "custodial" agreement to use only government-authorized news sources in the future, or face felony charges for webcasting content from unauthorized sources.

Winston sat at his desk, unable to move, ignoring knocks on his door from staffers. For a half hour he cried uncontrollably.

Now sitting, fourteen years later, in a director's chair in the immense corn field outside Siebert Colorado, Winston realized that his mind had drifted for so long that he had lost track of the commercial he was there to produce. He brought his attention back to the actors imitating well-treated farmworkers.

Smiling at the camera, Lester said, "Time for our scheduled work break!" The actor sat comfortably on the ground leaning against a cart, peeled open a big ear of corn and faked eating a large, satisfying bite out of it. "Best corn in the world," he said to his co-workers.

"CUT!" Scudder yelled. "Eat the corn. Don't just pretend to eat it."

Lester forced a smile. "I'm pretty careful what I eat, sir," he said. "But I can do a much better job pretending. Lemme try ..."

"Eat the corn or get the fuck off the set!" Winston demanded. The afternoon was wearing on, and he knew that his avaricious boss Roger Rex would force Winston to personally eat the cost of an extra day's shoot.

Lester nodded compliantly. A series of deep coughs rose through Winston's throat. He wiped his eyes and grabbed a respirator. He cursed the foul air for his shortness of breath, and then cursed the man he had become.

Chapter 2: Arrival

The sky was a radiant blue, the sun clear and strong. A soothing, steady breeze cooled the crowds that lined the roads since crossing Golden Gate Bridge to catch a glimpse of the First Family of the United Peoples of America.

The open car was filled with so many multi-colored flower petals from well-wishers that Dawn Souljah and Maria Sanchez, sitting in the front seat, could not see their legs. In the back, their daughters, Estrella and Sarah, were laughing and swimming in a flower petal bath as the electric Tesla turned into the National Intelligence Arboretum near Mountain View, California.

As their car pulled to a silent stop, the two founders of the young nation and their daughters brushed the petals off their legs and stepped barefoot onto the dirt ground of the parking lot. They greeted supporters, then walked toward the jasmine-covered trestles that formed the gateway of the Arboretum where their colleagues waited for them.

Estrella and Sarah exchanged glances and tried to duck out before the formalities began. Estrella, at 13, one year older than Sarah, led the effort. "Moms," she said anxiously. "I've heard over the group chat that my friends have been kicking it for two hours now across the meadow at the National Institute for Healing. You know there's tons of work to do!"

"Now, honey," Dawn reasoned. "You know we want you here for our opening song. Then you can both take off."

"But Mama," Sarah chimed in, impatient after the long, slow ride, "you know you're going to greet everyone and talk and talk and talk, which means by the time I get to the fields, the first half of the laser sword practice battle will be over."

"We do the opening ceremony as a family, as always," Maria replied gently. "You can use the restroom and say hi to the other kids joining the song, but be back and singing next to us in 15 minutes. Your mamas would be lost without you."

The girls laughed and took off in a sprint.

Maria and Dawn passed through the gateway, where they were greeted with hugs by the three other members of their country's Governing Council. The founding couple of the United Peoples of America were only 33 years old and by far the youngest members of the elected body. Former Washington State Senator Patty Murray, at 84, was the group's elder stateswoman. Native American rights activist Winona LaDuke, at 74, brought a lifetime of environmental and public interest organizing to government. Doctor Richard Wu, 51 and from Oregon, provided expertise in science and holistic wellness.

As they looked silently in one another's eyes for an impromptu check-in meeting, the five national governors opened their minds to a group telepathic communion.

Dawn had hoped that the other governors would join her enthusiasm to give the final green light for the long awaited Great Expansion. She was sad to instead hear, in their collective thought-sharing, only anxiousness and worry about the increasingly deadly missile attacks from Trump's United Enterprises of America.

Dawn felt relief when they were joined by Google founder Larry Page, who knew more than almost anyone about the force field that protected their young country from the violent vengeance of the Trump Regime.

Dawn thought back to her first meeting with Page and his fellow technology visionaries in the desert of Nevada at Burning Man in the late summer of 2023. She reflected on how much he had changed from the competitive billionaire she had met years earlier, and how much she had changed from the young woman who had been so intimidated when she entered the billionaires' enclave at Burning Man.

It had been a foreboding complex: a large inner ring formed by three dozen enormous ultra-luxurious recreational vehicles. She and Dawn had their musical instruments carefully searched as they passed through a security zone to a large open fire within.

The reputation of their two-woman band, Utopia Rising, and its ability to change the lives of those who listened to them, had reached the nation's leading tech billionaires, who had invited them to perform in their private inner sanctum.

Dawn recalled the conclusion of their concert, when their transformative song, "The Four Directions," sung with open arms and followed by the sound vibrations of a Tibetan bell, epigenetically activated Larry Page and his colleagues, Tesla founder Elon Musk, Facebook's Mark Zuckerberg and a dozen of their top managers.

After the concert, the titans of Silicon Valley pledged to do everything in their power to help heal their culture. Planning a technology blueprint for a breakaway utopian nation began the next day at noon. The first step, all agreed, was the creation of a one million-square mile force field that extended from the eastern borders of California, Oregon and Washington to a line hundreds of miles west in the Pacific Ocean.

It required three years of stealth development and the epigenetic Activation of all management teams and the labor forces of every technology company on the West Coast before the first iteration of the world's only protective shield technology was ready to test; it took another two years to perfect it. Finally, in early 2028, the force field was deployed, allowing the United Peoples of America to announce its independence from the tyrannical regime of President for Life Donald Jesus Trump.

By that time, California, Oregon and Washington had absorbed more than 40 million immigrants fleeing Trump's United Enterprises of America. Google's and Facebook's new mission, starting that day at Burning Man, was to transform the world's most widely used communication system and largest social network into its most effective collaborative organizing system. Groups were created for every city, town and large neighborhood across the new nation.

The most transformative revolution in human history began, not based on ideology, but on the peaceful evolution of the citizens of the United Peoples of America, as fear, competition and greed were displaced by compassion, collaboration and sharing.

The landscape of the new nation was transformed as spacious backyards, large farms and regional parks became the sites for millions of simple small homes. Food and herbal medicines were planted wherever land was arable. Pesticides and genetically modified food were banned, as nutrition and holistic remedies, along with Medicare for all, transformed a sickness industry focused on pharmaceuticals and surgeries into a wellness system focused on human health. Life expectancy soared to the highest level of any country on Earth.

With a widespread sense of sufficiency and safety, crime vanished. Taxes that had supported armies of police, prison guards, and prosecutors were reallocated to housing, educating and healing fellow citizens.

Full employment became a reality as state governments leased out tens of thousands of small organic farms on newly accessible and sub-divided land. More than a million jobs were created to build, staff and harvest thousands of kelp farms that stretched for hundreds of miles into the Pacific Ocean, sequestering carbon to save the planet from climate catastrophe, while providing sustainable bounties from forests of seaweed and the marine life that flourished in and around it.

As they reconnected now in the National Intelligence Arboretum, Dawn expressed gratitude to Larry and his fellow visionaries for helping create the world's most vibrant and equitable economy. And for building a network of protective shields that protected it from attack.

"Larry, would it be possible," Dawn asked, breaking the silence of the group around her, "to address the worry that my fellow governors feel about the recent missile attacks. Please tell my esteemed colleagues that we have nothing to fear except fear itself."

"I am afraid I cannot do that," Larry replied with sufficient discomfort to heighten the anxiety of the group. "They're stacking multiple Hellfire missile attacks repeatedly at the same point, just seconds after one another, trying to weaken the shield to allow the next one through. We had prepared for this sort of thing, in principle. But not for the sheer number of missiles, hitting in the exact same place, again and again. Their targeting capacity, and appetite to waste expensive missiles, is something …unexpected."

Larry noticed that General Serena Jackson was approaching the group. Relieved, he said, "But I don't receive intelligence briefings as they come in. Here is the woman who can fill you in on the latest."

General Serena Jackson, a tall ebony-skinned woman wearing a bright blue uniform, did her best to force a welcoming smile for Dawn and Maria.

"How is the shield holding up?" Governor Patty Murray asked, concerned.

"Today's been okay, so far," Serena reflected. "Better than yesterday, when we had five breaches and 824 unspeakably painful deaths, the most casualties since the Great Massacre of 2028—right before we had the force field."

They shared a reverent silence. Maria telepathically felt fear sweep through the minds of her fellow leaders like a foreboding wind. She looked at the empty blue sky and felt reassured.

Patty asked the question on everyone's mind. "Are you concerned about our meeting today?"

"Nothing around here at the moment," Serena said. "Reports are that today they are trying to breach our shield in the most populated cities—L.A., San Francisco, Portland and Seattle. We've increased the number of shield workers to up our game, cancelled leave, instituted mandatory overtime. But the breaches of the last few weeks are new; they're getting worse, and for the first time, I am worried."

"All the more reason to get started with the Intelligence Council meeting," Dawn said, changing the subject and searching for her daughters so that they could begin the opening song. "Shall we move toward—"

From out of the blue, a series of explosions was heard high above them, followed by a deafening burst nearby. The mushroom cloud of an immense fireball shot a ring of shock waves in every direction, knocking them off their feet and causing the Earth itself to tremble.

Chapter 3: The Protest

Monday May 1, 2034
2:30 p.m. Mountain Time
Good Foods Corn Plantation
Siebert, Colorado
Trump's United Enterprises of America

The director snapped a clapperboard and yelled. "Roll Sound… Action!"

This time, Lester ate the corn with gusto. The actors playing his fellow farm workers also pretended to enjoy snacking on the pesticide-laden corn during their seemingly pleasant work break.

"To think," Jennifer announced to the camera, "that in Indonesia and Vietnam, misinformed consumers claim that American corn is unhealthy and that laborers are mistreated." She laughed. "Our enriched genetically modified corn is the only way to feed a hungry world!"

"I didn't eat this well when I was poor and living on the streets," a well-fed actor replied. "Our corn is the best in the world, and Lord knows what would happen to us if –"

"CUT! Your hand holding out the corn is blocking your face," Scudder instructed. "We are almost there team. Let's take a ten minute bathroom break and then pick up at hungry world."

The actors rushed to the single portable toilet near the shoot and formed a line. Winston used the opportunity to move around. He walked briskly for a few hundred feet to an area of dead corn stalks, then stopped to relieve himself in the debris. As he did, he reflected bitterly on how his tightfisted boss had pressured him to produce commercials, even though it was never part of the employment contract Winston received when he sold TV1 to Patriot News in 2022.

As he zipped his pants, Winston felt his eyes burning from the toxic fog of pesticides. He wiped them with a handkerchief. Then he noticed the deer.

It had been years since Winston had seen a deer in the wild, and he never imagined one could live in the middle of Good Food Inc.'s 80,000-acre genetically modified corn planation, the largest in Colorado.

But there she was, plain as day, just 20 feet away, staring straight at him, unflinching, with enormous, piercing dark brown eyes. She stood perfectly still except for her large ears, which slowly rotated sideways, one at a time, like antenna tuning to a frequency.

Gazing deep into the deer's eyes, Winston suddenly felt himself falling through time.

He found himself back in 2022, 12 years earlier, at his first and only psychedelic visioning journey with the powerful entheogenic ayahuasca medicine. On a cool misty dawn, Winston was in a jungle in Maui, and he'd just stepped outside of a ritual hut to pee. A deer appeared out of nowhere and stared deeply at him, stopping time. He experienced a connection with the animal, a connection *through* the animal, unlike any he had ever felt.

He was the deer looking at his human form. He was himself looking at the deer. He was the crisp, moist morning air, the soft breeze, the song of the birds. The soft dawn-colored sky.

The ayahuasca ritual had been an unplanned detour from a short Maui solo vacation he'd treated himself to for his birthday to escape the stress of work. Just one hour after a shaman handed him the nauseatingly bitter green medicine and led him to his solitary bed in a small dark ritual hut, Winston had lost all sense of his body. At some point in the timeless night, thoughts of past experiences and warm gratitude shifted to a general sense of bliss.

The potent, ancient medicine performed its magic, stripping away Winston's thoughts and ego. Staring at the sky, he felt himself One with the cosmos, so empowered that he could move mountains, even stars.

As he stood in the ravaged field in Colorado, Winston was blissfully lost, re-experiencing that mystical journey and the joy he felt when his heart, so calloused and cynical, suddenly filled with a sense of wellbeing unlike anything he had ever imagined. A moment that opened into eternity.

Then he heard a voice that drew him back to 2034.

He could not tell where the voice came from, but the words were clear, forming in his head in a woman's gentle voice, a reassuring and loving voice.

"We are coming," the voice said. *"But very soon, you will experience darkness unlike anything you have witnessed. Know that this darkness will pass. Do no harm to yourself. You are needed. Wait for us. Thursday."*

Winston realized the deer was still staring at him. Then the animal's ear twitched, and it jumped away so quickly that it seemed to vanish in midair.

"Are you okay, buddy?" Scudder had walked over to get him. Winston was not sure how long he had been there. Silently, still somewhat mesmerized, he nodded and returned with the director to the set.

The actors were in position and ready. Scudder banged the clapper and an actor said, "I didn't eat this well when I was poor and living on the streets. Our corn is the best in the world, and Lord knows what would happen to us workers if —"

"STOP THE SLAVE LABOR!" a voice off-camera interrupted.

Winston looked at a ragged clump of people approaching the actors.

"WE'RE DYING IN THE FIELDS—PLEASE HELP US!"

"What the hell is going on?" Scudder asked. "CUT!"

A small group of a dozen real farmworker slaves, a couple of them mothers with sickly children, approached the scene warily and huddled close to one another, unsure of themselves. None had ever protested before, or even seen a protest, but they were driven by starvation, sickness and desperation. They were filthy skeletons, with bloodshot eyes, half-dressed in threadbare remnants of their convict uniforms. Their skin was a patchwork of rashes and open sores.

A ragged child, perhaps eight or nine, leaned on her mother for courage as she meekly held up a makeshift sign made of flattened corn stalks pressed together with mud.

"Boycott American Corn!" it proclaimed in thin letters, written in someone's blood.

"Please help us," her mother said as she fell to her bony knees and looked imploringly at the actors and crew. They watched, nervous and bewildered.

"Get rid of these people," Winston yelled desperately to Scudder. "This is suicidal. Get rid of them before Homeland Security finds them."

Scudder stepped toward the protesters with outstretched hands. "This is dangerous ... please leave immediately ... this is a restricted area and you were probably detected by sentry drones when you left the barracks. You can get killed for this!"

The actors watched with pity; a few joined Scudder, imploring the slave laborers to leave.

Two protesting children looked at their mothers unsteadily, then gathered around the girl with the sign and her begging mother, putting hands on their shoulders for support and nodding in agreement. "We will die soon anyway," the mother continued between sobs, "Please ... tell the world ... we are slaves, dying here from the chemicals and conditions ... no food, no medical ..."

A squadron of six drones suddenly appeared and hovered 10 feet above the heads of the protesting convicts. Winston recognized them as Homeland Security "Peacekeeper" drones, armed with small laser cannons. He slowly backed up to take cover behind the van. "They are unarmed and not threatening us," Winston yelled desperately to the drones. "Please just warn them away so we can get on with our work!"

The lead drone moved a few inches forward from the rest and announced, "Convicted debtors: You have violated Homeland Security provision 416-C and are guilty of terrorist incitement. Implementing security protocols."

Less than a second later, six laser cannons began rapid firing into the crowd of huddled, starving convict laborers, efficiently burning hole after hole through their bodies. It happened so quickly that they died wordlessly. In less than 15 seconds, as the putrid smoke from the seared victims rose around them, the drones regrouped, then blasted the other half-dozen protesting convicts.

A stench of burning flesh swept the area. The actors and crew members screamed in shock, "Noooo!" and "Stop!"

In a flash, the drones were above them. "Wait!" Scudder yelled. "We're U.S. Citizens, WE ARE NOT CONVICTS, NOT CON—"

Another round of laser cannons opened fire, shocking Scudder into silence while instantly killing a half-dozen actors. Scudder joined his crew members and two surviving actors, frantically raising their hands in surrender as they raced toward the van.

They were overtaken by the killing drones and shot to pieces before they got halfway there. George Scudder dodged for a few extra seconds and made it within 20 feet of where Winston cowered behind the van. Four drones approached from all sides, blasting Scudder with such force that his blood and innards sprayed the windshield. They shot him full of holes so large that Winston could see light coming through Scudder's body.

The massacre of two dozen people took less than a minute, the longest minute of Winston's life. He watched the drones begin to regroup and move in his direction.

Time stood still as Winston prepared for his death. He thought, *In a world so callous, so murderous, why resist? Why continue?*

Somehow, in the midst of the chaos, Winston heard the same soothing woman's voice he'd heard earlier. It was so loud that Winston's eyes darted around, looking for the speaker. *"This will pass. Do no harm to yourself. You are needed."*

Winston heard his own voice yell, "Wait! I am Patriot Citizen Winston Smith. Stand down for verification scan." With trembling hands, he held up his smartphone.

"Smartphone match for Patriot Citizen Winston Smith Number 846-7468-0021," the lead drone announced. "Stand down for Patriot retina identification," it ordered the drone squadron, which backed off a few yards.

"Please stand tall for the retina scan," the lead drone ordered as it hovered within two feet of Winston's eyes.

"Yes … right away," Winston assured it, gasping for breath. His senses were assailed by the stench of burnt human flesh. He tried unsuccessfully to restrain an impulse to vomit, then retched uncontrollably, nearly doubling over.

The drone's metallic voice grew more insistent. "Stand tall for retina scan or be eliminated!" it ordered. Three other drones, lasers aimed at his heart, moved closer.

Winston straightened his wobbly legs and forced his throbbing head toward the lead drone. He realized his eyes were filled with tears of terror and grief. He prayed they would not interfere with the scan.

"Verification of Patriot Winston Smith number 846-7468-0021. All threats eliminated. Further Homeland Security action unnecessary. God Bless Trump's United Enterprises of America and President for Life Donald Jesus Trump."

The drone squadron waited for Winston's response, recording every moment of their interaction. "God Bless," Winston gasped, "God Bless Trump's United Enterprises of America and President for Life Donald Jesus Trump."

The drones sped off, leaving an eerie silence and two dozen smoldering bodies. Winston collapsed to the ground. It was hours before he found the strength to get back in the production van. He drove slowly back to Colorado Springs, feeling terrified and alone.

Chapter 4: Trump's Ultimatum

Maria's powerful screams pierced the smoky haze. "Sarah!" she yelled. "Estrella!"

Sirens blared as ambulances raced across the arboretum to an area a quarter of a mile to the west where the Hellfire missile had struck. First responders rushed past assisting people on the ground, offering portable oxygen tanks and escorting the injured to a nearby disaster relief vehicles.

"Here mama, we're here," Sarah cried. "We're okay. We're okay."

Maria rushed to her daughters and hugged them tightly, sobbing between coughs.

'We've got to get to an RV," Maria said, leading them slowly to an expanding fleet of rescue vehicles lining the road. "Mama Dawn is okay; she was dazed and was just brought to one of these to wait for us."

It took two tries before Maria and her two girls, half-covered in soot, found the right rescue RV, which doubled as a command center. There they found General Jackson, the other three members of the Governing Council, and Dawn, who was stretched out on a bed.

Maria felt the filtered air in the RV cleansing her lungs as she opened her mind telepathically to the others, listening to casualty reports and rescue logistics while she crowded onto the bed and comforted her wife and daughters.

The Hellfire missile had struck the National Institute of Health summit being held at the far end of the arboretum a half mile away. The summit was scheduled to coincide with the Intelligence Council meeting. The young nation's most accomplished horticulturalists and healers had convened to assist the Great Expansion by preparing vast quantities of seeds and natural remedies to help their long-suffering neighbors to the east.

General Jackson telepathically requested an emergency meeting of the Governing Council and asked whether Dawn felt well enough to join them.

Dawn sat up on the edge of the bed and spoke. "I am fine, Serena. Just dazed from hitting the ground so hard. If it's okay just pull your chairs up around us."

Dawn and Maria sat on the side of the bed as Patty Murray, Winona LaDuke and Richard Wu joined them. Serena stood nearby, controlling a hovering video monitor that she positioned for everyone to see. "This message from President Trump," she said with severity, "arrived five minutes ago."

A video of President Trump, standing at his White House desk with his fists clenched, appeared on the monitor. Extensive plastic surgery had smoothed the wrinkles on his 87-year-old face. A fluffy wig composed of thin strands of 24-karat gold sat like a crown upon his orange-pink brow.

Trump said, "Here are the generous terms of our nonnegotiable ceasefire offer for your treasonous nation of traitors. You agree to pay me $200 billion now and $100 billion per month thereafter, as well as immediately sharing your force field technology with the Department of Homeland Security. In return, the missile attacks will cease 100% for as long as negotiations proceed in good faith on the terms of your surrender and the reintegration of your corporations and citizens into the greatest country on Earth, Trump's United Enterprises of America."

"We have stockpiled more than 200,000 thermobaric Hellfire missiles for this very purpose and will not stop the attacks until you agree with my terms and pay the restitution due to our great nation. Refuse this offer, and we will expand our force field-busting missile attacks and rain fire and agonizing death upon every man, woman and child in your country!"

The message ended. For a full minute, the listeners stared at the screen, shaking their heads.

Finally, unable to restrain herself, 12-year-old Sarah blurted out, "How is that man still alive?" She was standing on the bed behind her mother Maria, and directed her question to Doctor Richard Wu. "Trump is 87 now. After a lifetime of diet soda, junk food, and sedentary TV viewing, he should have dropped dead years ago!"

There was a short silence as the doctor answered. "We understand that his diet, like that of many aged oligarchs, has been augmented by suckling at the breast of new mothers whose babies have been taken from them. In addition, President Trump, like most oligarchs, receives full blood transfusions every week from so-called blood-bods, who are fed organic food and given continual exercise."

"Also," Dr. Wu explained, "Trump and the older oligarchs spend hundreds of millions of dollars each on life extension procedures, replacing almost every organ and body part except the brain."

"As a result, our scientists estimate that Trump and many of his oligarchs could live well past 100. Trump speaks of his family as America's royal dynasty, but instead of planning for succession, he has been pumping billions into a top-secret brain transplant institute. His objective is to remove the brain of a healthy blood-bod slave and transplant his own brain into the young body. And in that manner, achieve his dream of living forever."

Dawn felt a chill breeze blow across the circle as she and the Council members contemplated Trump's immortality.

Chapter 5: The Belly of the Beast

Tuesday May 2, 2034
8:30 a.m. Mountain Time
Patriot News Headquarters
Colorado Springs, Colorado
Trump's United Enterprises of America

It was only Tuesday morning, but as Winston rode the elevator 20 stories underground for a meeting with his dreaded boss, the CEO of Patriot News Roger Rex, it felt like the end of the longest week of his life.

Winston had been unable to sleep following the shattering experience of Monday's drone attack. Eight actors, as well as the video crew and his close friend George Scudder, had been massacred, and he knew their families were desperately awaiting word on their fate. But security protocols made it a felony for Winston to provide any information about what happened at the corn plantation without authorization from Roger Rex. Meanwhile, the ad for Good Food Inc. would miss the deadline for its international release and needed to be rescheduled.

Winston's stomach felt queasy from trying to force down food earlier that morning. He knew that a morning meeting with Roger Rex meant that Rex would eat while pelting him with demands. Sharing was not a part of Rex's vocabulary; he'd proven himself to be more avaricious than anyone Winston had ever met. Like many of the nation's 400 ruling oligarchs, Roger Rex resented having to fork over half the profits of his company to President Trump, the richest man who ever lived. Unable to protest even privately, Rex and the other oligarchs took out their anger on their armies of servants, slaves and employees.

Winston entered Patriot News Headquarters, a large office building almost entirely underground, and caught an elevator to Rex's private residential floor at the bottom, 20 stories down. As he exited the elevator, he entered the security airlock. Poison gas nozzles whirred into readiness while a security drone hovered a couple of feet from his head, its laser pointed between his eyes. He had only been to Rex's inner sanctum a handful of times in the 12 years since Patriot News acquired his company. Its reputation as a place of depravity and torture almost made him regret requesting the meeting. But he thought of his friend George Scudder's widow and son and felt an obligation to at least inform the family of what happened and to do his best to secure death benefits.

The expansive subterranean fortress within a fortress felt even darker and creepier than the underground offices a few levels up, where the TV1 offices had been moved from Boulder. Winston placed his finger DNA chip in the reading device and looked up for an iris scan.

A thick airlock door slid open, and he walked into a much larger security chamber. Two enormous guards with muscles about to burst out of their black uniforms were waiting for him. On the far side of the room, Winston assumed other guards were also monitoring him behind a one-way mirror with a laser cannon mounted in the middle.

"Good morning," Winston greeted them, taking off his shoulder bag, and emptying everything from his pockets and putting it all on a table. He placed his smartphone in a diagnostic box and was waved into a scan module.

"Where you hiding your dildo, pretty boy," the taller guard, who, with his combat boots, seemed close to seven feet, said. "Where's your eye-liner and your cunt-makeup?"

Winston maintained his composure, having heard it all before from the private army of security goons who made the Patriot News Headquarters complex into an armed camp. Rex's private guards were a class of crass unto themselves, he realized, because they typically had to deal only with delivery boys and slaves.

"Can I just head in?" Winston asked politely. "My appointment starts in three minutes, and you know Mr. Rex doesn't like to be kept waiting."

"What's this?" the tall guard held up a pen and small notepad.

"It's called a pen. You write things with it on that pad, which is called a notebook."

"Brainy dickweed lecturing us about books now, Donnie."

"Okay, pretty boy. Pull down your pants cause it's show time!" said the shorter guard, who seemed more brick than man. He pulled a device from a nearby box.

"You don't have to do this," Winston protested calmly. "You can see from my ID check that I am the Executive Vice President of TV1 and have worked in this building for—"

"Hey Donnie, twinkle toes here is telling us what our job is and isn't!"

"That's rich, comin' from Richie Rich here. Listen, snowflake, you got three seconds to turn around, spread your butt cheeks and let auto dickie have his time with you, or Bruno and me are gonna do it ourselves. And that robot probe is gonna seem like a sweet breeze after we get through probing you with our big prickies."

"Big prickies or auto dickie," Bruno laughed, placing the probe next to his groin. "Da choice is yours."

"I like that one," Donnie said, grinning, as Winston pulled down his pants. "Big prickies or auto dickie—that's a good one!"

Bruno put a lubricated casing around a small probe and pressed it a half inch into Winston's anus. A sharp pain and then a cold shiver passed through his body. The diagnostic results appeared in seconds on a screen hovering near Bruno.

"He's clear to go," Bruno said, disappointed. "Maybe next time it'll be my big prickie, snowflake. And it'll hurt a lot more."

"A lot more!" Donnie said. "And mine would hurt even more. Cause it's bigger. Much bigger!"

"Bullshit," Bruno said, grabbing his crotch and licking his lips. "You wish your tool was half this size."

The security monitors opened an entry door into a long, dark metallic hallway. Winston could hear the juvenile banter continue as he grabbed his briefcase and walked briskly.

As Winston made his way down the hallway, he recalled the promise he had made to himself as a younger man that he would never work for a huge soul-sucking corporation like Patriot News.

But what choice did I have? He now asked himself. By 2022, only the largest media conglomerates were able to resist the Trump Administration's intimidation and suppression of the media. Winston's small TV1.com web video network had been forbidden to webcast citizen videos or news, relegating the company he had founded to light entertainment and video organizing technology. So when the opportunity arose to sell out to the fast-growing media conglomerate Patriot News and provide himself and TV1's investors with a profit, Winston jumped at the possibility.

At their first ever meeting, Patriot News' founder Roger Rex took Winston to a lavish meal, praised TV1's technology and seemed to appreciate Winston's rebellious sense of humor. Winston did not share Rex's enthusiasm for President Trump, so he hoped that he could sell his company for its technology and audience, and find a new vocation.

But Rex made clear that the only way he would buy TV1.com was if Winston was bound by golden handcuffs. The purchase price was to be paid annually over the next 20 years, but only if

Winston remained to manage his company as a subsidiary of Patriot News.

With the Trump Family Enterprises as a founding investor, Roger Rex had begun building Patriot News in 2020 after acquiring Fox News and the Breitbart News Network. As Trump demanded that the media stick to cheerleading and stenography, Patriot News thrived, while other media companies faced escalating government lawsuits. Unlike other executives who had made the mistake of fighting to continue to report real news, Roger Rex's interest was propaganda, not journalism. He had been laughed at by his rivals as a fat suck-up to power, but in just a few years, he had the last laugh.

Winston hated the terms of the offer, and tried to shop around for another media acquirer, but by the end of 2022, he could see the writing on the wall and accepted the deal.

The Trump Administration had already announced its plans for the 2023 Constitutional Convention to gut the nation's Bill of Rights and allow the president to rule for an unlimited number of terms. Winston knew that Trump's revised Constitution would pass easily through the nearly all-Republican Congress and state legislatures, and it did.

Suddenly, the new Constitution, which renamed the country Trump's United Enterprises of America, abolished the First Amendment's freedom of speech provision, replacing it with severe criminal penalties for treason anytime the president, at his sole discretion, found that such speech defamed the military, the government, the president or anyone in his family, or any business that they had an interest in.

On January 1, 2024, as the new Constitution took effect, Homeland Security forces arrested hundreds of journalists, editors and even board members of the largest independent media companies in the nation. The *New York Times, Comcast* and the *Washington Post* challenged the arrests in federal court, but lost in one unanimous decision after another.

Within months, every newsroom in Trump's United Enterprises of America had been shut down, except for Patriot News. Its slogan, "The Only Name in News," had come true even sooner than Winston had predicted.

Winston's ruminations ceased as he heard a door that he was approaching slide open. Standing in the hallway, he knocked loudly against the entry area wall.

"Come in, come in," commanded a gruff, muffled voice.

Winston entered a cavernous, dimly lit living room. Rex's massive body sprawled across a wide leather lounge chair. Winston watched as Rex's broad, wrinkled head, bald with grey wisps of thin hair, pressed against the large breast of a topless young woman, whose light blond pigtails rolled slowly across her bare back. Rex's mouth, clasped to a nipple, made loud slurping sounds.

Like a number of older oligarchs (including, it was rumored, President Trump himself), Rex sucked the breast of new mothers to enhance his health and longevity. Winston had never seen anyone doing it before, and he restrained an impulse to vomit.

"I can step outside and come back after you've finished your, finished your … breakfast, Mr. Rex," Winston offered.

Runny white milk ran down the fat jowls of Rex's double chin as he pulled himself off the young woman's left nipple and yelled, "Sit the fuck down, Winston. I've got a busy day, made busier by your fuckup Monday. I've got no time for your pansy games." He gestured to a cheap folding chair in the middle of the room and resumed sucking and slurping, this time at the right nipple.

"My ... my fuckup, sir?" Winston asked.

"Yeah, your fuckup, snowflake," an accusatory voice interjected, startling Winston. He had not noticed the tall, deathly pale man leaning against a wall on the far side of the large room. It was Scoop Walters, the chief propagandist and news director of Patriot News and Rex's right hand man.

"Maybe you think you did a good job on Monday?" Walters sneered. At 30, he was a full 20 years younger than Winston, but through ruthlessness, loyalty and ambition, he'd risen quickly to the top of the Patriot News management team. Like Rex and his bodyguards, servants, assistants, blood-bods and a half-dozen milkmaids, Scoop lived in the corporation's massive 20-story underground fortress and broadcast facility. Unlike the workers and slaves, who were cramped into dormitories, Scoop occupied a luxurious private suite with rooms to house a few leased sex slaves of his own. Nobody had seen Scoop or Rex leave the premises in years.

"Or maybe we misunderstood you?" Walters continued. "Like, maybe you got the footage in the can and the corn ad will be ready to roll for Good Food's international ad campaign starting Thursday, our contracted deadline?"

"The cameras, the equipment, the footage—they were all destroyed in the drone attack. They went after everyone. Just massacred the whole team."

"Attack? Massacred?" Walters demanded. Then, in an aggrieved child's voice, "Da big bad Homeland Security drones killed innocent people. Wah, wah wah!"

Rex pulled his head off the woman's chest, wiped his face with an embroidered handkerchief and jumped in. "Whiny, fucking wuss! Maybe you want me to dig into our corporate profits to give the surviving families wrongful termination payments?"

Winston stammered, "I … I was thinking … I was hoping I might notify the families. They … they will be worried. I need your permission, sir. The director, George Scudder, had been working for TV1 for more than 15 years and perhaps there might be death benefits available. He's a friend of mine and his wife …"

"A what?" Rex cackled meanly. "Hear that, Scoop? One'a the deceased losers was Winston's friend! He's got all the time in the world for friendship, during his time off! Off having friends while we sweat our nuts off to protect the greatest country on Earth. Friends, huh!"

"Fuck-buddy friend more likely," Walters piled on.

Rex rose in outrage, pushing his milkmaid aside and almost knocking her to the ground. "You want me …" He paused to pick up a platter prepared with eight lines of methamphetamine.

He snorted one line up his left nostril, then another through his right. The drug added gasoline to the fire of his anger.

"So you want me to reach deep into my own pocket to give your fuck-buddy's surviving whore and little brats my hard-earned money ... MY HARD-EARNED MONEY, YOU FUCKING LITTLE TWIT!"

"No, sir, no ... I just ..."

"Holding me up in my own castle is what you are doing!" Rex pulled a huge Glock pistol from a pocket in the lounge chair, switched off the safety with his fingerprint lock, and trained the laser sights on Winston's head. Scoop took five steps to the side, while the milkmaid grabbed her clothes and quietly backed away.

Chapter 6: The Human Extraction Industry

In a bomb-proof underground meeting room beneath Google's International headquarters, the 72 members of the Strategic Intelligence Council of the United Peoples of America circled the gigantic round table with their heads bowed in deep meditation.

Council members, their eyes filled with tears, viewed each face of the 432 people who had perished in the missile attack as the images rotated on the screens hovering over them. They felt and celebrated each life. Collectively, through their telepathic hive mind, they then sent each departing soul on its way with prayers of love.

Maria telepathically guided the group back to the meeting about to take place. The Governing Council deferred to her natural mastery as a facilitator for opening and closing important events. She reflected on the relief she felt that delaying Estrella from joining the health summit had saved her daughter's life, and that this relief was the opposite of what hundreds of mothers and fathers were feeling at that very moment.

"There is a reason for everything that happens," she began. "We are living out the great prophecy of uniting our species in a harmonious Wetopia. That's what we call our nation, because it is all about *we*. *We* play our part in this eternal dance, our karmic struggle to bring light to the darkness. But destiny is not a preordained outcome. It begins with believing as possible something very different than what is."

Maria clasped her hand on her chest in prayerful intention. Instantly her motion was joined by 71 other pairs of hands.

"Today," Maria continued, "we decide whether we are strategically ready to take this long-awaited step. On Wednesday, the People's Council will make the final decision as to whether or not to support the Great Expansion. On Thursday, the Council of Mystics will consult with Spirit itself about the timing of our noble effort."

"We start our meeting with a report on the state of our protective shield by our country's Director of Technology, Elon Musk, who, along with Google's Larry Page, has committed much of the last decade to creating and enhancing our force field technology."

Elon Musk rose and greeted the circle with an optimistic look, still seeming more like a teenaged dreamer than a 63-year-old technology mastermind.

Elon, whose employee-owned Tesla corporation had become the world's largest vehicle, battery and solar-equipment manufacturer, accompanied his presentation with 3-D images on the overhead screens. "As you know, the million-square mile force field protecting the West Coast states was the largest technology challenge of the 21st century. We succeeded in creating devices that both collected and harnessed psychic chi energy to form a nearly indestructible force field seven miles above our country," he said.

"We have trained, equipped and hired two million chi energy experts, who work from their homes in two one-hour shifts per day to avoid psychic exhaustion. Only one in 40 humans possess the energetic capacity to be chi workers. Once trained, they channel their chi force into accelerators, which then funnel the energy to shield node devices along our borders and into the Pacific."

"We also developed airlock-like portals to allow authorized aircrafts in and out, as well as a cloaking system to thwart aerial surveillance. For more than five years, our shield has protected the United Peoples of America against incessant missile attacks. But starting with the Mount Olympia breach last September, 322 missiles have found their way through our system, killing 42,647 of our brothers and sisters. Today's attack here, we just learned, was one of seven major breaches, the most in any single day."

For the first time since his Activation at Burning Man 11 years earlier, Elon felt a sense of personal failure. He was comforted by colleagues through the hive mind and continued. "We are working 24/7 on strengthening the field and preventing further breaches by building secondary and tertiary shields deployable the moment an impact occurs. Our chi workers are on double overtime, and we are training thousands more each week. We can and we will do better. But Trump's army now sends dozens of Hellfire missiles in 15-second intervals stacked to hit a single point in our field again and again in as many as 50 locations simultaneously."

"It is hard to grasp how great their obsession to kill us is," Elon said, shaking his head. "Each of these missiles costs $120,000. This means that on a single day like yesterday, they spent hundreds of millions of dollars attacking us. I had wondered how they could justify this. But yesterday, hearing the $200 billion price of Trump's ransom terms, it makes sense, in the warped universe of criminality and tyranny that defines our former country. I know that I speak for most of us in tech when I say we must resist and transform this evil!"

Elon sat down. The round table was silent as the 72 members of the Council uneasily digested the news.

Dawn introduced the next presenter. "Everyone knows our Director of Intelligence, Edward Snowden."

Snowden, dressed in jeans and a white tee shirt, stood with enthusiasm. After 15 years in exile as the most effective and notorious whistle blower in history, he loved his new job.

"Our communications monitoring, aided by intercepted video surveillance, shows a Trump Regime resorting to increasingly barbaric tactics to expand their extraordinary wealth," Snowden explained. A graphic slideshow listing the logos of corporations appeared on the screens. "The consolidation of all major corporations in the country by the 400 oligarchs and the Trump Family was concluded four years ago, when the lead shareholders of a few dozen holdout businesses were assassinated. Every significant business in Trump's United Enterprises of America now partners with Donald Trump, providing him with 50% of all profits from their corporations."

"Our Pacific state secession brought with it a brain drain that removed the entire technology, aerospace and entertainment sectors, causing the Trump regime's economy to contract to half its size. That decline has been accelerated by Trump's destruction of what had been the American middle class. Now only 50 million working class families are left, most living from paycheck to paycheck. The rest of the population has been driven into prisons for 110 million slaves."

"Meanwhile, most nations are now unwilling to import any foods from Trump's United Enterprises of America because of their pesticide toxicity. The so-called human extraction industry is now the largest export earner for the T.U.E.A., followed by the most polluting mining operations on Earth and rental fees for mercenary armies."

Snowden continued, as holograms showed brochures in multiple languages for stem cells, kidneys and slickly marketed mother's milk. "The outlawing of abortion, combined with the criminality of giving birth without adequate means of support, has led to the confiscation of more than half the children born in the T.U.E.A., along with the lifelong incarceration of so-called *illegal mothers* in oligarch-owned slave labor camps. Babies fetch six figures internationally, while mother's milk and blood products are vacuum packed and exported, along with body parts like stem cells and kidneys. These are sold on the grey and black market to millions of affluent consumers throughout Asia and the Middle East."

"The Trump regime has added a new level of barbarity to this harvest of misery industry. It has authorized six American corporations to open *planned exit* centers at the 1,000 slave labor camps across the nation. During the past few years, in order to simply buy the medicine or food needed to prevent their loved ones from dying, millions of parents and grandparents and even children who are trapped in these camps have sacrificed their lives by selling their bodies for just a few thousand dollars."

"National intelligence estimates that Trump's United Enterprises of America now has a life expectancy of 34 years, the lowest on Earth. In the six years since our secession, the population of the states that comprise our former country has been reduced from 230 million to 160 million."

Snowden stood silently while bar graphs on the hovering screens gave way to a montage of skeletal corpses piled into mass graves and burned in huge mounds. He looked around the table. "As expected, many of us have a hard time believing what is happening. That's why we are showing you a video that we obtained by hacking into the twice weekly Patriot News broadcast made to the nation's 400 oligarchs and their families."

A holographic video of a cantankerous President Trump suddenly appeared. "There is a reason, my friends, that we renamed our great nation Trump's United Enterprises of America," Trump intoned. "What makes America the greatest country that has ever existed is our freedom to achieve, a freedom that, through the grace of God and men like us, has created the greatest wealth the world has ever seen. Nobody who ever lived has gotten even a fifth as rich as I am today, and I include our trusted ally Vladimir Putin. Nobody eh-ver! And we all agree on what it says in the Holy Bible: God helps those who help themselves. That's the winners; that's us!"

Trump paused, swigged some water, and nodded his head approvingly as a roomful of off-camera staffers applauded loudly and chanted, "T.U.E.A. T.U.E.A." He then went on.

"Now, there used to be a different philosophy among the communist Presidents who came before me, criminals like Barack Hussein Obama. Free health care and food stamps for the do-nothings, while government taxes bled folks like you and me who worked hard for our money. We were a nation of deadbeats, sucking our economy dry. But in making America great again, I have liberated our economy from these vampires!"

"God has blessed you and me with the best genes. Caucasian genes, Christian genes, genes that created the best business leaders the world has ever seen! Norman Vincent Peale's Prosperity gospel and Darwin both had it right. Our success comes from our evolution as white men and from God's blessing of the fittest. And it's not our job to care for the losers. Not our fucking job!"

"So, I've heard from my sources that some of you lucky duckies are complaining that you have no room left to house the deadbeats that Homeland Security has assigned to your slave labor camps. And that a few of you are griping to your fellow billionaires, "Send 'em to someone else's camp, we're full up, we can't take any more. Whine, whine, whine, wah, wah, wah!"

"Well you can quit your bitching 'cause here's the deal: I know that we have way too many debtors and not enough gold mines or slaughterhouses or factories or toilets to scrub. But I never said you had to keep these bloodsuckers happy, or give each family its own bed, or feed them, or keep them alive. Work 'em till they die, lease 'em out as domestics, gold miners, sex slaves, blood-bods, milkmaids, test tubes … these hundred fifty million deadbeat debtors are no longer citizens and our great country is overpopulated, so what you do with them has nothing to do with government. We're not regulating, we're not interfering!"

And if they can't pay their keep that way, we've got a permanent solution that pays out big time. Here comes the good news—the big opportunity. The international demand for their body parts is booming. Booming! The Russian Empire! China! India! Saudi Arabia,—it's hu-ge!

So starting next week, the origination royalty for every freshly harvested body doubles to six thousand bucks a head. Multiply that by 50 thousand deadbeats and it's a nice piece of change and yours to keep, untaxed. Just send 'em to the termination clinic that we've been expanding in all of your camps and leave it to our extraction companies. They'll manage the execution, sales and delivery. Our great nation collects billions in foreign currency while disposing of resource-sucking deadbeats. This is win-win. Everyone's happy! No complaints, right?

No complaints!

The image of Trump pointing a threatening finger faded to darkness as Snowden sat down. Like a fog, a sense of dread engulfed the room.

Chapter 7: Gratitude

Tuesday May 2, 2034
9:00 a.m. Mountain Time
Patriot News Headquarters
Colorado Springs, Colorado
Trump's United Enterprises of America

Training his Glock on Winston's forehead, Rex gnawed his lower lip as he took a step closer. "I should've snuffed you years ago, what with a name like Winston fucking Smith, for your Commie parents, treasonous opinions and sucking money outta my company every year. But it's not too late to do it now when you come here shaking me down for your imaginary victims!"

Winston had stared down the barrel of Rex's gun during drug-induced rages a half-dozen times before. He had also witnessed, or heard about, the murder of lower ranking employees almost every month. He could barely stand on his trembling legs, and he repressed a powerful impulse to vomit. He took a deep breath and tried to visualize calmness entering his body. "Of course, Mr. Rex, I would never expect you to compensate victims of a Homeland Security accident." Winston's voice was solicitous and reassuring. "Why should you, sir? It was not your fault."

"Fucking A it was not my fault," Rex concurred, lowering the gun a little.

"If anyone should pay, boss, it should be me. I … I am the one who fucked up, not you."

"Damned right you fucked up," Rex agreed. "And how do you intend to compensate me for your fuckup? Your *major* fuckup!"

Another shakedown, Winston thought to himself. As a "consideration in return for patriotic sacrifice," Winston, like every senior manager except Scoop, already allowed Rex to garnish 40% of his take-home pay. Perhaps, Winston thought, Rex would be satisfied with an even 50%. He hated the thought of it, but knew where this conversation was heading.

"Perhaps," Winston offered carefully, "perhaps 10% more for the next 12 months, bringing my consideration to 50%, would offset the cost of reshooting Good Food's ad?"

"Perhaps 10%," Rex replied in a mocking, girlish voice, "Perhaps I fuck you up the ass, bossman!"

The next moment Rex's gun was again pointing menacingly at Winston. "Ten percent would barely cover the costs, you cocksucker, much less the equipment we now need to replace, or your penalty because Scoop here will have to wipe your ass from this mess up and do the job right." Rex was frothing on both sides of his mouth. "Are we going to talk turkey, or am I going to put a cap between your eyes! Say 10% one more time, one more time, and so help me God, it will be the last word you ever say!"

Shoot me, you fat fuck! Winston thought to himself. *This is how it's going to end anyway. Why prolong it?*

A split second later, Winston heard the reassuring voice he'd heard the day before while staring at the deer. *"Your life is sacred.*

You are needed. Wait for us. We are coming." He again suppressed the urge to vomit and instead used every ounce of power to force an appeasing face and ask, "What would you suggest, sir?"

"One year!"

"One year's … one year's salary, sir?" Winston swallowed hard. His legs felt like jelly. "I can … I will accept that."

"Oh, you're a funny faggot, aren't you, Smith? A real comedian!"

"Sir?" Winston implored.

"I already get 40% of your overly generous salary. One year's pay PLUS one year's payout."

'That's … that's an extra $500,000, sir."

"You think I don't know how to count, shithead? Am I fucken playing with you?" Again, the gun pointed at Winston's face.

"I understand … please, Mr. Rex, I hear you and …"

"And WHAT?"

"And I agree. We have a deal."

'We have a deal," Rex said, triumphantly, returning the gun to its pocket. "Contract drone!" he bellowed. In seconds, a small recording drone with a screen appeared in the air next to him.

Rex dictated, "Winston Smith, Executive VP of Patriot News, hereby cedes to Roger Rex, CEO of Patriot News, next year's payout of $500,000 for the acquisition of TV1.com as well as one year's full salary starting Monday, May 1, 2034."

The drone scooted to Winston Smith. Winston placed his DNA finger chip into its reading device as it performed an iris scan.

"Positive identification of Winston Smith. Recording commencing. Patriot Winston Smith, do you hereby agree to cede next year's payout of $500,000 for the acquisition of TV1, as well as one year's full salary starting May 1, 2034."

"Yes, I do," Winston stated.

"Sign here, Patriot Winston Smith."

Winston signed the screen with his finger. The drone zipped away.

Satisfied, Rex looked around. His wet nurse had gathered her clothes and retreated toward a doorway, where she had quietly put her clothes on. She was dressed in a bright white schoolgirl blouse with a very short plaid skirt. At 16, she looked the part her boss had dressed her for.

Rex's eyes found her and he yelled, "Amber, where the fuck do you think you're going?"

"I … I'm sorry Rexie," she said, taking a cautious step closer. "I thought we were … finished … and that you had a meeting."

"WE are not finished till I say we're finished. Did I say you could go?"

"No."

"No—what?"

"No … Daddy," she said sheepishly, embarrassed in front of the other men.

"Do you want me to shop online for your replacement?" he said, menacingly. "I could have her here in time for tonight's feeding. And send you back to Tyler's mountain camp to starve to death, like the rest of 'em!"

"Please don't, Daddy!" Amber forced a pleasing smile. "Just tell me what you need me to do. You know I am always eager to serve … and service."

"Damn well better be eager to service," Rex demanded, sitting back down and unzipping his fly. "Bend over and take your spanking."

He grabbed Amber by the wrist, turned her around and pushed up her mini skirt. He slapped her buttocks hard, while addressing Winston and Scoop.

"This baby killer," Rex yelled, between slaps and snorting two more lines of white powder, "tried to get a back-alley abortion. As though the state wouldn't know. She got busted after delivering the baby in prison. Placenta gets sold, baby gets sold, and mom is facing execution for her capital crime. But she's got the looks, and the tits, to make the Milkmaid Catalogue's A-List. So I save her life, I save her fucking life by employing her, feeding her hungry hole, housing her. And she goes slinking off before the job is done."

"Now get to work, you trash whore baby killer." Rex grabbed the girl's neck and forced it into his crotch. "We're not finished till you finish me off."

Winston did his best to look away. He noticed Scoop staring with a disdainful smirk across his face.

"You still here, Smith?" Rex demanded, snorting the last two lines of white powder up his nose. "I'll see you at the meeting upstairs in a half hour."

"Mr. Rex, this has nothing to do with compensation or fault, but I was hoping you could provide verbal authorization for me to inform the families of the 10 men and women we had contracted with who died on Monday. Family members have been calling and texting me non-stop, and I would like to get them off my back."

"That ain't my problem, snowflake, and I would be a different kind of CEO than you know me to be if I allowed whiners like you to make it my problem. And you should know the law better than to be bothering me with this kind of request."

"The … law?" Winston asked.

"Scoop, tell him and get him outta here so I can enjoy a few minutes of pleasure before jumping into the meat grinder that is my work and national duty."

"Disclose and die, Smith," Scoop instructed. "Disclose and die. Where the fuck have you been for the past six years, old man?"

"I know that," Winston countered, trying not to get confrontational with his boss' favorite rising star. "That's why I'm just asking permission to make a limited private disclosure with—"

"Security protocols are there for a reason, Smith. Shit happens when you are protecting everyone from the most dangerous terrorists who ever walked the face of this Earth. There's bound to be some collateral damage. And the state never apologizes. Never. Our enemies would love it if we did—so we don't!"

"And we ain't gonna start today, fuckwit!" Rex chimed in. "Now get outta my face and outta my space, because this meeting is over!"

Winston turned and headed back the way he came in.

"Thank you—thank you for the meeting, Mr. Rex," he said with sober resignation when he reached the door.

Rex ignored him, focused on pulling Amber's golden hair. "Ungracious bitch!" he screamed. "Keep working it. You got a lot to make up for."

Chapter 8: The Plan

Tuesday May 2, 2034
10:00 a.m. Pacific Time
Google Headquarters
Mountain View, California
The United Peoples of America

Secretary of Defense Serena Jackson, the head of the National Intelligence Council, needed no introduction. She broke the chilling silence by standing and beginning her part of the presentation in a resounding voice. "Let me say this bluntly. "We have three options: to surrender, to perish, or to transform those who call us their enemy. I have no doubt that options one and two are the same. Option three is the only one that can save us. It is the only way to vanquish this darkness, for the benefit of every person on our planet, right up to Donald Trump himself."

Serena paused to listen to the hive mind. "I know," she said. "The decision does not rest on my shoulders. I am here to describe this third option so that this group can make its recommendation to the People's Council on Wednesday."

"We have been planning the emancipation of our enslaved neighbors for three years now," Serena continued. "This Great Expansion of our democratic utopia embodies a grand paradox: We are a people committed to non-violence, planning a war of liberation against the most murderous regime on Earth."

"The United Peoples of America is not going to war, as oppressive nations did for so many centuries, to kill enemies. We have no enemies. Our mission is to share our Activation, to transform our belligerent, fearful neighbors into the enemy-less state of Oneness that is our true essence."

"Our plan is to have as close to zero casualties as possible on both sides. For that reason, we carry no lethal weapons. Instead, our occupying army will be an all-volunteer army of love."

"An army of love!" Dawn declared, jumping from her chair to the table and into the wide circle around which the Council sat. She danced joyfully, springing lightly as she sang, "We are an army of love; we have no guns, we are an army of love, You and I are One!"

Maria glanced proudly at her partner as she felt the anguished spirits of those around the table lightening. Dawn spoke as she continued dancing. "Emma Goldman said, 'If I can't dance, I don't want to be part of your revolution.' I just want everyone to know that Secretary of Defense Jackson has assured me that all members of our army of love can dance at will."

"If we could stop the evil of the Trump regime without sacrifice, we would," Dawn said pointedly, slowing her movement to address her fellow Governors. "But let not our fear of death prevent us from living the miracle we are here to become. Tomorrow our daughter Sarah and I will be driving out to lead the first convoy to Denver. I know that we may never return. Each of us faces the choice whether to contract from fear or to expand from love. I realize the dangers that lie ahead. Yet I choose love, I choose to dance!"

Maria observed, with love, how Dawn's magic continued to impress her, 15 years after their wedding. Had their collective spirits, she wondered, discovered the first mystical Activation, or had Spirit herself chosen them, from birth, to fulfill their remarkable destiny?

After all, Maria reflected, both women shared the same auspicious birthday: November 11, 2000. And it was during their 20th birthday celebration, in 2020, shortly after their marriage, that they stumbled upon the key that unlocked the dormant Oneness gene.

It was during a sacred ayahuasca ceremony in the same ritual hut in the thickly wooded hills of Maui that Winston would later find his way to. It had been Dawn and Maria's first mystical journey into the cosmos. After a sleepless, soul-expanding night, the singers improvised the Four Directions gratitude song to greet the new day, standing on wobbly legs, watching the sun rise and ringing a pair of enchanted bells they found in the ritual hut.

A moment later, an evolutionary leap occurred that would forever change the lives of the two women, and the course of history.

For hundreds of thousands of years, the Oneness gene had laid dormant in Homo sapiens, switched off as humans established distinct personal identities, tribes, cultures, religions and nations. A culture of duality, one of separation, had allowed the human species to flourish, as civilizations rose and fell, while billions were born and died to experience their karma: light and dark, love and fear, joy and suffering.

In rare instances, enlightened masters, both known and unknown, had found their way to the spiritual interconnectedness and Oneness that exists as the true essence of all living beings. But even the great masters were limited in their ability to *share* their blissful awakening, to spread their sense of union with One Spirit and with all living beings.

That changed on November 11, 2020. Faced with imminent climate catastrophe and the rise of the darkest alliance of all time in Donald Trump's America and Vladimir Putin's Soviet empire, humanity stood on the brink of extinction. With the illicit reelection of a Trump Administration committed to ecological degradation and the poisoning of the planet, a species-wide evolutionary solution was required if the human race, and the Earth itself, were to survive.

That evolutionary solution was miraculously birthed by two love-filled women in that ritual hut on Maui. Tuned to a mystical vibrational frequency they'd tapped into, their discovery was as simple as it was radical: that the human heart, when flowing with love, was an Activation tool for Oneness.

From that day on, Maria and Dawn had become evolutionary Activators. They were capable of transforming almost anyone in their physical presence. By exposing their awakened hearts while chanting and clanging a bell to the vibrational frequency, they found they could switch on, like a key in a lock, the Oneness gene that lay dormant in every human being. They soon found other empaths who were also capable of leading Activation ceremonies. As their network of interconnected people grew, the process became easier, until, a few years later, any Activated being could perform the Activation ceremony to switch on the Oneness gene of everyone in their presence.

A hundred million human Activations later, Dawn, Maria and their new nation were ready to share their harmonious culture with their former countrymen and women long oppressed by the brutal Trump regime.

Sitting at the enormous round table in Google's underground meeting room, Maria felt her heart glow as she watched Dawn complete her dance and pop happily back into her chair.

Serena Jackson, a warm smile across her face, resumed her presentation. "Thank you, sister Dawn, for the enlightening support. Our Expansion forces are organized into one division for each of the 47 states that comprise the T.U.E.A. Each division is broken into regiments by task. The first wave will be the Activation facilitators, with soldiers to protect them, followed closely by the farmers, healers, teachers and administrators necessary to rebuild society.

"Only one fifth of our army will perform soldiering tasks. They have trained in nonviolent self-defense and martial arts and will be aided by a youth corps of N.E.W. Knights in Kevlar suits."

"Our ability to succeed without lethal weapons depends upon the success of the massive electromagnetic pulse disruption that our air force has prepared to accompany the Great Expansion. As you can see on the screens in front of you, the EMP sub-committee of this Strategic Intelligence Council has issued its recommendation that the disruption technology has been successfully tested and is ready to deploy." Serena finished with a confident thumbs up.

Dawn made the next introduction. "Our final presentation," she said, "is from our friend the Professor. As everyone knows, Professor Flynn Washington created our nation's wisdom frequency, the Informing to Empower network of 6,000 local websites that provide empowering information and coordinating logistics to every community in our nation."

Dawn smiled at a grey-bearded African-American man who wore a loose-fitting, brightly patterned African dashiki shirt and cap. "Thank you for the supportive words, Dawn," Professor Washington said with understated authority. The overhead screen displayed images of a sprawling cluster of buildings. "The Great Expansion will require the success of three core communications objectives: conceal, connect and collaborate."

"Concealment requires the hijacking of the most sophisticated surveillance system on Earth. With the help of our friend Ed Snowden and thousands of editors in Burbank, we will replace the footage sent from the N.S.A.'s national surveillance center in Utah with faux images that cover up the border crossing convoys of our expansion teams as they head to more than a thousand destinations across the country."

"Our second objective is to communicate to the terrorized people of Trump's T.U.E.A. that help is on the way. We intend to do this by replacing Sunday's noontime mandatory-to-view live Patriot News webcast with a specially tailored message of our own before our electromagnetic pulse attack turns out all the lights."

"Our third objective is to facilitate collaboration throughout our reunited nation. As we have done across the Pacific states during the past decade, we will integrate personal Facebook pages into tens of thousands of local Informing to Empower community facilitation sites."

"Which part of this plan concerns you the most?" Governor Murray asked.

"Access to the TV1.com broadcast is the most unpredictable component of our plan," Washington replied. "The security protocols guarding the broadcasts require the biometric and voice verification of two out of four of the top managers at Patriot News. These four are CEO Roger Rex, Executive VP Winston Smith, News Director Scoop Walters, and White House Communications Director Joseph Gerbers, who works embedded in the company's Colorado Springs headquarters. We have no way of knowing how Rex, Walters or Gerbers will react to our Activation. As we have seen, the awakening process can send certain people into a mental shutdown state resembling a coma for days or even weeks. This is where my friend Winston Smith enters the picture."

The holographic slideshow shifted from community websites to the cover of George Orwell's book *1984* and photos of Winston.

"Born in 1984 to Hal and Wendy Smith, Winston's parents named him as a protest statement against Ronald Reagan," Washington explained. "Twenty five years ago, Winston was one of my brightest grad students."

A montage showed images of Winston's past articles and websites. "Winston was one of the most motivated and purposeful students at Berkeley. Then, in 2018, during the beginning of the Trump regime, Winston founded a company called TV1.com, focused on videos created or curated by its users."

"Winston was a media visionary and he built a technology engine to match it. The TV1.com service exploded. But after the censorship screws were tightened, TV1.com was relegated to cute cat and celebrity videos. In 2022, Patriot News acquired TV1.com for its advanced web video delivery technology."

"In 2026, as we secretly planned our independence, I called Winston, urging him to join the good life in Trump-defiant California. But like most Americans, Winston never imagined how bad it was about to get. So he stayed put in Colorado, and I have not heard from him since. But I believe Dawn has had more recent contact with him."

Dawn smiled, then spoke. "Winston's destiny, and that of his mystic 12-year-old son Abraham are linked with our Great Expansion. I met him only once, during his shamanic journey, at which time I planted a secret seed of suggestion in his subconscious mind. My astral form spoke to Winston yesterday. This week, if Spirit and the Council of the People are willing, we will re-connect Winston Smith with his true purpose."

Chapter 9: Snowden's Revenge

Tuesday May 2, 2034
11:00 p.m. Mountain Time
National Security Agency Data Center
Bluffdale, Utah
Trump's United Enterprises of America

The sentry guards working the main gate of the National Security Agency's mile-wide data collection center in Bluffdale, Utah, were delighted by the donuts.

Four of their colleagues had arrived a half-hour early for the midnight shift bearing large boxes overflowing with dozens of Dunkin Donuts of every variety. The coffee machine at the guard building had been filled with fresh coffee for the night shift. Julia Braithwaite, one of the donut-bearers who had worked security for the N.S.A. facility since it opened more than 20 years earlier, had brought her guitar. It was an impromptu, belated birthday party for their manager, Chuck Benson, and all 18 people on duty joined them in the main entry monitor room to sing "Happy Birthday."

Everyone ate donuts and drank coffee and even the stiffest of the guards joined in the singing, at least mouthing the words. After that, Julia and her three fellow donut-bearers followed with a new song they had recently learned at the One True Church service in Salt Lake City.

"Don't worry," Julia said, laughing, "It's a short one!"

The four started singing, in less than perfect harmony, but with conviction. The song was unfamiliar to their colleagues, but that did not surprise them since few bothered going to church ever since the Mormon faith was outlawed as communistic by the federal government five years earlier.

They sang: "Gratitude … gratitude … gratitude … gratitude."

Chuck Benson, whose birthday was the next day, raised his eyes to the ceiling and busied himself selecting his third donut.

The two-minute song continued:

"The east breath
of gratitude
is to Creator for your light and sacred skies."

"The south breath
of gratitude
is to our Mother for your seeds and living lands."

"The west breath
of gratitude
is to our Teachers for your wise and ancient waters."

"The north breath
of gratitude
is to my Body, Mind, Heart and to my Spirit."

"For your light
and rising fire
breathing love and light With all as One.
With all as One, With all as One
With all as One, With all as One
With all as … Oooonnnne."

The four singers opened their arms wide and held the last note on the word "one." The singer next to Julia pulled a set of small bells from his pocket and rang them together as they sang the last note.

Just as Chuck and a few others prepared to politely applaud and begin the shift change, they found themselves unexpectedly frozen in the moment. All their thoughts, concerns, worries, fears, judgment, anger and plans dropped from their minds. Something deep inside stirred. The long dormant Oneness gene they and their ancestors had carried ever since humans first walked the Earth had suddenly been Activated.

With the exception of one man, who waved his gun aimlessly in the air and muttered incoherently before he fell to the floor in a state of mental shutdown, each of the guards experienced an energetic rebirth. They had never felt so contented, so grateful for the miracle of their lives. It was as though they had awakened to the moment for the first time.

Blissful smiles appeared on their faces as they looked, with tearful eyes, in gratitude at Julia and her three colleagues. They saw the gold, the divine presence in each of them and realized, with wonder, that they themselves were part of this divinity.

Then a voice spoke to them. It came not from any *one* of them, but from *all* of them, from the hive mind. Its first words, echoed in a dozen minds: *I have never felt such happiness.* A telepathic emotional sharing followed, each colleague receiving and expressing deep emotional histories, becoming familiar with colleagues they had worked with for years but had never really known.

When five minutes had passed, the hive mind became an internal organizer. Each person suddenly knew what he or she needed to do.

With almost superhuman speed, Chuck Benson sat at his desktop station and accessed the central security file. He opened a flash drive that Julia handed him containing instructions, then typed in their implementation. A handful of the other guards accessed their accounts and did the same. Within four minutes, the internal security monitors, ID checkpoint systems and drone feeds for the enormous facility were being fed prepared imagery from the Burbank headquarters of the Advanced Technology Agency of the United Peoples of America.

The other newly awakened guards joined their four previously Activated colleagues and practiced the Four Directions song for their 15 colleagues, who would be arriving promptly at 23:30 for the overnight shift.

By the time the overnight shift arrived and joined the earlier shift in the main monitor room to sing another happy birthday for their manager Chuck, the choice of donuts was limited. But no one cared.

Six minutes later they had all been Activated.

With a level of collaboration that would have been impossible as separate-minded human beings, the 40 guards split into two groups. One group would stay at the entry gate to provide sentry service as usual for the 5,000 workers who would be arriving between midnight and 1 a.m. to staff the overnight domestic surveillance shift. The departing gate team, with the facility's security manager, Chuck Benson, would drive down into the facility for a special training session that Chuck had just announced, via a text bulletin, to the in-building security staff.

As Julia followed her colleagues into the sprawling parking lot of the main buildings, a man in the back seat of her pickup truck emerged from under a blanket. Edward Snowden's small eyes glowed with enthusiasm.

As a young man, Snowden had joined the C.I.A. soon after the September 11 attacks and risen with record speed through its ranks. Snowden next worked as a high-level contractor for the N.S.A., where he lost faith in its mission after the Agency lied to the public and to Congress about its massive illegal domestic snooping operation. After carefully taking the news public in 2013, Snowden became one of the most important public interest whistleblowers in American history.

While a campaign by transparency advocates helped him gain a nomination for the Nobel Prize, right wing politicians openly called for his assassination. For 15 years, Snowden lived like an international fugitive, until he was welcomed by the new utopian nation to help build the most technologically advanced intelligence agency the world had ever seen.

Julia parked her truck in an area for security guards close to the main building. Snowden had only seen the massive facility in photos. From the truck window, he marveled at its size. Inside the series of connected buildings, he had read, was enough hardware to record, copy and store every communication made by every person in the United States for decades.

Julia felt Snowden's eagerness to join her in the main building, but both knew that her team would need to Activate the on-site building security first, and then the thousands of people working inside.

Because Julia had been Activated by an advance team of awakened facilitators from the United Peoples of America six months earlier, telepathic communication came easily to her. But she wanted to speak, because that still felt to her like a more caring form of communication. "I know you're keen to get started," she said to Snowden. "I'm sorry you can't come in with me in the first wave. Your California friends ought to be arriving soon, and then we can get working on awakening the full staff. Till then, anyone might recognize you, even with that blond hair."

"Thanks Julia. I'm accustomed to working remotely, as you may know." Snowden laughed. He made himself comfortable, stretching across the back seat with his tablet in hand, while Julia covered him again with the blanket. "Ping me when you're ready," he said. "May fortune smile upon you."

"And upon us all," she said, grabbing her guitar and heading into the building.

Chuck Benson had replaced the main building's entry guards with a handful of his newly Activated colleagues. Julia passed quickly through the biometric and iris-scan station and hustled down the hall into the main meeting auditorium. She unpacked her guitar and joined Benson on the stage. As they had planned earlier, he addressed about 100 main building guards from both the departing and incoming shifts. It was a huge hall, and they sat in the front rows, not even filling one-tenth of the auditorium's seats.

"Just in time for our presentation, Mrs. Braithwaite," Benson said smoothly, waving Julia to the stage. "Could I have a few other crew members join her in the presentation that we discussed? And Tim, set up a blackout system for this room. We're dealing with classified information here."

A dozen of the Activated guards from the front gate, including her colleague with the Tibetan bells in his pocket, joined Julia on the stage. They tuned into their hive mind to make sure they knew the lyrics and what to do next.

Benson spoke in the stern voice of the army drill sergeant he had once been. "We have received a top-secret advisory from Homeland Security about a new threat coming from a secret religious cult. They have been infiltrating military and intelligence communities and their families, possibly through drugs added to beverages."

"One way to identify them is to recognize a simple hymn they sing every time they gather. My orders are to make sure that this facility's security, as well as our army of listeners, recognizes this tune. To that end," he paused for a friendly smile, "we have forced a few members of our veteran entry gate team to memorize and sing this song for you."

Julia began strumming and the group sang the Activation song, "The Four Directions." Within 15 minutes, all but two members of their audience had been Activated and were filing out to take their stations with a newly interconnected sense of purpose.

A half hour later, Benson, Julia and a dozen singers were repeating the Activation chant with a full auditorium of 1,200 workers, a quarter of the overnight shift. They had been summoned for a special security briefing. When they were finished, 1,200 more employees were summoned, followed, in turn, by the third and fourth groups. Once these meetings were concluded, and Julia had retrieved Ed Snowden from her car, nearly all the workers in every building of the sprawling facility had been Activated.

Chuck Benson then sent out meeting notifications to the thousands of employees reporting for work at 8 a.m. and 4 p.m. In the meantime, he and Julia and their singing colleagues took long-overdue naps in a breakroom, resting up so they could repeat their performance the following morning.

Once he gained access to the building, Snowden wasted no time in meeting with the ranking duty director of the N.S.A. in the facility's cavernous central command center. The director introduced his top deputies and then Snowden went online and connected each of them to a managerial counterpart standing by at the United Peoples of America's Intelligence Agency in California.

By 4 a.m., every worker in the Utah facility had matched up with a counterpart in California, collaborating to replace, replicate, provide access to, or record and loop each of the millions of data sources that they monitored.

Snowden and the army of hackers and programmers in California next focused their attention on the drone feeds coming from the western borders of Trump's United Enterprises of America, as well as many of the nation's highway, bridge and road surveillance cameras. By 5 a.m., they had replaced all border drone feeds with loops of past surveillance footage. Soon after, to avoid detection by highway, bridge and tunnel surveillance systems, the license plates and identifier transmitters of hundreds of thousands of new vehicles were added to the T.U.E.A.'s central security database.

Snowden called General Jackson to give her a green light for the first "pulse" of the long-planned border incursions. On Wednesday at 6 a.m., the first vehicles of their convoy crossed into Trump's United Enterprises of America on a dozen border roads between southern California and northern Washington.

Dawn Souljah, her daughter Sarah and the advance team's vans were among the first to cross, heading on a thousand-mile drive to a forest west of Denver, Colorado. Over the next three days, Snowden's team would work to ensure these convoys would be able to transport without detection the two million volunteers of the Army of Love and their equipment into every city and town of Trump's United Enterprises of America.

Snowden felt surprisingly alert as he kicked back in a comfortable Aeron chair and continued the most satisfying all-nighter of his life. After four years of planning, he had succeeded in gouging out the eyes of the world's most terrifying ogre.

The largest, most important hack of all time was underway. Its consequences, he chuckled to himself, would be huuu-ge.

Chapter 10: Patriot News

Wednesday May 3,2034
9 a.m. Mountain Time
Patriot News Headquarters
Colorado Springs, Colorado
Trump's United Enterprises of America

After riding an elevator down to the meeting room floor, Winston had just enough time to rush to a toilet, puke his guts out, and wash up. Since Monday's massacre and Tuesday's encounter with Roger Rex, he had been unable to keep much food down, or sleep more than an hour at a time.

Winston was grateful that the security check outside the top-secret editorial meeting did not include another anal probe. He ignored the catcalls of the beefy goons in black body armor and darkened masks and entered the conference room at exactly 9 a.m.

Scoop was already there, along with Adam Dawkins, VP of Ad Sales, and George Johnson, VP of Operations. Scoop was arranging a new video shoot for Good Food's corn ad.

"I don't have to tell you," Scoop said, looking at Winston as though he were an annoying fly, "how important it is to make Mr. Dillon and his Good Food corporation happy. They spent $115 million with us last year. We took on this ad at the request of Dillon himself to help him out with their important new ad campaign for Asia. Sales there have dropped to shit because of the boycott by China, Japan and Korea. If Indonesia and Vietnam and India join them this year, which those slant-eyed pricks are threatening to do, it would be the end of American food exports and the beginning of the end of a profitable company advertising on Patriot News."

Winston tried to help. "That's why I thought we ought to outsource and collaborate with Patriot Advertising to get it done fast and well."

Scoop stood up and yelled, "Was I talking to you, snowflake? Was I?"

Winston thought of a nasty response but immediately decided to shelve it. This was not the time to go head-to-head with Scoop. In fact, Winston thought, given Scoop's growing power, the days of speaking up for himself were gone forever. He compliantly shook his head and stared down at the table.

"Do not interrupt me again, Smith, or I will wring your fucken neck until your Commie blood turns this carpet red!"

Winston sat silently. Satisfied, Scoop sat back down and continued. "This shit ain't rocket science. We've got the script. Take a news crew and producer and get out there tomorrow. This time," he glared at Winston, then looked at Operations head George Johnson and ordered, "this time, request a lock down and security perimeter around Good Food's dormitories and worker plants. Nip this shit in the bud."

Johnson nodded. "Yes, sir, Mr. Walters."

A door built into the wall slid open and Rex meandered in, arriving through a private tunnel and elevator system. He was accompanied by Joseph Gerbers, the powerful White House Communications Director. The Patriot News Headquarters contained a network of secret passages that only Rex and his top private security officers and bodyguards could access. Nobody knew when or where he or his fearsome goons might appear.

Gerbers oversaw the ever-shifting state propaganda that constituted news casts in 2034. Like President Trump, he was germophobic and rarely shook hands. He was a slight, fearsome-looking man with a coarse face and dead, dark eyes sunk into bony caverns.

Winston despised formality, but he joined his colleagues in rising and bending slightly, bowing to greet Rex and Gerbers.

Although he had never served in the military or law enforcement, Gerbers wore the black uniform of an officer of the Homeland Security Army, the ultra-loyalist force that had replaced all branches of the armed forces and the National Guard for domestic security. The uniform hung from Gerbers' spindly arms like the robe on the Grim Reaper. His chest was festooned with honorary medals for directing the propaganda campaigns supporting domestic and international wars, while his lapel sported a small bejeweled flag of Trump's United Enterprises of America.

"Before we start today's meeting, we have some human garbage to dispose of," Rex commanded, sitting at a wide lounge chair at the head of a black conference table. As everyone took their seats, Rex continued, switching on the video monitors that hovered in front of each of the six participants.

"Monitor present security camera for current incident at exterior security gate."

The monitors showed the security sentry station with a closed gate, and then zoomed in on two women standing on the lawn outside the gate holding large white signs handwritten in huge letters, "Wives of the Disappeared Vigil," over photos of two men. The camera zoomed in further, and Winston could see that the photos were of his friend George Scudder and an actor, both of whom had been massacred two days earlier.

"Driving into his office today," Rex continued, "Mr. Gerbers noticed that this May Day terrorist protest attempt has infected a few of the family members of the deceased. From what they told our security officers, the terrorist protesters claimed they would not leave until they learned the whereabouts of their husbands."

Winston considered putting in a word in support of this idea, until he saw Gerbers jump up, pound his fist on the table and scream, "We will NOT be dictated to by terrorists!"

"Of course not, Mr. Gerbers," Rex replied coolly. "Our only question is whether you would suggest that we deal with this ourselves or not? Our security army would be delighted to deal definitively with this human garbage, but this illegal protest is taking place on the shoulder of a public road. So should we leave it to Homeland Security to handle?"

Gerbers sat down and spoke with conviction: "With the imminent invasion of California to manage, I am sure that General Francis Baron has far more important work these days, Mr. Rex. I remind you that the public-private partnership arrangement that has shrunk big government across our great nation grants Super Patriots like yourself the complete authority—and responsibility—for keeping the peace on all public roads leading to your corporate offices."

"Thank you for that reminder, Mr. Gerbers. Phone!" Rex's smartphone hovered a few inches from his mouth. "External gate security," he barked, "this is Mr. Rex. Immediately implement restraint drone removal and permanent disposal protocols against the two illegal protesters."

"Right away, Mr. Rex," a military man's voice replied through the phone.

"This is going to be entertaining. Zoom in on the face of Scudder's bitch at the moment of termination," Rex instructed the security cameras.

The monitors showed two large drones suddenly appear directly behind the heads of both women holding the protest signs. Before they could move, a narrow steel restraint device dropped from the bottom of each drone over the back of the neck of each protester. One second later, the device frame unfolded around the neck, over the shoulders, down the spine, around the hips, and over the now-manacled hands of the two prisoners. They dropped their signs as the drones lifted them helplessly four feet into the air.

"This is the good part," said Rex excitedly, with a sadistic grin. "The idiots expect to merely be arrested and sent to prison. Watch their stupefied faces when they realize what is about to happen!"

"Are you watching, snowflake," Scoop chided Winston. "Your traitor friends are in for a big surprise."

"Their last surprise," Rex chuckled.

While watching the monitor, as he had been ordered, Winston tried to fill his mind with other thoughts in an effort to ignore what was happening to Valerie Scudder. Valerie had been married to his close friend for more than 20 years, and their son had been on a basketball team with Winston's son Robert for many seasons. But Winston's efforts to ignore what was happening on the screen in front of him were futile. The camera zoomed in on a small device holding a steel encased needle, which dropped from the drone into a harness at the back of Valerie's neck.

Valerie Scudder's eyes glowered with shock as the needle and its lethal poison penetrated deep into her skull.

"There it is!" Rex laughed jubilantly.

Valerie closed her eyes two seconds later. The actor's widow suffered the same fate. The drones hoisted the two dead bodies higher and carried them off.

"Garbage disposed of," Rex stated with satisfaction.

Winston felt numb, frozen in place. His only relief was that he did not have to speak right away.

Rex officially began the meeting with new commands. "Tuesday editorial meeting for this evening's Super Patriot broadcast, top security secrecy protocols, start recording." A small video scribe drone instantly appeared over the table.

"We begin," Rex stated in an ominous manner, "with every week's bottom line question: Dawkins, will you make your numbers this month?"

All eyes turned to Adam Dawkins. Winston wondered how anyone could sleep at night managing ad sales for Patriot News and working with a gun to his head every Tuesday morning. Dawkins had been on the job for 18 months, which was the longest any ad sales manager had lasted, Winston realized, since his company was acquired in 2022.

During Winston's time attending Patriot News weekly management meetings, advertising chiefs who failed to hit their sales targets were fired on the spot and blacklisted from the other two remaining media monopolies legally permitted to function in Trump's United Enterprises of America. Like Rex's Patriot News, the other two companies— Patriot Entertainment, which controlled all video entertainment content, and Patriot Sports—were run by other powerful oligarchs.

But Patriot News was more profitable than the other two media companies combined, placing Rex in the top 10% of the 400 billionaires in wealth. Because of the mandatory nature of its twice-weekly broadcasts to Super Patriots and to the 50 million ordinary citizens who managed to live outside of slave labor camps, Patriot News was able to charge a higher rate for each of its ads than Patriot Sports received from the Super Bowl. Its guaranteed viewership of the 400 wealthiest billionaires in the country, as well as a few thousand of their immediate family members, commanded $10 million a minute for the precious attention of an audience whose aggregate net worth was 10 times greater than the rest of Americans combined.

Dawkins enthusiastically reported the good news of an 8% uptick in Super Patriot ad sales over the previous year. The biggest sponsors for the broadcaster to billionaires, Dawkins reported, were the six human-extraction companies that had recently opened "harvesting clinics" in the remaining 100 labor camps that did not yet have them.

Despite the upbeat demeanor of his report, Dawkins could not avoid making involuntarily glances at Rex's enormous sidearm. Dawkins, like everyone at Patriot News, had heard the story of what happened to the unfortunate ad sales director who had presided over a precipitous fall in ad revenue in 2028 following the months of economic turmoil caused by the secession of the Pacific States.

Winston recalled the trauma of that late December 2028 meeting. Sitting in the same seat he now occupied, Winston had been splashed with blood from the ad director's exploding head while Rex waved his still smoking Glock pistol and ranted about the betrayal of those entrusted with protecting his company.

But that was then, Winston thought. Now, Dawkins spoke confidently of improving profits. He continued the report on the roster of advertisers from the mega corporations of Super Patriots. There was a campaign for ultra-exclusive life-extension medical treatments. Next, Dawkins shared a few ads from the companies that leased or sold desperate inmates of slave labor camps for milkmaids, blood-bods, sex slaves, child playmates or even human targets for hunting games. Another major sponsor sold advanced lethal weaponry that ranged from "auto kill" sidearms to helicopter gunships.

Patriot news had two major outlets for advertisers: one to oligarch families and the other to the general public. Weapons, Winston reflected, could be marketed only to billionaires because gun control had taken an unusual turn during the past decade. Under an emergency executive decree to fight the war on terrorism, gun purchases were now limited to the 400 Super-Patriots, their families, and the generals of their private armies.

Winston's thoughts drifted from Dawkins' review of ad revenue to how that emergency executive decree had come about. It followed the 2026 resistance from armed citizens following the shutdown of all government housing and the forced evictions of the working poor and debtors.

The resistance started soon after the Trump Administration decided to end all Social Security and welfare programs. The class of debtors stripped of their citizenship because they were "unable to compete in the new economy" suddenly included tens of millions of elderly and disabled Americans. Without the means to pay their rents and with law enforcement and Homeland Security troopers attempting forcible evictions, many destitute retirees were willing to risk their lives not to be shipped off in handcuffs to slave labor camps. Often their children and grandchildren took up arms and rushed to their side to defend them. Hundreds of thousands were killed in the armed rebellion of the poor, including thousands of law enforcers.

Pacification required declaring martial law and bringing the nation's mercenary armies home to assist Homeland Security troopers to forcibly remove weapons house by house in every state in Trump's United Enterprises of America. It took nearly two years, Winston recalled, before the rebellions ended at the end of 2028.

In a showcase trial, the Trump regime's hand-picked Supreme Court reinterpreted the Second Amendment to rule that "the well-regulated militia" named by the framers of the Constitution, whose right to bear arms could not be "infringed" by the government, referred exclusively to the private armies of the 400 oligarchs.

Winston's attention was jerked back to the meeting when he noticed Dawkins sitting down.

"On to content," Rex said pleasantly, his mood lightened by the ad report. "What have we got for the fat-cat news segment?"

Scoop answered, with authority. "I figure we'll start with the good news segment: Revenue for the Super Patriot pool continues to rise. Smith produced the April report and can give us the numbers."

This, Winston thought, was the only easy part of his work: doing the job he'd been hired for. He banished from his mind the execution he had just witnessed and read the main points of the segment, which was displayed on five hovering monitors in front of the five men at the table. "Tax Day means payday for Super Patriots! The economy overall continues to contract as the number of wage earning citizens dropped from 60 million to 50 million, with 10 million people entering debtor labor camps ..."

"Fucken deadbeats!" Scoop interjected scornfully.

Winston provided an obligatory nod. "Nonetheless, an increase in asset forfeitures for those unable to pay their penalties, fines or taxes meant that revenue for April 2034 increased 1% over last year, turning around five years of consecutive double-digit declines following the Great Betrayal of the Pacific States. This means $220 billion total in annual tax revenue, providing $110 billion for federal and state government operations, and $110 billion divided equally between the president and Super Patriot distribution."

"In addition, the royalties on unrestricted mining of natural resources from federal lands as well as government's revenue from the leasing to our allies of our army, navy and air force are both up significantly. The continuing Saudi and Gulf State financed war in Iran and Pakistan has kept American Forces Inc. fully occupied."

"The Super Patriot distribution for these segments will be limited this year due to President for Life Trump's decision to increase the Homeland Security budget by $30 billion to pay for the production of 250,000 updated thermobaric Hellfire missiles capable of breaching the diabolical force fields of the traitorous United Peoples of America. The president wants Super Patriots to know that this investment will be paid back a hundred times in the coming months, as the oppressed people of California, Oregon and Washington, as well as their high tech, aerospace, agricultural and entertainment industries, are once again reunited with our great nation."

"Patriot News extends a hearty thank-you to the greatest business visionary and political leader in human history, our courageous CEO and Commander in Chief, President for Life Donald Jesus Trump."

Winston switched off the screens and looked solicitously at Rex. "Any changes required, Mr. Rex?"

"Not bad, not bad, Smith," Rex said, nodding his approval of the report. "Good move, Scoop, to soften 'em up with promising news first. Remind the fat-cat 400 of the carrots they get from this great economy, and then ... then I hear we've got some tough love straight from the White House about a fat-cat wise guy who got whacked."

"Exactly, sir," Scoop continued, encouraged. "The second segment for Super Patriots is a very special message from the White House, a … a law-and-order advisory, if you will."

Rex guffawed. "Masterful term!" he said, smiling at Scoop's cleverness. "Law-and-order advisory—and the third one this year, those stupid fucks! Play it!"

The screens lit up with flashing letters, "EMERGENCY MESSAGE FOR SUPER PATRIOTS," followed by the talking head of Donald Trump in the Oval Office. The American flag waved in the background. The red stripes on the upper right of the old U.S. flag had been replaced with golden letters spelling TRUMP, and a modernized Nazi swastika rested in the blue of the upper left side, surrounded by a circle of 13 stars. The video started with Trump's stern face.

"Good morning, my friends and thriving business partners. Today's lesson is something they never teach in business school. The pigs get fat, and the hogs get butchered. Today's story is about John Roland who, before his premature death last week, was just like you. Lucky ducky Roland was one of the nearly 400 business leaders who thrive, as billionaires, BILLION-aires, in Trump's United Enterprises of America, the greatest nation ever created for capitalists like us.

"Roland owned Stem Source, a great business that sells placentas for stem cell cures and cosmetics. His business got even greater when we made abortion into a capital crime—with the execution coming AFTER murderous momma delivered the innocent baby—and its valuable government-owned placenta.

"Last year Stem Source did $20 billion in sales, mostly international, with profits, after finders' fees, of $8 billion. But

Roland had a problem—a big problem. See, he reported only $4 billion in profits to the IRS and paid just $2 billion in his profit participation tax to yours truly."

After a montage of images of John Roland and the Stem Source Corporation, a closeup of Trump's angry face appeared across the screen.

"That's right, friends. Loser John Roland stole $2 billion from his business partner, President for Life Donald Trump. He thought he could get away with it. Big mistake. Hu-ge mistake! And when we found out," Trump smiled craftily, "how much good do you think Roland's private army and mountain fortress with missile defenses and attack helicopters did for him?"

The video shifted to footage of a relentless aircraft and missile attack pulverizing a fortress castle.

"My son General Trump is a very good boy. As the head of Homeland Security, he does an amazing job protecting all of us. But when someone steals from his father, no matter who they are, no matter how much money they have, no matter how well they think they can keep it secret from the F.B.I. and N.S.A. and I.R.S, General Trump and I will hear about it. And we do not believe in second chances for thieving traitors.

"What we did offer Roland was a chance to come to a federal court, confess and be hung in public. Roland, hater and loser that he was, decided he was going to fight. Sad. Sad, because he knew how *his* story would end. But his wife? His children? His grandchildren? Hundreds of members of his staff, thousands of guards? Everyone? Did they all have to die with him?"

The video cut from Trump's face to footage of a burned-out shell of an enormous mansion, surrounded by a fortress of collapsed walls, guard towers and outer buildings. It then zoomed in on the charred remains of the corpses of adults and children.

"So think about it. We are in business to-gether. Too-gether. I get 50% of everything. Ev-ah-ree-thing. Short change me, and I will know it. Trust me. I will know it."

While an instrumental "Star Spangled Banner" played as background to Trump's voice, the screens showed the huge flag of Trump's United Enterprises of America billowing in the breeze.

Winston, Dawkins, and Johnson stared blankly at the screen in front of them, uncertain how to respond, knowing that their facial reactions and actions were all recorded and reviewed by the F.B.I. Scoop showed them the way, standing and clapping. "Standing tall!" he cheered. "Death to traitors!"

Rex put his hand to his forehead and saluted. "Well done, Mr. President! Hail to the Chief!"

Gerbers looked elated. Dawkins and Johnson stood to give the president and his broadcast a standing ovation. Winston hesitated for less than a second, wishing he were dead. He then pushed back his chair and, struggling hard to disguise his disgust, stood to join them in their enthusiastic applause.

Chapter 11: The Greenway

The hike to Armstrong Woods from their home in the Green Path agricultural commune would take more than two hours, but Estrella, Maria's 13-year old daughter, insisted on walking. She was eager to have time alone with her busy mother. She knew that once they arrived at the famed redwoods park, where the special session of the People's Council of the United Peoples of America was being held, they both would become absorbed in their responsibilities and not see one another again until they caught the shuttle home.

Estrella let go of her mother's hand and did an energetic dance twirl. She was full of energy and, after Monday's dismal tragedy, was excited to be joining the team of farmers and healers from around the North Bay preparing seedlings and salves and homeopathic medicines for what she liked to call Operation Johnny Healingseed.

The hikers left their commune's 100-acre field of organic vegetables and carbon-sequestrating cover crops and entered the bordering Greenway. The wide pathway was unusually busy with walkers. Delegates and their families headed to the historic Council meeting, joining the usual flow of morning trekkers. Maria telepathically welcomed those who passed, receiving glimpses of their excitement for the gathering and their recent memories of the previous night spent camping or couch surfing.

Estrella was delighted by the steady stream of animals that seemed headed in the same direction: squirrels, rabbits, quail, turkeys, raccoons, possums, skunks and deer, moving through the high brush and staying just far enough out of reach to avoid being petted.

When their grassy path converged with the Wheelway bike path, dozens of cyclists with loaded storage packs whizzed westward, heading to the same event.

Estrella heard her mother's thoughts and clasped her hands as they walked. "I'm anxious too, Mama," she said.

"She's driving now," Maria explained, trying to calm her worry by talking about it. "If Snowden's team was successful, Mama Dawn's convoy is on its way to Colorado. By this time tomorrow, she and Sarah will be napping in a tree sling up in the Rocky Mountains."

"If they haven't logged all the trees by now," Estrella joked. "Let's call them!"

Maria called Dawn and set her phone to hover in front of her as they continued walking. Seconds later, a holographic video of Dawn and Sarah in the back seats of a van appeared.

"Good morning, darlings," Dawn said, happy to see them.

"Did you sleep at all?" Estrella asked.

"Not a bit," Sarah answered proudly. "Too much excitement. We've been making up silly songs and stories the whole way."

"The tale that never ends," Dawn said wearily, smiling. "Really never ends."

"No, it doesn't, Mama!" Sarah laughed.

"So, when did you leave?" Maria asked.

"At 7 a.m. we got the all-clear from General Jackson and hit the road. We hear that Snowden's mission was a complete success!"

"Complete success!" Sarah repeated, waving the light saber that sat by her legs. "We are ready to stir things up and make shit happen!"

"Language?" Maria countered.

"Exactly!" Sarah replied triumphantly.

"We miss you," Estrella said. "We're worried about you."

"It's true, my loves," Maria said. "Now that you've crossed over to the dark side, how are you feeling?"

Dawn replied. "I'm fine. Eager to be doing the work we've waited a long time for. Anxious to get the green light from the People's Council so we can start. But I'm worried about you— both of you."

"We're still meeting at the giant amphitheater, but we've moved Operation Johnny Healingseed out of the park to a resort near Guerneville," Maria explained. "Estrella will be safe. And the shield should hold. The chi workers are super focused on protecting the Council."

"Have you spoken with the other Governors?" Dawn asked. "Are they still considering capitulation to that maniac?"

"We're waiting for the larger group to share in the dialogue."

"Are you worried?"

"I can only do my best," Maria said.

"Which is pretty damned awesome, Mama!" Sarah said, jumping in.

The call ended soon after. Maria put her arm gently around her daughter. "Moments like these, I need to remind myself that we each have our own special work to do in this life. And that we can only control what happens here." She gently touched her heart.

They walked silently for a while, appreciating the cool morning air and bird song. Telepathically sharing their feelings of concern, they focused their fears about what might happen to an astral space a few feet above their heads. As they had practiced for years, next they visualized loving light and an unconditional acceptance of the wisdom of the Divine One Spirit, focusing the light to flood the ball of worry and lift the darkness just as the sun was evaporating the morning fog that had started their day.

"Ahh," Maria and Estrella sighed in unison, expressing deep relief that their fears had dissipated, passing away like a cloud in the wind. They continued their walk through the Greenway.

A few hours later, as Maria and Estrella drew closer to Armstrong Woods, their path converged with another Greenway path, and the crowd thickened. The chatter of excitement, both verbal and telepathic thoughts shared in the common space, invigorated the hikers. All were eager to assist in the liberation of their oppressed neighbors.

Estrella noticed the absence of foreign helpers from Central and South America in the crowd. As their pace slowed, she thought of her dear friend's Christmas visit. "Mama, you run the Council. How come Ana and her permaculture group could not join me for the prep work for the Great Expansion? They wanted to come. How come it was so easy for me to visit Ana in Guatemala, but when she comes here, she has to go through a crazy immigration routine that takes so long and makes her feel like a criminal?"

"Ah, security protocols, even here. How we wish we did not have to have them."

Estrella's complaint was not finished. "Of course, she was Activated, like half the kids in her country."

"More like a tenth, Estrella," Maria observed. "Some day we hope to join with all the peoples in our hemisphere, and even the world. But first we need to make sure that our own country works well, and this means restoring unity with our hostile neighbors to the east. That's what we're working so hard to accomplish."

"Still," Estrella said, not ready to let the issue go. "Ana *is* Activated, and we know it, but when she got to SFO to visit us before Christmas, they took like hours and hours and went through all her things and clothes and every inch of her body, every inch of it—like, grotesque! She was like, 'What kind of terrorist monster do you think I am?'"

"Of course, it is too hard. And of course you know it has nothing to do with your friend or how we feel about Guatemala. But there are sick unloved people who spend their time creating nanotech and biological weapons that they can hide on people coming to visit us, even on their clothes. Look what happened yesterday. The missiles found and targeted the National Institute of Healing because a permaculture expert from Brazil had unknowingly carried a secret nanotech locator device, attached to his shoelace, into the meeting with him."

"Sick-O!" Estrella said.

"But this will change soon," Maria promised. "That's part of our work today for the Grand Council. No more war!"

Maria held out her hands and chanted it louder. "No more war! Peace to all. Love to all. Life to all!"

Estrella proudly joined her mother in song, pumping her fist in the air as they danced. Their enthusiastic chant spread among the Grand Council pilgrims and their families. First dozens, then hundreds and thousands joined in.

Their song was so loud that it was minutes before anyone had noticed the fleet of B52 bombers circling overhead. The singing slowly stopped as everyone heard the concern over the hive mind and looked to the sky.

A series of booms was followed by large fireballs that burned outside the forcefield seven miles in the air, leaving black stains of burned chemicals.

Maria felt fear spreading through the now joyless crowd. She stepped on a seating log and announced, in a voice louder than any her daughter thought possible, "A reminder, from Spirit, of our mission and the challenges that we need to overcome."

Balancing her athletic body easily on the log, Maria continued, in her grateful minister's voice, "Thanks to the Goddess that we get to rise to the urgent work that we are here to do. And thanks to the chi defenders for protecting us from harm."

She pointed up the path. "An abundant, nourishing meal and a restorative forest walk awaits us all. Afterward, Johnny Healingseed workers will be shuttled to their meeting space, and at noon the People's Council will begin in the Amphitheater. Know that Spirit blesses us all. Every one of us."

*

After lunch, Maria left Estrella and walked meditatively through the ancient redwood forest toward the Amphitheater. The century-old pathway felt like a cool valley through the towering canopy of redwood trees. Like others heading for the Council, Maria walked in silence, focusing her breath on the beauty of the moment.

The 1,000 members of the People's Council had been chosen in a special national election following the nation's founding in January, 2028. The Council included many of the elected officials from the three states that comprised the new Pacific nation, as well as indigenous tribal leaders, mayors, county supervisors and council members. It also included community leaders of all backgrounds and ages, from 14 to 108. One thing they all had in common: None had had an interest in holding elected office prior to their Activation.

The Activation of 100 million citizens had transformed both the nature of government and the nature of the people who ran for elected office. Gone were the days when a will to power, megalomania or greed motivated those who sought election. "We the People" took on new meaning as the role of government was transformed from a system in which elected representatives served only those who funded their elections to one in which the facilitation of the common good became the only objective. Political office had become an interim vocation for those with useful expertise like organic farming, climate sequestration and organizational science.

Each of the 1,000 men and women joining Maria in the People's Council had been chosen by their Regional Council of 100 representatives for their capacity and willingness to serve. In turn, each regional representative had been selected by their local community, often by consensus, during public forums, with all citizens over the age of 7 participating. Because an authentic enjoyment of engaging with strangers was a prerequisite for the job, candidates were typically extroverted. When opposed, they ran for office with an open mind, no attachment to the outcome of their election and a willingness to assist the winning candidate.

Maria arrived at the expansive opening of the Redwood Amphitheater a few minutes before noon. She observed a few dozen plant keepers, men and women whose job was to communicate with and protect the flora and fauna in Armstrong Woods Park. The plant keepers were busy sanctifying the space, some burning sage and other herbs while others meditated. All wore their hair in dreadlocks or long and wild, and they were barefoot with leather-like feet. Their sinewy bodies were either naked and covered in dried mud, like aboriginal New Guineans, or covered with coarse beige-colored hemp robes with wide hoods.

Because of the mission of the day's People's Council, Maria had made sure the plant keepers of Armstrong Woods had been advised well in advance of the meeting. The trees needed to be prepared to accommodate many more people than usual, and the animals and birds were to be made aware of the unique gathering as well.

As they completed the psychic clearing and holding of the sacred space, the minds of the plant keepers focused on all that grew there. Maria knew it would be disrespectful and unhelpful to interrupt their immersive journey with her telepathic thoughts. She focused her energy on joining the wavelength of the tree spirits and, as the spiritual leader of her people, intuited her way to her chosen place near the Ancient Witness.

The Ancient Witness, the black petrified remnant of a tree near the edge of the clearing, stood scarcely 20 feet high with a bramble of sinewy tentacles reaching in all directions. Above it towered a canopy of 300-foot redwoods, standing in a ring like a circle of gigantic elders.

The Ancient Witness had stood in its place since before the first human being or coastal redwood had arrived. At first glance, it seemed no different from the fire-scarred remnant of any small tree. Native people and then modern visitors gave it no notice, instead paying attention to the majestic old-growth forest surrounding it.

The eldest plant keeper, a shriveled mystic known as Yanni, stirred from her meditation, lifted her face from where it rested against the ground near the base of the Ancient Witness and waved Maria over. Yanni smelled of the moist earth. Her dark dreadlocks flowed over the ground around her, touching vines that reached from nearby trees to connect with her.

Yanni was a hermaphrodite; her wrinkled mud-caked skin revealed small woman's breasts, and both male and female sex organs. Legendary among plant keepers across the western states, Yanni never spoke, but her presence felt as powerful as a great redwood. It was rumored she had been born there, of the trees themselves.

Maria took a deep breath and sat close to the Ancient Witness, as Yanni nestled her legs and arms around Maria's back. Yanni drew the cool thin vines from her dreadlocks and wrapped them slowly around Maria's shoulders, letting the plants taste her skin.

Maria stared into what felt like the angular head of a petrified black skeleton. Her eyes moved along its body, stopping at the complex knots that seemed to connect every joint.

Welcome human sister, she heard. *We have been waiting for you.*

Maria memory-travelled to 2020, when she first discovered the Ancient Witness, shortly after her first Activation. She had been in the middle of a solo vision quest with magic mushrooms, spending a summer afternoon among the towering redwoods in the park. The psilocybin's powerful capacity to help her feel part of nature had expanded with the opening of her Oneness gene. As she rested her cheek against the redwood bark of a massive tree, she felt a transspecies connection that she would never have believed possible.

On that day, she first heard the call of the Ancient Witness as she noticed the petrified tree nearby. A vision filled her mind, of the plant species revealing their medicines to more and more people, reaching out with magic mushrooms, ayahuasca, cannabis, peyote and hundreds of other natural substances to help heal the insanity of the human species before all life on Earth was wiped out.

Now, 14 years later, she was reconnecting with the Ancient Witness and the plant species to ask for even more help. She looked deeper at the Ancient Witness. There, in a dozen knots, she saw human faces looking back at her.

The faces flowed in and out of the tree knots. The first she saw with clarity was a 16th century Florentine-period artist, Da Vinci himself, she intuited, wearing a velvet cap with a feather in it. Nearby was a grinning, toothless, wise-looking Asian woman of 80 or 90 who looked thrilled to meet her gaze. Each time Maria constructed a clear image and felt who was present, the tree knot would reshape itself into another face. These long-dead human spirits, Maria felt, were taking turns as they again experienced the world of the living through the Ancient Witness, and, she realized, through the knots in countless millions of other silent trees.

Maria felt the presence and support of the other 1,000 representatives of the People's Council, as they joined her in silent meditation around the Redwood Amphitheater.

"Oh Ancient Witness," Maria said, in a voice so powerful it could be heard by everyone in the circle as it carried to the top of the canopy of massive redwoods above them. "On behalf of our human species, I come first to ask forgiveness for the destruction that we have brought to this blessed planet that we share with you, for the disrespect of Gaia's land, for the logging of your majestic trees, and for the poisoning of our nurturing earth and flowing waters."

A thousand voices spoke in perfect unison. "Forgive us, oh Ancient One."

A deep, reverent silence, like a steady, gentle breeze, came from the east and cascaded through the tree tops. They swayed slightly, then glowed as they offered forgiveness.

"On behalf of all human beings," Maria continued, "we come to you this day to request your help. We ask, you that were here first, you that have persevered and survived millions of years through ice and fire, to help us in our struggle today as we arise to prevent the extinction of all life on the abundant planet that we all share. Please aid us and the plant workers among us that you have called to be part of our mission to spread the bounty of your precious food and your abundant medicines to those in need."

"Help us, oh Ancient One, we humbly beg you," a thousand voices echoed.

Maria continued: "In return for this request, we offer our sacred promise to live our future in harmony with the abundant nature that Great Spirit has blessed this planet with, to act as sacred guardians, not destroyers, of the abundance that you share with us."

The words "This we swear" resounded through the amphitheater.

As they opened their eyes to a sky of brilliant blue and their senses to an air fragrant with the moist life of the forest, the members of the People's Council telepathically shared an awareness of a luminous glow that emanated from the tall redwood trees around them. At that moment, hundreds of crows, hawks, owls, doves, blue jays and song birds filled the surrounding trees and let forth a symphony of bird calls, volunteering their participation. These were followed by howls of packs of dogs, coyotes and wolves, and then the screeches of fox, squirrels and wildcats.

Bright sunshine warmed Council members as they basked in the power of their interspecies alliance.

The magic of the moment was interrupted by a series of massive fireballs directly above them. The hive mind filled with Council members expressing concern. Some noted the fleet of emergency vehicles standing by, ready to deal with fires, while others questioned the wisdom of remaining gathered in a place where their presence had been detected. A few expressed a sense of panic and asked that the Council put an end to the danger by acquiescing to President Trump's terms of surrender.

Gazing upward, Council members watched as the fireballs smashed against the force field, penetrating to a second layer of the protective shield. Maria offered a collective prayer for the power of the chi workers to resist. As though in defiance, the blasts erupted even more rapidly than before and penetrated the third and final layer of the protective shield five miles in the air.

A chilling sense of panic swept through the hive mind as a missile whistled through the force field and plummeted down in their direction. Some Council members jumped to their feet, but Maria knew it would be a matter of seconds before impact. Unless …

Maria instantly offered a new prayer through the hive mind and it spread in the hearts of the thousand council members assembled. "Oh Ancient Witness, protect us all."

A glow above the circle of redwoods grew in its luminosity and expanded outward, ever higher, until it reached a thousand feet in the air. There it met the incoming missile, which was deflected slightly by the ring of light and sent howling over a nearby hill into the empty Bullfrog Pond campground.

The missile exploded in a thunderous fireball in a field near the campground. Sirens from fire trucks and the hum of helicopters filled the air. But the Council members were unharmed. As they looked skyward, they noticed the barrage of missiles had slowed, and the first level force field was once again resisting the attacks.

Maria felt a sense of relief, while hearing the chatter of those around her. She spoke loudly at first, causing the Council members to quiet down and return to their focus.

"We thank Gaia, the Ancient Witness, and our friends that grow for your help here today. Fellow members of the People's

Council: Let us begin the work that we have come so far, and risked so much, to accomplish. Gaia herself is with us on our urgent mission. Let us move forward with our plan, today! You have all read the recommendation to proceed from the Strategic Intelligence Committee, and you have heard President Trump's terms for surrender. I now open the floor to debate."

For the next five hours, representatives spoke passionately of their hopes, concerns and strategies. Some questioned the capacity of their untested Army of Love. Others, including governors Murray and Wu, wondered whether a negotiation to pay the ransom fee but not surrender might satisfy Trump. They pointed out that the treasury of the United Peoples of America ran a significant surplus. They might pay the initial fee and raise a dedicated tax for the monthly payments.

Most Council Members agreed that time was running out on their defensive force field. There was consensus that the Great Expansion would have to happen rapidly to be effective. But even after repeated polling and pooling of the hive mind, for the first time since the People's Council was formed, there was no consensus on rejecting Trump's proposal and approving the plan. Nor was there consensus among the five-member Governing Council about what to do next.

Maria, with Winona LaDuke's help and the support of fellow governors Wu and Murray, proposed a solution. They would delay the decision one more day and support the expansion plan only if the Council of Mystics, through its first-ever Grand Summoning process with Spirit herself, received a clear signal that their efforts would succeed.

If there was no clear sign from Spirit the following day, they decided, they would postpone the Expansion plan and negotiate a counteroffer with Trump.

Maria and her daughter didn't get home until close to midnight. She tucked Estrella into bed and, exhausted, found her first free moment since the attack to call her wife.

Dawn was appalled by the news of the Council's indecision. "Haven't they read the intelligence reports?" she asked incredulously. "Trump does not negotiate. He has plans to kill every leader in our country and our families, including every person on that Council, and to literally hang our bodies from light posts."

"I reminded the Council of this," Maria replied. "But a number of our elected sisters and brothers believe they must maintain peace, regardless of its cost. They cannot deal with feeling responsible for the deaths of so many others."

"I am concerned for you," Dawn said. "I am sure you read the intel that Homeland Security has other nanotech trackers on our leaders and may target your meeting tomorrow. It's not safe."

"Very little is these days."

Dawn smiled with resignation. "Tomorrow is a big day. You need to sleep. Rest knowing that nobody on this green Earth is more likely to make this work out than you, my love."

"I can visualize, I can pray, I can speak, I can sing, I can love, I can do my best," Maria reflected. "Beyond that, it is out of my control. May Spirit bless our sacred effort as we live and die, doing the work we are here to do."

Chapter 12: Advertorial

Thursday, May 4,2034
9:00 a.m. Mountain Time
Patriot News Headquarters
Colorado Springs, Colorado
Trump's United Enterprises of America

Thursday morning and only 9 a.m., but Winston's head already ached as he sat down for yet another Patriot News editorial meeting with top management.

In previous years, Winston had thought of himself as indispensable. Patriot News relied on technology that he created and, for a while, even deferred to his editorial input for user-created videos and news.

But, Winston realized with dread, circumstances had changed. When the TV1.com personalized video-newscast system he'd created was first sold to Patriot News, it required either he or Rex send the daily broadcasts that soon became mandatory for all citizens to watch. That was amended in 2031 to also allow Scoop and Gerbers to take Winston's place. Nobody was indispensable, he thought. Any Citizen, even affluent 1%-ers like him, could be murdered whenever an oligarch that employed them decided they were not doing their job well enough.

Winston knew that if Rex could have evaded paying him the remainder of his buyout contract, he might have found an excuse to murder him years ago. But because Winston's ex-wife worked as an attorney for a huge corporation owned by a different oligarch in Denver, she had the legal power upon his death, as executor of his estate on behalf of their children, to get the courts to enforce TV1's buyout arrangement. It gave Winston a small sense of comfort knowing that he wasn't worth more to Rex dead than alive.

But Tuesday morning's encounter highlighted the growing insanity of his boss and increased Winston's sense that he could not survive much longer.

This growing fear was somehow diminished when he recalled the curiously reassuring voice he had heard twice earlier in the week. *'Wait for us,"* the voice had promised. *"We are coming. Thursday."*

Her words, Winston thought, were inexplicably specific, down to the day. Yet it was obviously impossible for anyone to ever be rescued from his violent, security-obsessed country. Even a managerial Patriot like himself needed the approval of the oligarch who owned his corporation to travel outside Trump's United Enterprises of America. Just searching for information about border areas or emigration had caused colleagues to suddenly be disappeared.

The meanderings of Winston's mind stopped when he heard Rex call his name. "Smith," his boss commanded, "let's get started with the news segment of the Citizen broadcast!"

Winston stood to narrate the short news segments as they appeared on the hovering video screen. "Tomorrow's broadcast," he explained, "starts with Pharma Cure's advertorial turn for the weekly mandatory vaccine rotation, defending against the deadly Norwegian flu. This one is safe for infants and seniors, so Pharma Cure's blood port-ready snap-on vaccine will arrive for all 50 million citizens via Patriot Mail delivery on Friday morning. We'll let citizens know that $80 per dose will be debited from their checking accounts at Patriot Bank, and that they have until Saturday morning's broadcast check-in to take their vaccine. This will be followed by the Health Minister's explanation about the necessity of herd immunity from another deadly flu. As well as the standard warning about the need to protect everyone from lethal communicable diseases that originate from biological terrorists, most probably from the separatist nation along the Pacific."

"Motherfuckers!" Scoop yelled.

Winston did his best to look appreciative. He realized that Scoop manufactured his anger not only for their boss, Rex, but for those monitoring the room on behalf of the White House.

Producing news segments for the four rotating pharmaceutical oligarchs who controlled all the nation's drugs and vaccines was becoming increasingly upsetting for Winston. This was the seventh flu vaccine in less than five months of 2034. The segment was followed by an ad for expensive pills to counteract the potentially lethal impact of a flu that people had been vaccinated against—and charged for—in February. He longed for the days when dog, cat, child prodigy and jackass videos were his most annoying distractions.

Winston gritted his teeth, forced an outward smile and continued. After the pharma advertorial came footage of the top reality show in the country. "The next paid advertorial segment," Winston said, "is for Patriot Entertainment, announcing the four semifinalists for the 'Human Hunt.'"

The reality show segment appeared on the video screen, featuring finalist photos of hardened men with sharpshooter rifles dressed in camouflage. Each had "25 kills" below his name, next to 25 tiny figures with X's over their bodies. Flashing letters announced "$1 MILLION PRIZE" as highlights from past hunts played. The backdrop, the Yellowstone Hunting Preserve, had once been a massive national park; it was now privatized as an expensive hunting destination for billionaires. Debtors who participated as "prey" each received a thousand-dollar reward to feed their families in slave labor camps. The segment reminded viewers that of the hundreds of prey who started, only 50 young debtors remained alive. These had become experts at camouflage, hiding, stealth and survival. Any prey who managed to survive through the final rounds of the season's competition was promised $10,000, a release from all debts, a job with Patriot Entertainment, and a place to live outside the labor camps. Nobody, Winston knew, had ever survived a TV season to collect his bounty.

Dawkins followed Winston's presentation with a slideshow featuring advertiser logos and revenue figures for the Thursday and Sunday mandatory Citizen broadcast. "There's big news to report this week, Mr. Rex," Dawkins said enthusiastically. "This week's International Society of Laser Combat Knights championship competition in Denver has brought with it the first international advertisers we've had on our networks since our country pulled out of the Olympics and World Cup four years ago."

Winston wore an inscrutable poker face while he silently reflected on language in the age of Trump. Trump's United Enterprises of America did not "pull out" of the Olympics and World Cup competitions. In 2030, Winston recalled, his country had been banned from the events, at the same time that it was banned from every other international organization and association.

The eviction of the T.U.E.A. from all world sporting events followed a relentless series of C.I.A. and Special Forces-directed assassinations and bombings of athletes and officials representing the United Peoples of America. Within months of the Pacific states' secession, trained killers had joined the ranks of every T.U.E.A. sports team, diplomatic mission and trade association to kill "enemy traitors" from the United Peoples of America on whichever nation's battleground they were found.

In 2030, after the World Court labelled Trump's United Enterprises of America a terrorist nation, every country except for the Soviet Union and allied oligarch-controlled puppet states in the Middle East and Africa, banned the T.U.E.A. from international events and competitions.

During the four years since then, laser combat, a sport that originated in the United States, was the only competition that contenders from modern democracies still participated in with the T.U.E.A., provided the events happened outside of their countries in one of the dozen allied dictatorships that maintained relations with the Trump Regime.

The Denver-based championship match culminating that afternoon was a rare opportunity for the pariah nation to receive more than a thousand foreign athletes and their families, as well as media representing 40 nations in Europe, Asia and Latin America. The White House had ordered roads repaved, hotels restored and city parks beautified. Coal plants and smelting operations for 50 miles around Denver were shuttered for two weeks to minimize air pollution.

Dawkins continued his rosy report. "Patriot News has the exclusive broadcast rights for all laser combat matches. Under the strict supervision of Mr. Gerbers and Scoop Walters, international media is focused on censor-approved stories of the competition results, interviews with their country's top contenders and Denver's thriving economy in the age of President for Life Donald Jesus Trump."

Winston nodded approvingly to mask the shock he felt each time he heard Trump's revised middle name. It had been nearly a decade since the president had changed it, to coincide with the renaming of the country, but Winston was still unable to get used to it.

"Starting last weekend," Dawkins said pleasantly, "Winston's TV1.com crew has been doing a great job of covering and streaming all laser combat matches, which have become the most internationally viewed Patriot News videos of all time. Ad buys have poured in from 30 countries. Incremental revenue for these videos alone, after commissions, has exceeded $90 million, nearly all of which is profit."

For the first time in many months, Rex applauded Winston's work. "Good job, Smith. You said it would be big, and you were right. I guess you have an inside track on this one, eh?"

Winston nodded and said, "As you've proudly heard me say in the past, sir, my son Abc is the U.E.A champion for the 11- to 12-year age group. He loves the sport. Been playing since he was three. He has a decent chance of clinching the gold medal at this afternoon's match in the Mile High Stadium."

"Well, I see you have some surprises up your sleeve that do not include terrorist protesters," Gerbers said, with a wry smile. "Laser combat is, as you know, the most patriotic of sports. Many of the young rising stars in our officer corps for Homeland Security, the Marines and the Special Forces had previously excelled as laser combat knights. Has this boy of yours considered a career in the military?"

"It's still early for that," Winston said sheepishly. "He still needs to get through 7th grade. But he's already earned enough endorsements to pay for his equipment and some of his college, too."

"If he wins the world title this afternoon," Gerbers offered, "I might put in a good word for him at West Point."

Shoot me first, you Gestapo bastard, Winston thought. But he smiled appreciatively and said, "Thank you, Mr. Gerbers."

"This competition has drawn the attention of President for Life Donald Trump himself," Gerbers explained. "One of his grandsons, who enjoys laser combat, will be in the audience tomorrow. In total we expect more than 20 Super Patriots and their families to attend the event, as well as hundreds of top military brass who have enjoyed the sport. Security will be very tight."

"As planned, I will be heading to the stadium right after this meeting to manage the coverage and the web video distribution," Winston explained. "Meanwhile, we have a lead news segment for web release tonight that profiles America's top competitors in each of the six age groups."

"You are on a roll, Smith!" Rex exclaimed. The incremental ad report had given him 90 million reasons to be in a good mood.

Chapter 13: The New World

Thursday, May 4, 2034
8:00 a.m. Pacific Time
Bodega Bay, California
The United Peoples of America

As she completed her sunrise meditation overlooking the Pacific Ocean from Bodega Head, Maria breathed deeply and drew solace from the tranquility of the still water. She had slept only five hours, but starting her day with deep meditation always provided her with the energy she needed to face the challenges ahead. It was hard for her to imagine that at any moment, the calming pink sky, kissed by the sunrise to the east, would again endure the relentless fireball attacks of deadly missiles. Hard to imagine that just 500 miles to the east, garrisons of soldiers were waking and preparing their deadly weapons for the green light to assault and murder hundreds of thousands of peace-loving fellow humans.

Hard to imagine, Maria thought, but impossible to ignore.

She took a long reflective walk to the Spud Point marina, where workers were loading food and tableware onto a large electric boat. Two other ships were also being prepared for the 50-minute voyage to the Sonoma Coast Ocean Farm Community Center 10 miles offshore. One was a kelp-harvesting vessel, and the other, which Maria headed to, was a ferry to carry 77 distinguished passengers who comprised her country's highly revered Council of Mystics.

Because she lived closer to the marina than the other participants, Maria was the first to arrive on the ferry, except for the pilot Leah Tarkan, who was busy preparing the vessel. Maria introduced herself to Leah, an introverted young woman who laughed shyly and rejected telepathic communication. Leah's resistance made clear to Maria that she was not interested in sharing back stories, even with the spiritual leader of her nation.

Or perhaps, Maria thought to herself, *especially* with the spiritual leader of her nation. She thought of herself as an accessible facilitator, not an intimidating presence, but even in an Activated state of Oneness, everyone was different. Maria knew that some found her overwhelmingly intense and avoided the telepathic sharing that was customary upon meeting another person.

That was okay, Maria reflected. It took all kinds to make the world the Garden of Eden. *Vive la différence*, she thought with appreciation.

"Is there anything I can do to help?" she asked.

"You wouldn't know where to begin," Leah replied, then caught her sarcasm and quickly added, before heading below deck, "No, thank you."

Maria sat on an outdoor bench watching seagulls dive for fish. She observed that like many of the two million Pacific Americans living offshore, Leah had branded the skin around one eye and much of her body with the flowing Polynesian tattoos of the multiethnic Water Tribe. Even through layers of warm fleece jackets, Maria could see her pilot's muscular shoulders and arms were characteristic of the swimmers, surfers, kayakers, kite boarders, canoers, sailors and fisher folk who chose to live and work upon the ocean.

It was a compliment to the new economy of the United Peoples of America, Maria reflected, that their nation could pay living wages to so many sea-loving citizens. She and Dawn often laughed at the innovative systems that had emerged in the new nation they had helped to create, in spite of the fact that neither of them possessed any technical or organizational skills.

The ocean farms were one of their proudest examples of this. The world's leading scientists had long agreed that manmade carbon in the atmosphere had brought about the warmest weather in human history. This had triggered unprecedented weather catastrophes and the near annihilation of life in the ocean, while placing the human species at the precipice of extinction.

Millions of concerned citizens and thousands of organizations around the world had worked tirelessly to align the public policy of their governments with the desperate needs of the planet. During the first part of the 21st century, they won the commitment of every modern nation on Earth to begin the effort to reverse carbon emissions from the burning of fossil fuels.

In the United States, slow progress came to a screeching halt with the 2016 election of Donald Trump. His administration dismantled all attempts at regulating carbon emissions, while banning decades of climate science as "fake news."

While most advanced countries in the world embraced the solar revolution and breakthroughs in battery-storage technology, the United States by Trump's second term had veered hard in the opposite direction. Major federal agencies fell like dominos as the budget lines for the Environmental Protection Agency and the Occupational Safety and Health Administration vanished.

Trump bragged that his administration would create jobs by "unshackling industry." America quickly became the world leader in toxic extraction industries such as gold and coal mining, hazardous chemical manufacturing and pesticide-reliant agriculture. Abandoning job safety and pollution controls allowed mines, coal plants, refineries and chemical factories to operate at the lowest cost on the planet. The only new jobs created were replacement positions for the tens of thousands of workers without health insurance who died each year from cancer, poisons, pesticides and mining accidents.

In the decade that preceded the birth of their Pacific nation, the western states used what legal powers they had to regulate pollution and counter climate change.

Big changes began happening in California, Maria reflected, with the 2022 gubernatorial election of the woman who was to become a political mother of their new nation, Winona LaDuke.

A few years after being Activated by Maria and Dawn in the summer of 2021, Winona and her grassroots network of earth activists began the most important environmental movement of the 21st century. They joined with scientists at the Woods Hole Oceanography Institute to create an evolutionary effort called the Campaign to Rescue Our Planet, internationally known as CROP.

Maria turned from the water and looked at the ferry's gangplank just as Winona LaDuke stepped on board. Maria waved her over and gave thanks to Spirit for the magical synchronicity of her life.

Winona was followed on board by the youngest member of the Council of Mystics, a 12-year old Hawaiian-born girl named Tenzin Keawe. Tenzin was better known as Her Holiness the 15th Dalai Lama, the first female Dalai Lama and the reincarnation of Tenzin Gyatso, who died peacefully in 2020.

Winona and Tenzin made their way to Maria, who welcomed them with hugs and an invitation to talk about the urgent matters of the day before the ship departed.

While the ferry filled with exotic passengers, some clad in simple monks' robes, others in ornate minister cloaks, Maria shared the importance of the Great Summoning and the challenge of how to balance the meeting with the potential danger of more missile attacks.

Tenzin was undeterred. "We all heard the intelligence report, and, judging from the full attendance we see around us, we all made the same decision. I spent yesterday in consultation with the leading astrologers of the Tibetan-Mongolian tradition. Today is an auspicious day, and our effort is destined to end in success. Not with ease, but with success."

"Thank you, young sister," Maria said, tuning in to those around her. "The sense I hear is that many of our 77 Council of Mystics have gone through a similar evaluation process and have found that the stars are indeed aligned with the Great Expansion."

"If only it were that simple," Winona said. "You and I, Maria, carry the authority of the People's Council, which has asked for guidance from the Great Spirit itself before we can proceed. Hence the Great Summoning, the first of its kind in generations. It is a bold undertaking, and the outcome has not yet been ordained."

"This is true," Maria agreed soberly. "This is true."

As the benches around them filled with other spiritual leaders and shamans, Maria, Winona and Tenzin made room and greeted them warmly.

Other crew members, including the top-ranking Admiral of the sea farm fleet, Michael Van den Berg, joined Leah. They helped pull in mooring ropes and backed the ferry into the bay as the ship departed.

The supply boat and seaweed harvesting ship led the ferry slowly from the bay into the Pacific Ocean. Admiral Van den Berg, a tall, thin 62-year-old ex-New Englander with a grey goatee and slight Boston accent, was eager to act as a tour guide for his distinguished passengers. It was not every day that he had two of the five members of the Pacific nation's Governing Council on his ship.

Michael spoke with passion and force, his voice rising above the purr of the electric engine and the sound of the rough waves slapping against the ship. "Good morning, friends," he bellowed. "My name is Michael Van den Berg, but my colleagues in our world of ocean farming call me Admiral Seaweed!"

Michael waited for laughs, but none came, so he settled for a few smiles and continued. "This voyage will take just under an hour. I will be your tour guide to the magnificent world of ocean farming, habitat restoration and carbon sequestration. How many of you have been on an ocean farm before?"

Maria and Winona were the only two to raise their hands.

"Excellent!" Michael said, eager to teach newcomers. "As you might know, the vision of our Campaign to Rescue Our Planet, which Governor LaDuke and I helped start in 2023, was to create an expansive array of floating kelp and fish restoration farms across the Pacific. They use the inexhaustible resource of photosynthesis to suck carbon out of the air and sequester it in underwater vegetation."

"Imagine," Michael said excitedly, "that, within one decade, by building such ocean farms across just 1% of the Pacific between California and Australia all of the excess carbon created by humans since the dawn of the Industrial Revolution can be removed from the atmosphere, and the future of life on Earth will be saved! Instead of diminishing the amount of carbon-sequestering vegetation in the world by cutting down or burning the rain forests, as humanity has done for centuries, our Campaign creates new forests under the sea."

"Today, we are a quarter of the way to making that vision a reality. At this moment, PVC pipes a half mile below us are using deep sea currents to bring cooler, more plankton-rich water to the surface. The small structure you see to the south of our boat right now houses the work crew for this sea farm. For every 50 ocean farms, there is one floating community center similar to the Sonoma Coast Community Center where we are heading now."

"These new ocean farms," Michael continued with pride, "require no fresh water or arable land. They provide easily harvestable bounties of ultra-nutritious, pesticide-free food for people, livestock and marine life, all the while drawing down massive quantities of carbon from the atmosphere. Our country has now built more than 100,000 of these farms, creating the most effective climate-change solution of all time. It has been financed by more than $200 billion worth of green bonds and your carbon taxes. Our kelp habitats have restored marine life to levels not seen in centuries. The lead boat to our north is a kelp harvester," Michael observed, pointing out to sea. "It rides—"

Michael halted mid-sentence as the repeated thud sounds of explosions seven miles above them drew everyone's eyes to the sky. Fireball after fireball, only a few seconds apart, burst into mushroom flames in the same spot.

"Perhaps we should all head below deck," Michael advised, but he was unable to stop looking at the sky. The fireballs penetrated one force field, then another layer a mile closer, then a third.

Maria was impressed by the composure of the spiritual mystics around her as she waited for those in front of her to file calmly through the narrow doorway to the deck below.

Suddenly she heard a loud whistling object speed toward the water. A moment later, a powerful explosion demolished the harvest boat 200 feet ahead of them. This was followed almost instantly by a second explosion, this one with a fireball that spread and consumed everything in its path. As she watched the supply boat burst into flames, the force of the fireball swept her, and everyone else on the deck of the ferry, into the freezing waters of the Pacific Ocean.

Chapter 14 One True Church

Thursday, May 4, 2034
10:00 a.m. Mountain Time
Patriot News Headquarters
Colorado Springs, Colorado
Trump's United Enterprises of America

As the Patriot News Citizen broadcast meeting entered its second hour, Winston helped himself to a third cup of coffee to keep from falling asleep or slitting his wrists. As he guided the other executives through the news and video segments that his team had prepared about the international laser combat competition, which he would get to cover once the meeting ended, he struggled to dredge up an appearance of enthusiasm around his work and suppress what he really felt: despair, disgust, fear and helplessness.

Scoop Walters felt no such reticence as he followed Winston's presentation with glee. "Now for my favorite part," he proclaimed, grinning at Rex. "This Sunday's Weekly Hate is going to focus not on the Islamic terrorists, or their spies and traitors among us, but on the terrorists on our West Coast, the Pacific States of Betrayal. Mr. Gerbers' team and I have been working on this new segment for three weeks. It also leads seamlessly into our biggest solicitation campaign of the year, with paid advertorial segments following the weekly hate all the way through July 4th."

The video monitors lit up with the flag of the United Peoples of America, which depicted colorful hands circling a photo of planet Earth. The flag immediately caught ablaze and disintegrated into flame and ash. This was followed by footage of emaciated cadavers, including many children, being stacked in a mass grave and covered by a bulldozer. Winston recognized the stock footage from one of the enormous labor camps in Texas.

The voiceover of an enraged President Trump played over visuals of death and deprivation. "This is the living hell the Great Betrayal has brought to the suffering people of the traitorous Pacific States. The lunatic communist leaders of this so-called nation hide behind an illegal wall that provides a safe haven to their deadly terrorist forces. Like the cowards they are, they hide from our military behind a force field while their army of terrorists and killer drones sneak across the border to sabotage our thriving industry and massacre American families, men, women and many, many children. Now, tell me, patriotic citizens and Patriots of the greatest nation on Earth, what should we do about these traitors?"

The visual shifted to Trump, who held his hand cupped to his ear, while crazed voices in his studio screamed at the top of their lungs: "KILL THEM! KILL THEM!"

"I can barely hear you! Is that the best you can do? Remember, our great freedom, the freedom of the freest people who ever lived on this planet, is not free. It must be defended by every citizen, by every Patriot. Now, tell me, what should we do with these murderous terrorists? Remember, we are listening. We are always listening."

As Trump held his hand to his ears and grinned approvingly, the off-screen screams of "KILL THEM!" were deafening. Winston dreaded this part of the mandatory viewing broadcast. At noon every Sunday, he had to stand before his two-way video screen at home and scream his hatred at whatever target the government was singling out as the enemy. On alternating weekends, when Winston's children stayed with him, they had to join him in summoning a convincing degree of anger. Every citizen's screams of "patriotic hate" were monitored and analyzed. Tales of entire families disappearing for the felony crime of "unexplained absences" or "traitorous comments" circulated widely.

With "Kill Them" screams providing an audio track, the presentation flashed the names of a half-dozen rural counties in Trump's United Enterprises of America, each dissolving into images of civilian carnage. Winston noticed that the ethnic clothing on the dead bodies contradicted the premise that this took place on American soil; he recognized it as the B-roll of newscasts showing successful American attacks in the decade-long, Saudi-financed Pakistan War. But Winston had learned to keep his mouth shut about such things. Even constructive feedback was regarded by Scoop—and Rex—as seditious.

After the yelling died down, Trump's voiceover continued, pivoting to what Winston had accurately guessed would wind up as a national shakedown. Trump's began with a softer, explanatory tone, while the screen shifted to images of starving, ragged Americans standing in endless food lines, each with the name of a different state expanding across the screen: "California, Oregon, Washington."

Trump said, "Patriotic Americans can never forgive the cowardly, murderous, traitorous leaders for their Great Betrayal. But we are a generous people, a Christian people. We can forgive—and we can help—the victims trapped in that hellhole."

"We can provide food and medicine, warm clothing and diapers to these impoverished people, enslaved by their crooked leaders in what was once the beautiful state of California. This is what Christians do: We care. That's why today I am announcing that for the next two months, I will personally match, dollar for dollar, every contribution made by citizens and Patriots for our continuing Pacific Victims' Relief Fund. Even if it's $100 million, $200 million, $500 million: Every dollar you give gets matched by a dollar from the Trump Family Foundation."

"My fellow Americans: The need here is so great, the deprivation so vast that Minister Shepherd Powers himself, the leader of America's One True Church, the only patriotic and legal church we have during these troubled times, wants to address you directly."

Looking into the hovering screen, Winston concentrated on keeping a compliant and obedient face, while thinking: *There is no depth to which this man will not sink.* Winston knew not a single dollar was ever matched. In fact, no donation went unstolen. The Pacific Victims' Relief Fund, along with the Trump Family Foundation and the video that Patriot News had been paid to produce, were all fictions of marketing. Just well-polished lures to attract contributions.

The video jumped to an image of Shepherd Powers, a tall, tanned and handsome man in a finely tailored business suit standing at a pulpit. In the background, a flag of Trump's United Enterprises of America filled a gigantic wall. A large statue of Christ crucified on a cross stood 10 feet behind Powers, and hovering between this and the flag were the words in 3-D letters: "ONE TRUE CHURCH."

Minister Powers spoke with the charismatic conviction of the megachurch TV evangelist that he had been before partnering with the Trump family. "You know, my sons and daughters, that ours is a nation of winners. But you also know what our gospel values almost as much as wealth, almost as much as the phenomenal success that free men in our country enjoy. Our gospel also values Christian charity. And this means charity even for losers."

"That's why today I am joining our God-blessed great leader, the biggest winner of all time, President for Life Donald Trump, in asking each of you to reach deep into your soul to determine how much money you have available for this important campaign. Yes, we know that many of the losers suffering and dying of starvation and disease in that traitorous nation to the west were the very haters and losers who deserted our country in time of need, the very traitors who aided in the betrayal of our great nation. In one sense, they are getting exactly what they deserve."

"And yet, Christ teaches us to care for the needy: We, the people, must personally bear the burden of the poor on our shoulders. Now, children of God, nowhere in the Bible does it say that our government has a responsibility to care for the needy. Instead, it commands us to render unto Caesar what is Caesar's. Trump's United Enterprises of America is not, thank the Lord, a communistic state. It is no longer a state that exists to redistribute the hard-earned money of the winners to losers and debtors unwilling to pull their own weight. And our One True Church is not like those communistic religious cults of yesteryear, like the Mormons and Catholics and Jews and Muslims and Buddhists, the loser religions that, thankfully, have been relegated to the dustbins of American history—and to the prison camps where their unrepentant followers have deservedly been sent to die."

"No, it is not our Great Government that is called upon by God Almighty to contribute funding for the Pacific Victims' Relief Fund. Instead it is each of us, each true Christian follower of the One True Church, you and me. We are called. Our enlightened leader, President for Life Donald Jesus Trump, has just made the most generous offer ever made. And we, like our president, we must each of us answer this call. Listen, my children, to this call …"

The video cut to a ragged, starving white man and woman, each holding a child in their arms, all four of them appearing to be on the verge of death. They stood near a line that formed around a truck marked in fresh paint "Pacific Victims' Relief Fund" from which volunteers handed hungry-looking people trays of wholesome prepared food and three-gallon containers of water. Two menacing-looking guards with assault rifles and riot gear stood near the relief line beneath the flag of the United Peoples of America.

The woman holding her infant spoke to the camera. "We believed the lies and moved to California in 2027, never dreaming of the misery we would find here. The commissars and their cronies keep all the good food to themselves, and most of the people here are starving. Without the Pacific Victims' Relief Fund, without the generosity of American Christians, all of us will die. Our lives, and the lives of millions like us, depend on your generosity. Please, please give." The toddler in her arms weakly joined her, begging, "Please save us."

The video returned to the sincere face of Minister Shepherd Powers. "Remember those words: 'Please save us.' From the mouths of babes," he said solemnly. He paused, looked downward for a few seconds of silence and wiped a tear from his eye. "How could this not touch our true Christian hearts? I am personally pledging $1 million to this effort. Praise the Lord! My donation, like your generous gifts, will be matched by the munificence of our great and blessed leader, President for Life Donald Jesus Trump. God bless President Donald Jesus Trump, God bless the One True Church, and God bless Trump's United Enterprises of America!"

Once that segment was over, the words REPEAT expanded across the screen, followed by the words, one screen at a time: **God bless President Donald Jesus Trump! God bless the One True Church! God bless Trump's United Enterprises**

of America! The video ended with the text advisory, "Each adult in your household may now authorize a donation on your monitor, which will be conveniently deducted from your checking account or next paycheck."

"Good wrap-up," Rex concluded. "Great job on the suffering victims, Scoop! What grave did you dig them out of?"

"We stayed local," Scoop answered, proudly. "Mulligan's West Colorado mining operation, the third largest labor camp in the state. We shot it with our most trustworthy team. It's amazing what starving debtors will say for the promise of a few weeks of food rations," he said, laughing.

"Did you leave any ... loose ends?" Rex asked, glancing at Gerbers.

"Dead men tell no tales, sir. Dead and buried, everyone in the scene except our security agents and production crew."

"Attaboy, Scoop, attaboy," Rex said, rising to pat him on the back before leaving. "You were born for this work!"

Chapter 15: The Eternal One

Thursday, May 4, 2034
3:00 p.m. Pacific Time
Sonoma Coast Ocean Farm Community
Pacific Ocean off the Coast of California
The United Peoples of America

"I don't know whether I can do this alone," Maria confided to Dawn's hologram. Her hair was still wet; her eyes stung with smoke and a residue of salt and grime felt caked into every pore of her skin. An extra-large Ocean Tribe sweatshirt draped her body and some stranger's worn out sweatpants were cinched with a rope around her waist. "How I wish you were with me!"

"I wish I were there too, my love. I would hold you and warm you and brush the goop out of your natty hair." Dawn's 3-D image looked at her wife with adoring eyes.

"Ugh," Maria replied, the trace of a smile piercing her dark mood. She sipped from a hot mug of restorative tea. "It is a testament to the ocean rescue teams that everyone on the ferry was saved, and a tribute to human evolution that every member of our Council of Mystics, even those with painful burns and bruises, are willing to proceed with the Great Summoning."

"We have no choice," Dawn said simply.

They stopped to listen to a telepathic group chat with General Jackson and Admiral Van den Berg, then resumed their private verbal conversation.

"We were fortunate that the missile hit the lead boat and not ours," Maria reflected, shaking her head in sorrow, "though that means 59 more deaths. The chi workers are focusing enormous energies to protect us. But the missiles just don't stop. Now they are right above us. It sounds like a slow machine gun that never stops shooting. It would drive a lesser woman crazy!"

"One more reason I am glad that I didn't marry a lesser woman." Dawn laughed, then added with concern, "They know where you are."

"We all know what needs to happen today," Maria said. "It is part of our prophecy, written in the stars. We have faith that the Eternal One will support us."

Both women breathed deeply for a few minutes, attuning to the Oneness they shared and the One Spirit they prayed to.

"So much depends upon this Council of Misfits," Maria reflected.

"You said misfits," Dawn said, smiling.

"Did I?" Maria replied innocently, then smiled back. "You should see what we look like."

Maria heard a telepathic call to gather, said her farewell, and followed the hive mind directions through the sprawling vessel of walkways and decks. As she walked, Maria understood why people referred to ocean farms as the world's largest "virtual" boats. Most of the boat was an array of thick horizontal ropes that floated, secured to pontoons, two-kilometer-square, just below the surface. Thousands of smaller ropes with kelp and shellfish growing on them formed a vertical comb 100 feet below the surface, creating a food oasis for sea creatures.

Maria arrived at the end of the walkway and marveled at the design of the theater-in-the-round that made the Sonoma Coast Community Center the best offshore meeting space in the

Pacific. Attached to a small dormitory building, a four-foot-wide swim platform formed a perfect circle 50 meters wide out to sea. A series of small pontoons secured the circular walkway and provided mooring for participants who arrived by kayak, canoe, paddleboard, wind kite, or sailboat. In the center of the circular walkway, a floating stage pontoon was large enough to accommodate a panel of speakers, a band or a theatrical company.

Maria took her place standing in the circle, alongside the 76 other members of the Council of Mystics. A few were in wheelchairs, others leaned on canes. Maria noted with sadness how very different they looked than earlier in the day. Gone were the ornate robes, beads, headpieces, and sacred jewelry that had delighted her eyes at the beginning of their ill-fated ferry ride. Now their bodies seemed vulnerable and frail, clad in blankets, towels, spare clothing and bandages.

"As we begin the Great Summoning," Maria announced, "we evoke our ancestors and the ancestors of all living beings on this planet."

They joined in the Four Directions song, with young Tenzin ringing the Tibetan bells for their ending "One" chant.

The Council of Mystics then checked in, silently, to the hive mind of their sacred circle.

Maria felt grateful that advanced practitioners of more than a dozen different religions were present. All had been Activated and all had been born in the caul, giving them the mystical vision and disposition to facilitate the Great Summoning. Maria reflected inwardly that although they had had little food and no rest since their ship's hull splintered and sank from the shock waves of the nearby missile, every woman and man present was focused on their mission, not food or comfort. She thought how fortunate they were that this was a group accustomed to fasting and to focusing.

Maria began the meeting by addressing the hive mind thoughts that might interfere with their sacred mission. "Yes, they know we are here, and they hope to kill us," she acknowledged, hearing, as they all did, the dull thuds of missiles striking the force field overhead. "They want us to be afraid. Their power over others depends upon their ability to manipulate fear. Our power is the power to love all beings, to feel our Oneness, and in that feeling, to be fearless."

Winona spoke next. "My ancestors the Ojibwe people have a prophecy that speaks of a time during the seventh fire when our people will have a choice between two paths. The first path is well-worn and scorched. The second path is new and green." She paused before adding somberly, "Our work today is to summon the One Great Spirit to help lead all people along the path that is new and green."

Tenzin spoke next, solemn and clear, expressing the intention of their scared circle. "We summon the Eternal One," she said.

The Council of visionaries opened their arms in silence and tuned their hearts to the One Spirit within and without. They waited.

After half an hour, the stillness in the large circle of water in front of them was broken by 11 bottlenose dolphins, as they popped their noses curiously in the air. Then the heads of a dozen more dolphins broke the surface, looking purposefully at the people around them. The dolphins made progressively smaller rings around those standing on the platform, and their numbers kept increasing. Within 10 minutes, their numbers were exactly 77, each one swimming near the feet of one of the assembled mystics.

Maria felt telepathic messages from the hive mind that the 77 shared. *Stoop down to touch the dolphins*, she heard.

Almost as one, the 77 council members squatted on the edge of the narrow gangway and reached their hands, palms open and low, over the sea water in front of them. The bottlenose dolphins appeared and each placed its nose, for just two seconds, into each person's outstretched hands.

Maria felt a jolt of energy surge through her body as her dolphin, whose name was Soo-elle, touched her and connected across species. Time stopped as a telepathic exchange between her and the dolphin reached her mind and heart. It felt different, Maria observed, than the exchange of experiences she shared with humans upon Activation or Reconnection. She was thrilled to feel, through Soo-elle, the swift sensual movement in water and the shared identity of the pod. But Maria was attuned to something else happening to her and her 76 fellow mystics.

The dolphin was psychically inspecting her aura and even her emotional history. Maria felt more naked and vulnerable than she had ever felt before, as though she were baring her very soul, as though Soo-elle was examining deep secrets and scars and memories that Maria herself could not access.

When the inspection ended, Maria felt a warm, ecstatic pulse pass through her body, and a sense of **Yes.** Soo-elle and the other 76 dolphins flipped playfully back toward the center of the circle. They swam in elegant loops, as though they were security guards around the partially submerged pontoon.

Suddenly, the water near the pontoon stage began to move. What started as a ripple quickly turned into waves as a massive creature broke the surface.

Maria felt her skin tingle. This was the moment they had prayed for. *The Eternal One has arrived*, the hive mind buzzed. Impulsively, Maria bowed her head.

The form of a sea turtle five times larger than ever witnessed by any human emerged slowly from the water. Its battered shell was the size of a small house, and its protruding neck was an intricate web of deep wrinkles. Emerging from its home miles under the sea, The Eternal One, using the strength of its elephantine flippers, pulled its massive body onto the stage, causing the surface of the pontoon to drop into the Pacific.

The Eternal One looked upon Maria with large, kind eyes. She melted into a loving Oneness. Tears of ecstasy streamed down her face as Presence filled her soul.

Maria tried to speak, but her throat suddenly felt parched; no words emerged. This had never happened to her before.

The Eternal One waited patiently. There was no hurry. Maria felt the perfection of all experience.

When Tenzin spoke, it was not with her voice, but with the voice that some in the circle had last heard decades ago: the melodic, playful Indian-accented voice of Tenzin Gyatso, the 14th Dalai Lama.

"Oh Eternal Creator," Tenzin said. "On behalf of all living beings of this green Earth, and of our ancestors and those to come, we humbly ask for your support in this our time of greatest need."

The Eternal One's giant eyes looked intently at the young girl. Then it slowly moved its head with an almost imperceptible motion as it stared into each set of human eyes, wet with bliss,

and peered deeply into the soul of each of the 77 mystics
standing around the circle.

In the silence, they heard something moving slowly from
beneath the swim platform on which they stood. They did not
look down but could see the shimmering green kelp growing,
inches each second, onto the platform and around the bare feet
and legs of the people standing across the circle from them. The
moist snugness moved up their legs and over their midsection,
conveying a visceral awareness to each of them that the kelp
was enveloping their bodies. It grew over their arms and
covered their hands like mittens. It encompassed their necks,
then the back of their heads, and wrapped around their cheeks,
leaving only their mouths, nostrils and eyes open.

The 77 kelp-enveloped mystics felt a sense of deep presence
pouring into all the cells in their bodies. Those who had
suffered burns and cuts felt their skin pulsing and within
seconds, healing fully.

A paralyzing, all-encompassing stillness followed. The Council
members were unable to speak or move or even think, as
though they had been transported to a place beyond their
physical and mental states.

Tenzin felt her lips part and a powerful voice she had heard
only in vision dreams spoke through her to the assembled circle
of 77 mystics, shamans and spiritual leaders.

"Behold!" she proclaimed, looking to the sky.

The eyes of the Council of Mystics looked skyward. The
greatest barrage of Hellfire missiles ever unleashed had burst
open three layers of shields, and half a dozen missiles had slid
through the breach and were whistling toward them.

The gigantic turtle-like creature tilted its head upward to meet the missiles, then made a slight nod. The six missiles, and the four that followed them, instantly disintegrated and turned to dust. The force field glistened for a moment and the breach was repaired.

The Eternal One lowered its head to the area in the ocean where the missile dust had fallen. As the 77 members of the Council of Mystics watched, a glorious rainbow arched its way from the spot where the missile dust had fallen to the enormous shell of the ancient being at the center of their circle.

The spiritual masters had journeyed into mystical realms before, yet each remained paralyzed in wonder.

Time expanded into the richness of the miracle.

Finally, Presence expressed itself simultaneously in their 77 minds: ***Spirit is with you.***

With that, the Eternal One blinked its ancient all-seeing eyes, slowly nodded its head two times, and dived back into the ocean.

Chapter 16: The Tiger

Thursday May 4, 2034
4:00 p.m. Mountain Time
Mile High Stadium
Denver, Colorado
Trump's United Enterprises of America

Winston was relieved to spend Thursday afternoon away from the office and his rabid boss. After winding up work interviews with the league director, sports pundits, top contenders and their families from other countries, Winston settled into his V.I.P. seat, ready to enjoy watching his agile younger son, Abraham, compete in the annual championship of the International Society of Laser Combat Knights.

But Winston did not relax for long. A top-ranked contender called the Siberian Shark was closing out the quarter round finals by mercilessly demolishing another boy in the ring. Winston was close enough to the playing field that he could hear the sound of the Shark's laser sword smash across his opponent's back. The savage blow ended the match, and its recipient, a swarthy competitor from Sweden, had to be carried off the combat court in a stretcher to a waiting ambulance.

Winston's heart raced as he worried about what such a blow would do to his smaller-boned 12-year-old son if he ended up, as sports pundits had predicted, facing Mikhail Ivanoff, the notorious Siberian Shark, in the finals for the 11- to 12-year-old age group.

As the referee held Ivanoff's mighty arm in the air to announce his victory, a group of 100 cheering fans jumped from their V.I.P. seats, blew air horns and chanted the name of their homeland: "SOVIET! SOVIET! SOVIET!"

The Siberian Shark's father, whom Winston had interviewed for Patriot News that afternoon, was Nikolai Ivanoff, one of the most powerful oligarchs and Putin cronies in the restored Soviet Empire. Ivanoff controlled the mineral mining for much of Siberia. He was so wealthy that he had rented out the entire top floor of Denver's most exclusive hotel for the week of the tournament and arrived from Novosibirsk in a private jet large enough to bring him, his son Mikhail and an entourage of more than 100 friends, relatives, bodyguards and cronies.

On cue, the Siberian fans illuminated their holographic shark helmets. Suddenly, the closing-in-for-the-kill music of the film *Jaws* blared from stereo speakers attached to their helmets, while life-sized 3-D holograms of four-foot-wide jaws brimming with dagger-like teeth were projected over the cluster of cheering heads. It looked to the 40,000 other spectators in the stadium like a horror movie was being filmed in the front rows.

The M.C.'s announcements about the next round could barely be heard over the din of Mikhail Ivanoff's fans. They were egged on by their employer, Nikolai Ivanoff, who swigged and shared vodka while surrounded by a few friends and family members, as well as a dozen hulking bodyguards.

Winston had heard of the thuggish antics of the Siberian Shark's fans from a Patriot News camera crew. They told him a possible local news story on Ivanoff had been killed at Rex's orders, after a rumored payout of a million dollars and a call from the White House.

Rex's hush money, Winston learned, was the smaller of Ivanoff's payoffs from his mob's wild night. At a popular local sports bar, the Siberian Shark's oligarch father had led his entourage into a drunken fistfight with a group of off-duty Homeland Security troopers. The fight left the bar in tatters, and when the dust cleared, four troopers were dead and more than a dozen hospitalized.

Looking to his side at a section of seats closest to the court, Winston saw the top security area of American oligarch families, Homeland Security officers and high-ranking military brass. A half-dozen rows, with heavily armed guards standing at either end, hosted a sea of dark uniforms, adorned with insignias and medals. Winston could make out Homeland Security General Francis Baron, Commander of the Western Forces, sitting next to White House Communications Director Joseph Gerbers. Like the other military officers surrounding them, the two men sat companionably, as though nothing had happened the previous night.

Money before country should be their motto, Winston thought.

Ivanoff was said to have paid out a total of $10 million in American cash, which, he had bragged, depleted just one of the three currency-packed duffel bags he'd brought with him. As usual, rumors followed the payoff. It was assumed that most of the money went directly to the top. That would have been to General Baron, to be shared, as with all payoffs, with President Trump himself. But a portion of the payout also trickled down to the victims' families for medical and funeral expenses.

That part was unusual, Winston reflected cynically, thinking of Monday's massacre in the cornfield.

Also unusual was Mikhail Ivanoff's claim to be 12 years old. Winston's Patriot News team had interviewed the kid earlier in the day, along with dozens of other top-ranked competitors. Mikhail's voice was as deep as a man's, and he was already shaving. At 230 pounds and a height of 6-feet 3-inches, he was easily the largest "12-year-old" Winston had ever met.

Although the International Society of Laser Combat Knights checked the passports of participants to verify ages, Winston knew that for Mikhail's powerful father, falsifying a birth certificate and passport could have easily been managed by the assistant of his assistant. Winston was convinced the boy was a ringer, but he also knew there was nothing he could do about it.

As the Shark fans finally took their seats, the M.C. introduced the next quarter-round finalist competition between Winston's son Abraham and the top 12-year-old contender from China. Winston watched with pride as his boy entered the combat field. He tried to find comfort in the thought that Abe had gone undefeated for the past two years, with only minor injuries. Abe, Winston knew, had the sixth sense of a giant cat, which is why he was known as the Colorado Tiger.

After bowing to greet his opponent, Abe lit his supple Kevlar combat armor into bold tiger stripes, holographic fur and tail, and a tiger helmet and visor that sealed and protected every inch of his small, well-muscled 5-foot 2-inch body.

Winston stood to applaud his son and felt proud when more than a thousand local Colorado fans also rose from their seats in welcome. Many of them were dressed in stylish tiger hoodies, a big seller from Abe's sponsor, Combat Armor, Inc.

The sponsorship money, $200,000 over two years, seemed like a lot when it was offered, but it barely managed to pay for the expensive high-tech armor, laser swords, training and martial arts classes for his son.

Abe's fans recited a favorite call that Winston had heard in regional matches, "Go Tee-gray, T.U.E.A., Go Tee-gray, all the way! Go Tee-gray, T.U.E.A., Go Tee-gray, all the way!"

Abe's opponent was known as the Cobra. The hilt of his illuminated 3-foot-long laser combat sword took the form of fangs, and his armor hologram was a standing snake. The Cobra had turned out his own sizable fan base of countrymen. Hundreds of them cheered and waved Chinese flags, while projecting holograms of cobra jaws clamping shut.

As the first round began, the Cobra did a standing backflip against the high trampoline wall behind him then flew straight at the Tiger's midsection like an arrow.

Abe fell on his back to avoid the Cobra's extended sword. Like lightning, he extended his own laser sword upward just in time to miss the Cobra's helmeted head and swiftly swipe his vulnerable underbelly.

The digital receptors in the armor registered a major hit. The enormous overhead video monitor/scoreboards registered 340 points for the Tiger and Abe's fans rose to cheer him.

The points were based on the damage that a real sword would have done to a real body. At 340 points, the sophisticated armor suit calculated that the wound would have gravely wounded its recipient, but not quite incapacitated him.

The Cobra returned with a series of spins and kicks so fast they seemed a blur to Winston. The Tiger got caught in the Cobra's signature move, a high kick immediately followed by a low sword stab from the opposite direction. The scoreboard registered 250 points for the Cobra. His fans flew to their feet, extending their fang hologram and yelling, "Cobra Strike! Cobra Strike!"

The score was fairly close as the third three-minute round neared to a close. Then the Tiger came in for the kill.

Abraham fell to the ground with a high kick to the side of his head from the Cobra but he suddenly rolled, sprang up, and in midair, neatly swiped his laser sword across the Cobra's neck.

The receptors in the Cobra's armor registered the power and placement of the blow and concluded that a real sword would have sliced his head off.

In giant letters, **DECAPITATION!** flashed across the overhead monitors, followed by **TIGER WINS!**

The audience jumped to its feet in a standing ovation.

Winston joined them, then walked out to check in with his camera crew and get a snack. He returned to his seat eager to rest his legs. The next few matches passed by in a blur as he felt his deep fatigue from the long workday and the week's restless nights.

He hadn't slept more than a few hours since staring down the barrel of Rex's loaded Glock pistol Tuesday. Winston knew that as an oligarch, Rex could murder him or any of his other employees at any moment.

A fantasy about quitting his job was interrupted by the entrance of his ex-wife Suzanne, their 15-year-old son, Robert, and Rick, Suzanne's second husband. They all wore tiger hoodies. Winston rose, shook Rick's hand and smiled politely as the group edged past him into the seats Winston had reserved next to him.

He noticed with satisfaction that his older son, at six feet, stood an inch taller than him. He also had a clear complexion and sported a trendy haircut. *When did all that happen?* he wondered.

"You're in time for the semi-finals," Winston told them. "Abie was amazing in his last match—decapitation in the third round."

"He's gonna kick ass today," Robert said, sitting between his mother and Winston.

Winston thought wistfully of the days, not too many years ago, when his sons hugged him when they met. But they didn't even let their mother kiss them these days.

He was genuinely pleased that Suzanne had found a supportive second husband and a well-employed stepfather for their children. Both Rick and Suzanne worked as attorneys for oligarch Ted Collingsworth's Patriot Minerals Corps in Denver. The company, in partnership with Trump, had a monopoly on all mining in the Southwest United States, making his wife's boss one of the top ten percent wealthiest oligarchs.

No matter what Rex did to him, Winston knew Suzanne, who he'd made sure was granted full custody, would retain the beautiful home she'd received in their divorce and keep their children safe under the legal protection of her powerful employer.

Glancing sideways, Winston noticed that Rick held Suzanne's hand, something he'd stopped doing well before the last four sexless years of their marriage. He reflected on something their couple's therapist had said to him about their split: *You have a part in it, too.* Indeed, he reflected, the stress of running a media company in the age of Trump and then the integration of his company into Patriot News had distracted him from holding hands, or doing anything else with Suzanne.

He'd come to accept that their breakup was more about him than her. And the proof of that was sitting next to him: Suzanne had a healthy relationship with somebody else. But with the exception of the occasional sexbot rental, Winston had not felt the desire to go on a second date since his divorce five years earlier.

Prescribed anti-depressant drugs did nothing to ease the cause of his anxiety, which was a job he hated and the omnipresent fear of his boss' boot smashing down on his head. And worst of all was the self-recrimination of having brought this world of misery upon himself.

Winston played the tired movie again in his memory. What choice had he had but to stay in Colorado and sell his company to Patriot News? *How was I to know,* he asked himself for the 100th time as he sat in the stadium, *that it would all turn to shit?*

"Dad!" Robert said, shaking his head with teen disgust, poking his arm to tell him to stand up. "Where *are* you? You can at least *pretend* to pay attention," Robert hissed. "You are so fucken out to lunch!"

"What have I told you about cursing in public?" Winston replied. Robert just rolled his eyes.

Winston *was* embarrassed. When the M.C. announced the contestants' final championship round for the 11- to 12-year-old category, he realized he had daydreamed through the Shark's semi-final victory round. After a short break, the Siberian Shark would face off against Abe.

Winston was all in for the big final match.

As the competitors entered the court and lit up their armor, the cluster of Siberian Shark fans unleashed a new amplifier for their *Jaws* movie theme song that drowned out Winston, his family and thousands of Americans chanting "Go Tee-gray, T.U.E.A.! Go Tee-gray, all the way!"

The competitors bowed to one another, lit their armor, and the contest began. Winston tried not to let his worry show at how impossibly larger the Siberian Shark was than his son. Robert noticed Winston gnawing on his clenched thumb until the skin wore thin. "Dad, Abie has this. He's beaten bigger opponents before."

Winston gave him a serious look. He did not have to mask his worry. "No, he hasn't," he said.

"Welllll," Robert answered, with a rare look of respect into his father's face. "*Almost* as big as the Siberian Shark."

"Nowhere near, Robbie, and you know it. That boy is no boy."

"And our boy Abe is no ordinary boy!" Robert countered. "My money's on him."

"So is mine," Winston said, turning back to the match with a prayer in his heart. "So is mine."

The first round was hard for Winston to watch. The Colorado Tiger moved like a swift feline to avoid the Siberian Shark, who managed to chase him down twice and pound his smaller opponent's defensive sword. Every time Abe came close for an offensive blow, he was met with a frenzy of powerful parries from Mikhail Ivanoff that shut down his attack.

The second round started with little score, as neither fighter managed to inflict more than a few small virtual flesh wounds on his adversary. Both boys tried using the trampoline walls followed by tumbles to standing attacks, only to be repelled with expert sword defenses when they arrived.

The Shark had reserved an effective trick that Winston had not seen before. Mikhail started with a relentless attack of hammering blows. As Abe was busy defending and ducking, the Shark saw his opportunity and suddenly grabbed Abe's sword hand and pulled it toward him in one deft judo motion.

To avoid having his arm snapped in two, Abe dropped his sword and dived forward, extending his body as far as he could lunge, then tumbling toward the trampoline wall.

The Shark rushed toward his unprotected adversary to finish him off, placing his giant body between the Tiger and his fallen blade. The Russian fans erupted from their seats, lit their shark helmet holograms into the air and blasted the *Jaws* song. In giant letters, the scoreboard monitors screamed:
***TIGER DISARMED**.*

Winston gulped. Abe was already losing by 200 points. The Shark had only to land a clear blow to win the match.

Abe bounced high off the wall, over the Shark's head, and landed on his feet in an Aikido pose. The Shark thrust his sword forward and missed. He swiped down to where the Tiger had moved to and missed again. It was as though Abe knew where the next blow would fall a millisecond before it started, as if he could read the Shark's instincts before they turned into actions.

The Shark took a vicious swipe at his opponent's head, but Abe deftly pivoted on his heels and backed away just enough to avoid it by a quarter inch. The Tiger pivoted forward on one foot and followed with a perfectly timed karate kick into the spinning back of the Shark, knocking him flat onto the mat and scoring 150 points. The Russian knight instinctively focused on retaining his sword and rolled into a defensive ground posture, forgetting for a second that his adversary was swordless.

It was the opening Abe had been working for. He did a double roll to where his fallen sword laid and scooped it up, then jumped to a standing position.

TIGER RE-ARMED! the monitors flashed.

A guttural tiger roar came from Abe's mouth as he attacked in a flurry of sword spins so fast the Shark found himself on the defensive, sustaining a virtual slash on his side. As the second round ended, the Colorado Tiger had caught up and the match score was tied.

The competitors rested and drank water while a slick commercial for the Tiger's sponsor, Combat Armor, Inc., played on the overhead monitor. It featured Abe and other American champions fighting in their high-tech holographic suits.

Robert waved to his brother on the bench. When Abe made eye contact, Winston joined Suzanne and Rick in waving back and giving the thumbs up sign.

"Where does he get that ferocity?" Winston quipped to his ex-wife nearby. "Not from my side of the family."

"We're lucky he saves it for the laser combat court," Robert interjected, pleased to see his divorced parents talking to one another.

As the final round began, Mikhail rushed forward immediately, swinging his sword relentlessly and using his superior strength to put Abe on the defensive. The Russian champion had embarrassed himself during the last round by failing to dispatch an unarmed fighter half his size, and he was determined to bring an International Laser Combat gold medal back to his homeland.

Abe worked hard to find an opening, but it was all he could do to keep a step ahead of his longer-limbed foe, whose martial arts skills and swordsmanship matched his own. He glanced at the scoreboard and could see that he had only one minute of the final three-minute round remaining, and that he was down by 50 points.

Acting a bit more fatigued than he was, the Colorado Tiger tempted his opponent by wandering closer than seemed prudent. Thinking he had a championship-winning opportunity, the Siberian made a faux thrust and lunge, which turned into a sudden elbow to the back of his opponent's head.

Abe had sensed the blow as it was coming, but allowed it to connect just hard enough to fool his opponent into thinking it had knocked him out. He fell hard to the mat, face first. Believing he was about to end the match with a decapitation of the famous Colorado Tiger, The Siberian Shark swung a wide arc downward.

At the last moment, the Tiger rolled slightly to one side, and the Shark's sword barely scraped his neck. In the same movement, Abe's legs darted out in a scissor move, tripping the Shark just as his body was following through on what he'd thought was his lethal blow.

Mikhail started falling backward as Abe, finishing his body roll, sprung to his feet and thrust his sword against his opponent's heart. ***LETHAL BLOW!*** appeared on the monitor, with a 1,000-point bonus added to the Tiger's score.

Robert screamed to his dad, "I *told* you Abe would do it, I told you. YES!" Robert pumped a fist in the air. He gave Winston a powerful high five and, without protest, received a big hug from his father.

Words flashed on the overhead screen as the M.C. held Abe's tiger-striped fist in the air and announced, "The champion of the International society of Laser Combat Knights for the 11- to 12-age group, Tiger Abraham Smith!"

Huge words flashed across the stadium's overhead monitors.

CHAMPION!!!!

THE COLORADO TIGER

ABRAHAM SMITH

TEE-GRAY T.U.E.A. ALL THE WAY!

Next came a replay of the ten seconds leading up to the final blow, followed by the words:

THE TIGER WINS WITH EYES IN THE BACK OF HIS HEAD!

And then, mixed with images of the waving flag, a looped series of celebratory text:

WORLD CHAMPION!

FROM TRUMP'S UNITED ENTERPRISES OF AMERICA!

ABRAHAM SMITH!

THE SIXTH SENSE KID!

Winston waited in his seat for the crowd to thin out as the announcer promoted Friday's final round competition for the 13-14, 15-16, 17-18 year-old age groups. He realized how exposed he felt witnessing his son's sixth-sense powers on display for the world to see. He found himself consumed by deep worry about what the military might do with such unusual abilities—and those who possessed them.

"Da-ad. Earth to Dad!" Robert sang, snapping his fingers in front of Winston's face. "I think we can now head in to congratulate my famous brother."

The crowd had thinned sufficiently to allow Winston and Robert, with Suzanne and Rick following right behind, to head through the combat court into the locker room area. For the first time since he could remember, Winton was glad to see a swarm of uniformed Homeland Security heading in the same direction he was. The Siberian Shark's oligarch father, he reflected, might not find the second-place silver medal sufficient to redress the pain of watching his son's defeat by a boy half his size.

Once inside, Winston relaxed with Robert in the meeting space off the locker area, watching from across the room as Abe's burly coach carried the exhausted fighter around on his shoulders. The champion had illuminated his tiger hologram and, sporting a huge gold medal around his neck, took selfies with friends, fans, oligarch kids, laser knights and military officers.

Joseph Gerbers, wearing a formal Homeland Security military officer's uniform with even more medals and insignias than usual, edged his way across the room with a video crew and a handful of troopers. They cleared supporters away for a few minutes to shoot a video of Abe for national news.

Gerbers beamed as he presented the young champion with an honorary flag pin and personal congratulations from President Donald Jesus Trump himself.

Chapter 17: Abraham

Thursday May 4, 2034
7:00 p.m. Mountain Time
Hana Restaurant
Denver, Colorado
Trump's United Enterprises of America

Abe's celebration dinner, at Denver's best Japanese restaurant, had delighted him, not just because sushi was his favorite food, but because his father and mother had sat next to one another and nobody had argued. To top it off, on their ride home his brother Robert, for the first time ever, had relinquished his usual spot next to Winston in the front seat to let Abe ride shotgun.

Abe reflected on what an awesome day it had been. And tomorrow, he sensed, could be just as good.

"Something big is about to happen to you, Dad. Real soon," Abe said. "The biggest thing ever."

"That's saying a lot," Winston quipped, his driver's seat pivoted to face his 12-year-old son. He noticed Abe's piercing bright cat eyes, an emerald green, just like his mother's, that seemed even greener than before. "Something big just happened to *you*, Mr. International Champion!"

Abe smiled modestly. "Not big in a prize-winning way, or a business way," he continued. "Big in another way ... in a spiritual way."

Winston nodded politely, unconvinced.

"It won't be an easy thing," Abe warned. "But you won't die. It's your destiny, so don't worry about it, because you won't die."

"That's reassuring," said Winston sarcastically. He had a low opinion of people who talked about destiny as though it were preordained. "And how do you know all this? Does your laser sword double as a crystal ball?"

Abe ignored this. "You know, Dad. It came to me in a vision," he continued with sincerity.

"Taking drugs at an early age, are we?" Winston quipped.

"Dad, listen to us for a change!" Robert chimed in loudly from the back seat.

"Oh, now it's *us*?" Winston said, pivoting in his seat to face the back, where Robert's body was tugging at his seat belt harness as he half stood up in defiance.

"Abie had this same vision the last three nights in a row," Robert yelled. "That has NEVER happened before!'

This is getting out of control, Winston thought, aware of his frustration that the celebratory mood was deflating. He thought back to Abe's unusual birth. It was hard to believe that it was more than 12 years ago—November 11, 2021—when the boy suddenly dropped out of his mother's body.

He and Suzanne had expected something completely different, something similar to the challenging 20-hour process of pushing, waiting, leaning and yelling that had brought Robert into their lives three years before. Instead, this time their doula had not even taken off her coat at the Boulder natural childbirth center when Suzanne screamed, grabbed the wall for balance and went into labor. Winston and their doula rushed to Suzanne's side, took hold of her trembling hands and immediately heard liquid gush onto the floor. Seconds later, the doula had fallen to her knees and caught the infant before his head hit the ground.

Abraham's head was still enveloped in the bubble of embryonic membrane that had protected it in the womb. The doula had been helping deliver babies for more than 30 years, but she told them she'd never seen a child born with the amniotic sac still over its mouth, nose, ears and eyes. Fortunately, she had read of this remote possibility and knew what to do. With soft fingers she parted the fluid from the newborn's eyes and mouth before the baby suffocated. Then she said a silent prayer.

Winston had never heard that the enveloping embryonic sac was called a "caul" until one week later, when a stranger arrived at his doorstep. It was Saturday morning, and Winston was expecting food deliveries for a family luncheon to honor Abraham's birth. The bell rang, and Winston was surprised to see a slender, intense-looking man standing in the doorway.

The man apologized for the interruption and said he had something important to tell Winston about his infant son. He asked for ten minutes. Winston stepped out onto the front porch. "My name is Dr. Timothy Simon," the man began. "I am a psychotherapist who has practiced in Boulder for the past 40 years."

"What does this have to do with us?' Winston asked impatiently. Thirty people would be arriving in three hours, and he had a lot to do.

"I heard about your son's unusual birth from a client who works at the birthing center," Simon explained. "Like your son," Simon explained, "I, too, was born in the caul—the embryonic sac around my face, 62 years ago. The only person still living who knows this is my sister, and now you."

"Look Doctor Caul, whatever," Winston replied, irritated, stepping back toward the door. "I don't know what you're selling but—"

"Please bear with me for just two minutes," Simon continued, undeterred. "There is something special about being a caul bearer, something very different. It is said that Jesus was born in the caul, as well as the Buddha. And every Dalai Lama reincarnate. During the Spanish Inquisition, the church burned all babies born in this manner, believing they would grow up to be witches and warlocks."

"I'm not sure where this history lesson is going," Winston said, puzzled. "What does any of this have to do with my son?"

"Being born in the caul—it brings unusual abilities … unusual powers," the visitor said. "You see, for my entire life, I have been able to see things … without my eyes. When I was 5, I could watch my parents sleep ... as a spirit on their ceiling. And then there have been the dreams, the visions. Knowing just what would happen before it happened. Meetings. Accidents. Deaths."

"So," Winston stammered, "so you've come from nowhere to tell me that our son is going to have dreams that … that come true?"

"You are blessed with a son who will be very special. Cherish it. It is a rare gift. Take it from one who knows."

With that, the stranger clasped his hands together, bowed slightly, and walked off.

Winston never heard from him again.

Sitting in the car with his sons, Winston stared at the road ahead of him and considered what to say next. He thought of his ex-wife's advice in dealing with teenage rebellion: *Don't take it personally. Look at the cause of their anger. Listen and let them know you are listening. You are the adult. Breathe deep and de-escalate.*

He started over with Abe, this time with curiosity. "But I thought you regularly had these … premonition dreams?"

"They're visions, Dad, and I always have just one at a time," Abe replied. "This one was three nights in a row, clear as day from the mountain top."

"But your dreams don't always come true," Winston noted.

"Visions, Dad, not dreams. And they *do* always come true when they are clear like these were."

"Not all the time," Winston said evenly.

"*All* the time," Robert interjected from the back seat. "And you know it! Grandma Nancy and Grandpa David and those 25,000 other people in South Lake Tahoe, in the middle of the night firebomb attack. Abie told us the day before. You couldn't have forgotten that. He was six years old. Only six fucken years old!"

"Let's change the subject."

"Let's not!" Robert insisted scornfully. "Nobody knew it would happen. It had never happened before, even during the Civil War! Our own government, wiping out every man, woman and child in an American city—25,000 people—with thermobaric Hellfire missiles!"

"You think I want to talk about that right now?" Winston asked, feeling riled up again. "We are celebrating your brother's biggest win ever, and you are reminding me of my parent's tragic death and talking about something that you know you are not allowed to talk about!"

"Abie knew! How did he know?" Robert demanded. "And why do you keep calling it a tragedy. It was a massacre; a government massacre of its own peo—"

"Watch your tongue!" Winston yelled, jabbing a warning finger within inches of his son's face. "Everything is recorded. That includes this conversation!"

"Fuck them!" Robert shouted defiantly. "It's all about to change."

"Do not talk like that. You do not know what you're talking about, and you are not allowed to talk like that about our government."

"Dad, take the pus out of your ears and listen for the first time in your life." Robert nodded to his brother. "Abe, tell him."

"No turning back, Dad. It's already started."

"*What* are you talking about?" Winston demanded.

"That lady, the singer … I've heard her voice too. I know what happened Monday with the drones, and you being the only survivor."

Winston looked incredulously at his son and Abe stared right back.

"You're going to meet her soon. She's already in Colorado."

The auto driver announced, in a sleek woman's voice, "Five minutes to destination."

There was a minute of silence. "What else?" Winston asked.

"Two more things," Abe advised. "First, I am ready for this, Dad. I have been waiting most of my life for what is about to happen."

Winston stared at his son.

"It's true, Dad," Robert joined in. "Abie's ready, and so am I. We talked about it."

"Ready for what?"

"To do what it takes," Abe said. "To help her."

"To help who?" Winston asked.

"That lady whose voice you've been hearing."

"Du-uhhh," Robert added.

"How do you ... what's the second thing?"

"Don't freak out, Dad. But I'm going to help her rescue you."

"Rescue me? I am right here. I don't need any ..."

The car announced its arrival at Suzanne's home and pulled into the driveway. The outdoor lights came on as Winston and his sons stepped out.

Winston looked at Abe as the three of them walked to the back of the car to unload the large duffel bags filled with sports gear. *How could this be happening to my 12-year-old?* he wondered.

"This isn't from me, Dad," Abraham said, as though reading his mind. "It's not about me, and it's not about you; it's about *us*. It comes from where everything comes from, the divine source. We are all part of it. And we're all gonna be part of the change. Every one of us."

"Except me," Robert said, lightening the mood. "I'm gonna stay the same cause someone's gotta be an apathetic teenager."

"I appreciate you covering that base," Abe said, stretching to meet his brother's hand and elbow for a fast, intricate series of bumps and motions that comprised their secret handshake. "Bestie bro ever!"

"No, you are!" Robert laughed, completing the handshake.

It took all three of them to lug the bags of gear from the car to the front door.

"I love you and I'm proud of you," Winston said, setting down the gear and hugging his son.

For the first time in a year, Abe did not pull away, but hugged him back.

"I love you, Dad," he said. "And don't sweat it. We got this. All the bases covered. Even yours."

"Especially yours," Robert laughed, joining the hug jam.

Chapter 18: Crossroads

Thursday May 4, 2034
10:00 p.m. Mountain Time
Golden Gate Canyon State Park
30 miles west of Denver, Colorado
Trump's United Enterprises of America

A person wearing a huge grey full-body bunny suit and a tall top hat waved a yellow light stick to direct Winston's car to the pay booth. After handing over four crisp $100 bills to an attendant and having his car searched for stowaway gate crashers, Winston parked in a huge grassy field amidst a sea of other vehicles.

He stepped out of his Cadillac SUV, stretched his back, and took a deep breath. It was the freshest air he'd smelled since he had been to last year's Burning Man rave in the same location. It had taken less than an hour from the Denver suburb where he'd dropped his sons to get to the former state park. A few times each year, a well-connected event organizer rented a section of the park from his ex-wife's employer, Ted Collingsworth, who had privatized it for mineral mining with one enormous bribe to President Trump in 2027.

It was only 10 p.m., and it would take just an hour to get home, Winston calculated. He didn't need to be at work till 9 o'clock the next morning, so he could party as hard as he liked for at least three hours, or four if he met someone. He was jonesing to dance with wild abandon. All he needed were some drugs and a costume.

Opening the back of his car, Winston looked at the optical scan to unlock his safe box, then considered his choices. The clothes were the easy part. The hologram-aided Tiger hoodie he'd worn to the tournament would provide a basic foundation, made brilliant by his prized pair of tall, furry tiger boots with built-in springboards and a custom light set. He paused to narrow his drug choices from six Ecstasy brand legal pharmaceuticals in prescription containers down to two: RAVE89v2 or HOT328v7.

He thought about it for a moment and then chose the Rave option for its energy boost with manageable side effects. Turbocharged dance energy, not sex, was on the evening menu.

Winston popped two capsules out of the container and downed them both with a few swigs of water. It would be so good to dance out the horror of Monday's massacre, to forget the wretched, unchangeable past. To focus on the grooving vibrations of the moment and, afterward, on surviving in the future.

Survival is all that truly matters, he was thinking when a loud object suddenly smashed onto the roof of the car next to him, creating a THUNK sound so loud Winston involuntarily jumped back two feet in panic. His head spun around seeking the cause of the noise.

A smashed surveillance drone sputtered on the roof of the nearby car. A huge eagle perched over it, holding it still with its powerful claws while tugging out circuitry and chips with its razor-sharp beak as though they were the innards of its prey. The eagle twisted its head to confront Winston's eyes.

As the eagle's wide eyes glistened with intensity, the words *Welcome, we have been waiting for you* flowed assuredly into Winston's ears. He looked around for the source of the sound. It was the same delicious woman's voice he'd heard already three times that week. He spun around to find her, but once again was alone.

As he watched the eagle fly off, leaving behind a wreckage of steel and wires, Winston realized he was about to experience an unusual evening. He locked up his car safe, hit the illumination switches for his costume and headed down the forest service road toward the thumping music and pulsating lightshow.

As he walked on the bouncy party boots, Winston wondered: *Why would an eagle attack a drone and pick out its circuits? The eagle wasn't going to eat those wires? And why had an eagle downed a drone in the first place? Birds never attacked drones. And where did the eagle come from? They hadn't been seen here since half the park became an open pit mine. It makes no sense.*

The deafening music drowned out his thoughts as he entered the central dance area and started moving to the powerful beats. Winston made his way along the costumed crowd to where he could see springboard ravers like himself popping high above the heads of others.

The rave featured the popular DJ Star Power, whose signature booth, with brilliant rays of pulsating colors shooting out in all directions, floated from side to side in the air over the thousands of dancers. Star Power played a popular hit that kicked in with the Ecstasy as Winston's veins began to feel as though they'd burst.

Now he was ready to join the party. Winston's bounces increased in velocity with the energy around him. He admired the double flips and back spins of the younger, more acrobatic springers and was mesmerized by the near-naked professional go-go dancers, their bodies adorned with wild tattoos, floating above the dancefloor stages as they gyrated to the music.

*

Dawn stepped away from the small team of plant workers who had joined her convoy from California and found a quiet spot on a nearby hillside. It had been a busy day since arriving at the park. They had successfully tapped a well of clean groundwater and set up a filling station and a PVC pipe system to bring it closer to the Burning Man Party. A small irrigation drip was also set up. With the magical assistance of nature, the seeds had already grown into the herbs that their healers would need that night.

Without Gaia's assistance, their plan would be impossible, Dawn reflected gratefully. But everything seemed to be working out fine. Now they needed one last green light from the Council of Mystics.

Dawn rested for a few moments to calm herself and visualize a Yes! She laid down in a patch of tall grass and called Maria.

Her wife's face floated in a hologram above her. Dawn realized she was relieved just to see her alive. "What news, my love?" she asked anxiously.

Maria's face glowed. "It is hard to even speak of it," she said, awestruck. "We are good to go. The Eternal One itself has blessed our plan. The miracle is unfolding."

*

An hour had raced past in a blur when Winston became aware of a desperate need to rest and get some water. He reminded himself that he was not 25 years old anymore, and that at 50, pacing himself had become an essential element of partying without regret.

Winston handed a $100 bill to an attendant to access the V.I.P. area, grabbed two bottles of vitamin water and flopped down on a massive inflatable sofa. He gulped the first bottle, kicked up his legs and laid back.

He could feel his chest pounding. He recalled the danger of heart attacks from this iteration of party drugs and was grateful to be off the dancefloor—and to have chosen RAVE89v2 instead of the notoriously hazardous v1. He closed his eyes, focused on his breath, and in less than a minute had fallen asleep.

It was a short nap, just 20 minutes or so, but a lot happened in his sweet dreams. He woke slowly, trying to recall everything. There was a feeling of empowerment, of flying freely, untethered by fear of sudden violence, unworried about his boss, or having his hidden thoughts or true self discovered. How liberating it had seemed! The mysterious voice had appeared in the dream, too, the siren whose call he'd heard only a few hours earlier.

Winston sat up with some effort and tried to conjure what she had looked like in the dream. Nothing came to him. He gave up, looked out toward the crazy lights and began to summon the energy to return to the dancefloor.

And then he saw her. She was standing right outside the V.I.P. area, staring at him. Her lithe bikinied body was painted a robin's egg blue. She wore a white feather mask, glitter makeup and an impressive pair of white feather angel wings across her back. Despite her costume, Winston knew with 100 percent certainty that this was the woman of his dream, the siren whose voice had comforted him during the past week, and as he now saw her, his guardian angel.

Dawn Souljah smiled with a loving gaze and eyes that seemed to peer deep into his soul. Winston looked behind himself for a second, thinking she was probably looking at someone else she actually knew.

The blue angel nodded assuredly, then turned slightly and pointed in a direction up the road away from the dance area. With some effort, Winston pulled himself to his feet and headed out of the V.I.P. area to meet her, only to see her heading up the trail.

Winston quickly realized the blue angel was a fast walker. He followed the angel wings from 100 feet behind. Eager to catch up, he increased his pace along a forest service road up a long, steady hill. The music and lights faded behind him, so he switched on his tiger hologram to help light the way. Within ten minutes, they had passed a smaller cleared area with a large "Wilderness Stage" sign along the trail. Winston briefly noticed a few hundred people watching fire dancers and acrobats, but he did not stop to watch.

Winston followed Dawn for another half mile, at which point the gravel road flattened out and became a dirt road. He broke into a sprint to catch up. Just as he got within 20 feet of the blue angel, she cut off onto a tiny side trail through the bushes.

Winston found the narrow trail and followed it through the tall brush until he stumbled into a clearing where a small wood fire burned brightly, surrounding by hot, glowing stones.

A 20-something man dressed in a festive clown costume squatted near the fire. His long red hair fell loosely around a face adorned with white makeup, zany colored stripes, and a red clown nose. The clown was busy filling the largest, most intricate glass water pipe Winston had ever seen. The central area of the pipe had a deep chamber for water and ice, which was surrounded by a sphere of glass colored and imprinted to replicate the Earth. Around the planet was painted a circle of multi-colored hands clasped together. Winston realized it was the flag of the United Peoples of America.

How did they get this here? Winston wondered. Just being seen with the flag of the secessionist nation could get someone drone-blasted or disappeared, Winston thought as he looked around to see if this was some sort of entrapment or shakedown scheme.

Winston looked for Dawn, but she was not there. Instead, a grey-bearded, dark-skinned older man whose body was covered in an owl costume now stood next to the clown.

The man, whose face seemed familiar to Winston, opened his arms to offer a hug and said, "My old friend and collaborator, Winston Smith, at long last."

The voice provided a memory trigger. "Professor Flynn Washington!" Winston recalled with joy. He stepped forward impulsively and received a strong hug from Flynn's long arms.

Then a sense of worry surged through Winston's body. He pulled back and looked around suspiciously. There were only three of them around the fire. "What are you doing here?" he asked. He had never heard of anyone visiting from the United Peoples of America since secession, much less that country's most famous media visionary. "How did you get here? And where is that woman in the angel wings?"

"You must mean Dawn," Flynn said, smiling. "She is busy with the plant workers, tapping a new underground spring and growing herbs for our revival concert, which we are hoping you can join. It starts in just 20 minutes. Did you notice the Wilderness Stage on the hike over?"

Winston ignored the offer. "But I saw her! I followed right behind and didn't lose sight of her. How could she not be here?"

"Ah, the powers of the Goddess," Flynn said, with a knowing grin. "Astral projection. It takes a special kind … and Dawn is so special."

"So special" the younger man agreed. "My name is Ridley. Sit a spell and relax, Winston."

Ridley waved Winston closer as he opened a small glass jar and extracted a sticky bud of green and purple marijuana. Ridley placed it into the large chamber of the water pipe.

"Flynn and I have been waiting for you to start the peace pipe ceremony," Ridley said. "This strain was bred with inspiration from Gaia herself, using your DNA, formulated for where you are and what you need right now. It will help you reduce the fear."

Ridley stood up next to Winston, held a lighter up to the bowl of the water pipe and extended the mouthpiece toward Winston's face.

Winston hesitated, took a step back, and waved away the offering. "Reducing fear sounds like a sucker's choice to me," he countered. "Maybe you're too young or stoned to have gotten the main memo of the last 20 years, but only the paranoid survive!"

Flynn looked at Winston with soft eyes. "You are among friends," he said simply.

Winston thought back to the last time he had smoked marijuana, five years earlier. It was in a protected venue at the party of the playboy son of a local oligarch: a lavish, walled pool deck outside a sprawling mansion. But marijuana, unlike pharmaceutical party drugs, was a felony in Colorado. If tested or busted, Winston could be forced to pay hefty bribes to Rex and a dozen law enforcers and judges up the line to keep his job and avoid long jail time. Or, knowing Rex, it might be used as an excuse to halt the TV1 purchase payout and shoot him. He put nothing past his avaricious boss.

And, Winston worried, if that weren't bad enough, a Peacekeeper drone might hear their voices and swoop under the dense tree cover, then spot the pipe shaped like the enemy's flag, which, even without the marijuana, could trigger a laser attack on everyone in the immediate area.

Recalling the horror of Monday's massacre, Winston's eyes looked upward in terror and his body lurched forward. "I'm outta here," he murmured and took off in a rush down the narrow path.

Winston had only taken a few steps when he bumped into Dawn with such force that she had almost been knocked to the ground before he was able to stop her fall. To his surprise, Dawn slid gracefully through his hands and gave him a warm, stabilizing hug. Winston felt a tingle of energy surge through him.

"Don't worry about the drones, Winston," she said easily. "The eagles and crows have disabled them all. We are safe here for a little while longer. Come back to the fire with me. Come back to the light."

Winston's mind raced to process the questions: *How did she know that I was worried about the drones? Why would eagles disable them? How had the professor and the stoner with the crazy pipe travelled across three states and avoided detection?*

The oddness was tempered by the familiarity and comfort of the angel's voice. Dumbfounded, Winston allowed Dawn to lead him back to the small fire ring, where she squatted alongside him and beckoned for the water pipe mouthpiece.

"It would be helpful for you to smoke this special medicine. You will need it for the dark night and challenging days ahead."

"I thought you were here to help me, not get me into trouble," Winston protested.

Dawn smiled. "The trouble, as you noticed Monday, is with us, whatever we do. Our choice is to fear it or change it. Plant medicine, used judiciously and in moderation, helps us reduce our fear and be that change."

Ridley lit the packed bowl. Winston inhaled deeply, pulling in the fire. The bud burned with tiny embers. A cylinder of smoke bubbled through the water and rushed through the glass tube into Winston's mouth.

He held the smoke in for long seconds, then pumped it out of his mouth in a short fit of coughing. He felt first a head rush, then a lightness. It tasted stronger and fresher than any marijuana he'd ever tried, and it had an odd herbal flavor that he found appealing. He took a second hit, caught his breath, and then a third.

By then, everything around him seemed to be happening in slow motion. Dawn, Flynn and Ridley packed a few things, as though preparing to leave. Winston, deciding that gravity had become too challenging, plopped down to the ground and leaned his back against a nearby tree, staring into the fire.

The embers were glowing hypnotically; he could discern patterns and, to his surprise, what seemed like glowing faces. Familiar faces. He shimmied to his knees and drew his face so close to the embers that his cheeks turned red. It seemed impossible, he thought, but he could make out his mother's eyes, nose and mouth. Then his father's. Their forms dissipated for a few seconds as the flame flickered, but as soon as the embers began glowing again, their faces returned. Their eyes gleamed love.

A thought, not a voice, but a thought that came from them, appeared in his mind: *We are proud you have found your way.*

"Hey, old buddy," Flynn said kindly, putting a light hand on Winston's shoulder. The voice seemed to come from far away, as his awareness slowly returned. "We need to make a move soon. We need you with us."

Winston looked up. The light of a full moon flooded the small clearing, making everyone look as though they were on a movie set illuminated by an aerial spotlight. He wondered how he had not noticed the beautiful moon earlier.

Winston watched as Ridley, looking like an animated clown in a psychedelic comedy sketch, packed the gigantic pipe into a padded bag.

"It's time for the concert," Dawn said, interrupting Winston's mental movie. "I think you will find it a very special show."

"Always is!" Ridley agreed, closing the bag's zipper. "A once-in-a-lifetime opportunity. You wouldn't want to miss it. Need a hand getting up?"

Winston nodded. Ridley held out a hand and pulled him to his feet. His legs felt wobbly. He watched as Ridley shoveled dirt from a nearby pile to extinguish the fire.

Dawn stood close and brushed her hand softly across the side of Winston's face. He looked into her caring eyes and tried to think of the last time someone had touched his face. "How are you feeling?" she asked.

"Fine," Winston said. He felt an easy lightness and a sense of hyper awareness. "Really well, thanks. Brilliant, in fact!"

Winston watched Ridley pull himself 15 feet up a nearby tree, like an expert coconut tree climber, where he unwound a rope attached to a pulley. Ridley hoisted the bag containing the large pipe and another bag high into the tree canopy. To Winston's astonishment, the branches parted. The bags moved through them to an area above and then the branches closed again, camouflaging the gear. Ridley tied the rope and jumped down from the tree.

"Did … did those branches just part open and then close for you? How…"

Flynn answered for Ridley. "Down the rabbit hole," he said, smiling. "And we're just getting started."

"But how?"

"By following the angel," Flynn said, pointing toward Dawn.

Winston followed the others out of the small park and back to the main trail. Walking quietly in the beautiful moonlight, he noticed that Dawn was carrying a guitar case and that Flynn had put on his owl head, completing his costume and assuring his anonymity.

Sounds of drumming grew louder as they approached the Wilderness Stage. The trail opened to a small field, illuminated by the moonlight and whirling fire dancers.

Sounds and noises greeted Winston as he walked into what felt like an outdoor circus with hundreds of participants. He was enjoying himself, going with a wild flow, following an angel he had heard but never before met. For the first time in ages, he hadn't the slightest concern about what would happen next.

Chapter 19: Activation

Thursday May 4, 2034
11:55 p.m. Mountain Time
Golden Gate Canyon State Park
30 miles west of Denver, Colorado
Trump's United Enterprises of America

Winston followed Flynn, Dawn and Ridley along the edge of the costumed crowd of 300 ravers circling the small Wilderness Stage. Dawn set her guitar down and leaned against a tree along the circle's perimeter to watch.

Winston stood near the others, but instead of watching the fire dancers, his attention fixed to an odd sticker covering Dawn's guitar case. The design was of a radiant human being with tree-like roots. He recalled where he'd seen the symbol before: on the wall of the ritual hut in Maui, during his ayahuasca ritual a decade ago.

An M.C. announced the next act as "Sizzling Sarah the Sword Girl." A 12-year-old girl with a gymnast's body tucked into a fireproof, ocelot-colored Kevlar body suit stepped onto the small stage and began dancing with a fiery sword, as the music took a Middle Eastern turn.

Continuing to stare at the symbol on Dawn's guitar case, Winston barely noticed the act. The symbol was like a key to a door into a rarely visited past. He felt himself tumbling back through time to that night in Maui, seeing the mysterious symbol in a simple frame on the wall. He recalled stepping outside into the cool night air on legs that did not feel like his and violently vomiting some of the powerful bitter medicine onto the grass outside his hut.

Winston's recollection had been that the administering shaman had left him entirely on his own in the ritual hut in the Maui jungle for an endless, soul-expanding night. But suddenly additional memories surfaced, like a layer of forgotten dreams. *Dawn was with me that night! What was she doing there?*

He heard Dawn's voice again, as though he were back in the hut a decade earlier, patiently explaining to him, "Mother Ayahuasca gives you the exact amount of medicine you need; the rest is returned to Gaia."

It was all connected.

Winston found himself back in the present, staring at the intricate patterns of light and the expert martial arts moves made by the young fire dancer. He suddenly thought of his son Abraham, who had moved in a similar pattern during the tournament. It was only eight hours ago, he thought, but in his state of marijuana-induced immediacy, it felt like weeks had passed.

He turned to speak to Dawn, but his words disappeared at the sight of the two ethereal figures leaning on each side of her as she stood propped against a nearby tree. Dawn's arms wrapped lovingly around what appeared to be the ghostlike astral form of a dark-haired woman in a brilliant white tunic, whose own arms held a teenage girl who resembled her. The teenager's eyes glowed adoringly as she watched the performer dance with her fiery sword.

Winston watched as Dawn's eyes glistened with appreciation and tears; tears appeared in the eyes of the specter in her arms as well. Winston could not restrain his curiosity.

"What ... who?" he asked, incredulously.

Dawn turned to him calmly. "My wife Maria and our daughter Estrella are watching my younger daughter's spirit soar. It is a sight we want to share."

"But ... how?"

"The same way you followed my astral form when I was not there."

"But," Winston protested, "That's ... it's ... not possible."

"So much is possible," Dawn offered.

Maria's apparition turned and looked straight at Winston. "Is this the one?" she asked.

"Yes," Dawn replied.

"What does she mean *the one*?" Winston asked, bewildered.

Dawn held a finger to her lips to request silence, then pointed to the stage as she refocused her attention on her daughter Sarah.

Sarah held two fiery swords now. Somehow, she managed to work one of them with her foot as she created luminous designs that drew a round of wild applause. Winston placed his smartphone camera on hover mode, floating it in the air to capture the impressive act. He called it back and texted his sons the video he wanted to share, with the word: "Fantastica!" He also took a photo of the intriguing symbol on Dawn's guitar case, as well as one of her and her astral visitors, curious as to whether they would show up in the image. They didn't.

Glancing at his phone a few seconds later, he felt frustrated when an alert notified him the video did not send. He sighed.

Satellite service had been better in the park in earlier years. He resolved to try again on the drive home.

Sarah finished her act and the M.C. bowed. "Give it up for Sizzlin' Sarah!" he said. The crowd cheered.

"Wow," Winston said to Dawn, noticing that the astral figures near her had vanished. "That daughter of yours would make a great laser knight if they ever allowed girls to compete. My son is …"

"I know," Dawn smiled. "We are looking forward to meeting Abraham soon."

"How do you know my …"

Dawn just smiled as she pulled her guitar from the case and slung it around her shoulder. "I am up next," she said. "Please, for the sake of your children, for the sake of us all, please be present for our song of Activation. The Oneness gene is in you as in all of us. We are here to help you take the evolutionary step of switching it on."

Dawn spoke with a crystal clarity that brought his mind to silence. "Remember that you alone are the architect of your destiny," she continued. "You alone can choose to unlock the higher purpose hidden in your DNA. Imagine, Winston, a world guided by love, by forgiveness, by freedom from fear, by the Oneness that is our essential being-ness. Imagine that this is the next stage in the evolution of our species. Imagine that this is happening right now."

A dozen new questions swam through Winston's head, but before he could say a word, Dawn had climbed onto the small stage nearby with her guitar and the M.C. was already introducing her. "Our last act of the night for the Wilderness

Stage is called Utopia Rising. Afterward, the dancing continues till dawn on the main stage. I'll be there after about a dozen more drinks … have a great night!"

The M.C. stumbled off the stage while Dawn was joined by Ridley, costumed as a clown, who started juggling four holographic balls above his wild red hair. Large three-dimensional letters appeared above his head that said, "I Am You." He was a masterful juggler and the balls flowed through the "o" in "You" every time.

Dawn began to chant with hymn-like reverence, "Gratitude … gratitude … gratitude … gratitude." Flynn and their Activated colleagues dispersed around the crowd and joined her. The audience grew silent.

Dawn turned to the east and her allies joined her, modelling the direction, breath, and song for those around them. "The east breath, of gratitude, is to Creator for your light and sacred skies." They paused, took a deep, calming breath and turned, in unison, to the south.

The song continued: "The south breath of gratitude is to our Mother for your seeds and living lands."

Winston watched Flynn, who was standing next to him, take a long breath, eyes closed, as though in a trance state, then turn to face west.

The song continued: "The west breath of gratitude is to our Teachers for your wise and ancient waters."

Winston breathed deeply, thinking of Flynn and other teachers he had known, especially his mother, whose presence he had felt by the fire.

A wave of panic swept over Winston's body and the air suddenly felt very cold. He had a discomforting premonition that the life he knew was about to change forever. Part of him welcomed it, but another part felt deep dread. It was a fear that he would be branded as different, that he would stand out as part of a pathetic rebellion that would be snuffed out as quickly as the lives of the protesters he had seen massacred during the past three days.

Dawn had spoken of a choice: Was it suicide? Winston trembled as a voice in his head asked: *Why should I sacrifice my life for a symbolic gesture against the Trump dynasty?* His heart beat faster. *I can just walk away, right now,* he thought. *I can be gone before anything happens. Show up at work tomorrow next morning, get congratulated for Abe's victory. After all, the president himself had sent congratulations to my son. Gerbers might warm up to me, perhaps even convince Rex to give me a bonus for the high tournament ratings. What could possibly be gained by resisting the iron fist of government?*

Winston slowly backed up as Dawn sang, ""The north breath of gratitude is to my Body, Mind, Heart and to my Spirit. For your light, and rising fire, breathing love and light, with all as One."

They repeated the last words of the song again and again. "With all as One. With all as One. With all as One."

Winston could see the main trail as he neared the edge of the clearing. He took a last look at Dawn on the stage, concluding the song. She stared right at Winston, freezing him in his tracks. Her arms, like the arms of two dozen others planted among the crowd, were held wide open as they slowed down their final, "With all as …" and chanted the last word of the song, "Onnnnne" in a continual wall of harmonic sound. Ridley rang a Tibetan bell he held high, and its crisp clang soared through the air to merge with the human voices into one vibrational note.

The night fell still. It was a silence unlike any Winston had ever experienced. Not only was it silent around him, but, he realized with wonder, it was silent *within* him. For the first time in his life there was no chattering mind, no concern about what had happened in the past, no fear about what was happening then or what might happen in the future. There was only stillness.

In that stillness, he felt a tug, like a magnetic pull drawing on his heart. He heard it beating rapidly as something opened deep within his chest, responding to the pull as though it wanted to burst out of his body. He felt a deep warmth, a warmth that quickly spread until it seemed to awaken every cell in his body.

Winston felt a divine presence flowing deep within. He was aware, fully aware, that he was at a crossroads. He could choose to say yes to the soulful urge, to move forward into the light of his divine truth, into Oneness. Or he could remain in the dark, terrifying world he knew, the fearful life of his past.

It was the easiest choice he had ever made.

"YES!" he answered, in a space beyond words.

Instantly, an image swam through Winston's mind of an ape rising to stand. The image morphed into millions of outstretched fingers stretching to a magnificently blue sky, followed by a blazing ocean of brightness.

A warmth emanated from within him, soaring out in every direction.
Winston's mind felt at peace, as though floating in a sea of tranquility. At the core of this peace was a deep sense of knowing that everything that was happening was absolutely

perfect. Everything that would happen would be absolutely perfect. Everything that had ever happened had been absolutely perfect. The "good experience/bad judgment" he had clung to as long as he could remember dissolved into the clarity that it was all the will of the One Spirit that was part of all living beings. He and everyone else existed to experience exactly what they experienced, and evolve, some sooner, some later, from these experiences.

It felt as though a dam had burst open, releasing an all-knowing, all-accepting love, drowning his ego, his attachments, his judgments and his fears. He felt his old identity surrendering to a deeper ease after a lifetime of self-induced suffering.

As he lifted his arms wide, his inner eye saw waves of rainbow-colored light opening around him. Then, for the first time, he sensed a voice in his mind, not from Dawn, but from the larger mind of those around him. It was the wise voice of the Divine We: The Hive Mind.

Heal the past, love all that you have experienced and awaken to your true purpose, it said.

Like the hundreds of newly Activated people standing all around him, Winston's body remained still, while his memory travelled through years past to relive the vivid experiences that had scarred his soul with the greatest pain.

First came the conscious guilt. He blamed himself for his mother and father's deaths by fire missiles during the South Lake Tahoe City massacre of 2028.

Winston's parents had been socially conscious and caring. They raised him as an only child in Berkeley and supported his passion for journalism and new media. They even took out a second mortgage on their home so he could focus on unpaid writing and tech projects instead of working at menial jobs to pay his way through college and journalism school at U.C. Berkeley.

In 2017, when Winston moved to Boulder, Colorado to plan TV1.com as a web-video startup company financed by a wealthy friend, his parents took time off from work to drive halfway across the country to help him furnish his modest apartment.

For years they supported Winston's decision to move to Boulder, until the political divide between the West Coast states and the rest of the country worsened. By 2024, Winston's parents began pleading with him to return to California with his wife and two young sons. There was room in his childhood home for all of them, they said, and he needed to leave Colorado where the government, unlike California's, had been unable to resist the Trump regime's police state takeover.

Call after call, Winston ignored his parents' pleas. He said he owed it to himself and to his investors to build TV1.com to the highest value possible. Besides, he explained to his parents, he and his wife had bought an expensive home and her work was based in Colorado. They could not just walk away from so sweet a lifestyle.

Then, in 2027, as millions of Americans fleeing the brutality of Trump's America emigrated to California, Winston's parents sold their house to make room for a large family and two new small homes in their yard. They retired to a small condo in South Lake Tahoe so they could stay in California but be nearer to their grandchildren in Colorado.

Six months later, just before the western states announced the formation of the United Peoples of America, Winston's parents and the 25,000 other residents of South Lake Tahoe were incinerated in a rain of Homeland Security "Peacekeeper" missiles that arrived just hours before the new nation's force field could be launched.

Winston had carried the guilt of knowing that his parents would be alive had he heeded their request and moved his family to join them in their spacious Berkeley home. While on one level he knew this was the greatest tragedy of his life, he had avoided facing the shame of it by clinging to the story that he'd had no choice.

Now, as he stood outside in the cool air, tears of sorrow for his lost parents streaming down his face, he faced the reality that he indeed had had a choice, and that his choice had resulted in painful consequences.

At that moment, Winston became aware of an even deeper layer of shame, one that was so submerged that, like an emotional iceberg, he had never felt it surface. His flawed choice, he realized, was not in 2022, when he decided to sell TV1 to Patriot News and stay in Colorado. It had happened a decade earlier, when he'd sold out his youthful idealism, rejecting Professor Washington's offer to help build a public interest media network and choosing the allure of great wealth instead.

He had let himself down. Yet it had happened with such subtlety that until his Activation, he had never been aware of having made the choice.

The road not taken was the greatest pain of his life: the unwillingness to find the courage to live in integrity with his ideals. But as Winston touched his stomach, he felt a well of acceptance and forgiveness cleanse the shame that he had avoided facing for so long. As though naming it dissolved its power over him.

The voice in his head spoke again. *Love all that you have experienced. Spirit was with you then, as you experienced what you came here to experience. And Spirit is with you now, as you awaken to your true purpose.*

Winston felt a new power surge through him. It was the power of fearlessness, a fearlessness born of knowing himself as an eternal, interconnected divine being.

"I am ready," he heard himself speak.

"We are ready!" he heard a voice proclaim, this time in his ears. It was Dawn. As she spoke, people began moving around her. Winston and others were returning to their present consciousness and looked up at her.

Within ten minutes of the song of Activation ending, 300 people in the small clearing were busy working. Like a flock of birds flying in synchronized formation, every person instinctively knew where they needed to be and what they needed to do.

Winston walked to an area a few hundred yards from the clearing, where Dawn had tapped an underground spring. Two 20-something Burners still dressed in their flashy Burning Man costumes closed the groundwater spigot and hoisted a five-gallon container onto Winston's shoulders, then began filling a new container. Winston carried the water to an area where Flynn and Ridley were supervising the mixing of a strong herbal tincture into hundreds of paper cups of fresh water.

"Freshly grown herbs," Flynn explained, "to provide a cleansing, natural mineral antidote to the toxic foods and chemicals that have polluted American bodies for too many years."

Flynn handed a cup of the green liquid to Winston. "Drink it slowly and breathe in between sips," he advised.

Winston took a sip of the medicinal brew. It did not taste good or bad, he noticed with satisfaction. He felt the healing liquid flow through his throat into his mineral-starved belly. He took another sip, and another, until he had finished.

Then he returned to work. The elixir making and drinking was complete, so Winston helped others fill the large water containers and load them onto strong folding carts. A nearby group of helpers were harvesting herbs and filling hemp bags with them.

Dawn returned to the small stage. She nestled her daughter Sarah under her arm. The 12-year-old looked like an ordinary girl, having stored her flaming swords and traded her ocelot suit for a warm hooded jacket. She and Dawn carried large backpacks and seemed prepared for a camping trip in the mountains.

"We welcome you to our shared divinity," Dawn began, warmly. "You have just made history: You are the first citizens of Colorado to be Activated. By the end of the month, with the support of the One Spirit inside us all, 150 million of your fellow citizens will join you, as we end the nightmare that has been the Trump regime and replace it with the state of connected bliss that each of us feels right now; a state of being that once experienced, never leaves us."

Dawn paused as her listeners opened their minds to a vision they had never before imagined. "We have arrived," she continued, with elation. "This ... this is our rebirth, as human beings. As humans whose being, whose thoughts, whose words and whose deeds radiate our One Spirit!"

Dawn held her daughter Sarah close. The moon glistened on their faces. The onlookers basked in the healing energy of the happening.

Dawn paused to join the others in silence as they breathed into the bliss. Then she continued. "I know that sharing our One Mind and One Heart is new to you all. I will speak with my voice tonight, but as you have already experienced, our connection to one another and our capacity to communicate are far simpler and more powerful than this."

Each of us may also share like this! Winston heard these words in his mind. He looked around at the 300 people who had become Activated with him just a half hour earlier. Many nodded appreciatively; most had looks of deep contentment on their faces, which glowed in the moonlight. Instead of reacting with judgment, with opinions of approval or disapproval, attraction or repulsion, instead of projecting, he accepted and loved, appreciating the beauty and the wonder of every face. As he accepted and loved himself fully for the first time.

Witnessing the transformation of what Winston had long thought of as his personality, he was aware that monumental changes were indeed possible. Consciousness creates reality, he realized, and a miraculous transformation beyond anything he might ever have imagined was underway. He was part of it. A willing, capable, empowered part of it.

"The time has come to step forward despite the challenges, which are many," Dawn continued. "We will now disband into two groups. Those of us who came from the west will move deeper into the mountains, which will require hiking for seven hours until dawn. If you have been conditioned to survive such a march, you may choose to join us. For everyone else, know that this magnificent change you feel will be detected by Homeland Security. The ruthless powers that rule this country will be threatened by you. They will arrest you and hurt you as they try to learn what has just happened to you. In a few days, we will free you as we liberate those who incarcerate you. And everyone else."

A minute later, Dawn and her crew, joined by a handful of the fittest Colorado Burners, were off blazing through the woods. Winston followed the main trail to his car. The parking lot attendant was dispensing travel information "Bad news," he advised. "The road you came in on is closed. Freak accident: two ginormous trees collapsed three miles down. The only way out is 25 miles west to Highway 116, then a short turn left before circling back east."

Winston didn't mind the detour. In his mind he saw a bird's-eye view of the massive fallen trees, and behind them, a long line of police and emergency vehicles, their lights flashing helplessly as black uniformed storm troopers surveyed the roadblock, cursing and shaking their heads. He thanked Gaia for delaying the troopers' access, which allowed the Activation to take place.

His celestial vision soared up from the roadblock to witness hundreds of destroyed drones around the perimeter of the gathering. Intermingled among them were the corpses of a few large birds that had been killed by the drones on their way down. As he watched, a fast-moving armed drone sped into the airspace, its lasers shooting in the air around it. Within seconds, a dozen crows attacked it from all directions, clawing at its wiring and cannons, knocking it from its trajectory. In less than a minute, it had been smashed into a rock.

Winston drove slowly along the back road. After a half hour of cautious gravel-road auto driving, Winston ordered his car to pull into a wide shoulder so he could urinate. His Hive Mind eye could not tell the future, but it could see the road ahead.

In about ten miles, his car would hit a Homeland Security checkpoint. Scores of army and police vehicles lined the road, and they had commandeered a field where they were pulling over every vehicle that tried to exit. Winston knew he was about to be captured. The awareness, he observed with amusement, was not met with fear, or even apprehension. He welcomed it as part of his destiny. He thought of his smartphone with the video and image he had taken earlier, and he considered smashing and burying it.

Let them see what they are meant to see, the hive mind instructed him. *And do what they are meant to do.*

As he continued driving, Winston felt comforted by this insight. Like most people, he had always harbored an unspoken hatred for the functionaries of the brutal, repressive Trump regime. His disdain for his boss Roger Rex, his deputy Scoop, and the cruel Gerbers was so deep that their very presence made him nauseous. Now when he thought of them, he felt a new compassion, an understanding of the tragic, heartless existence they each led.

This understanding, however, did not minimize his powerful new resolve to stand against the brutality of his country's dictatorship, to risk all to end the suffering and degradation of the Trump regime before it destroyed their species and the Earth itself. Winston's heart brimmed with an excitement he had never felt before, a sense that peace, the deep peace that had been awakened within him, was not only possible for the world around him, but inevitable.

A series of flashing lights and a squad of troopers with heavy rifles directed Winston to pull his car into a field off the road. He noticed a dozen other drivers being interrogated at gunpoint.

Winston rolled down his window. A trooper shoved the barrel of an assault rifle and a bright light into his face and ordered: "KEEP YOUR HANDS BY YOUR FACE AND STEP THE FUCK OUT OF THE CAR OR YOU ARE A DEAD MAN!"

Winston stepped outside his car and looked in the faces of the men arresting him, remaining calm while one of the soldiers performed an iris scan and frisked him electronically for weapons. He recognized the child in the eyes of each soldier, despite the hostile charade that he understood to be their role.

The older soldier, with an officer bar beneath the flag on each shoulder of his uniform, held out an unfamiliar device and looked at it with a confused expression. "Patriot Winston Smith: Where are you coming from?" he demanded, with a meaningful nod to his partner. Winston realized that he had seen something in the second device, something that necessitated a response.

"Burning Man party up the road," Winston replied.

"What were you doing there?"

"Celebrating," Winston answered truthfully.

"Wiseass! Corporal Jeffries, show dickweed here what we think of wiseasses!"

"With pleasure, lieutenant!" The younger officer smashed a rifle butt into Winston's spine. He collapsed to the ground.

The lieutenant kneeled over Winston's face and ordered an arrest drone to drop an incarceration cage over Winston's head and shoulders. An injector needle pressed lightly against his jugular vein.

The lieutenant clasped Winston's face roughly by the chin and said, "Let me make this brief, Smith. You are officially under Homeland Security arrest. Whatever rights you enjoyed ten minutes ago have disappeared. You are about to disappear into a black hole, and big shots way above my pay grade will decide whether or not you ever climb out of it. You are in a position to do one thing and one thing only right now. That is to decide whether I let Jeffries here have his sadistic fun before taking you in, or whether you order your phone to sign an agreement to turn your nice new car over to me personally, as a consideration for my generous treatment of you. Then it's a painless sleep until you wake up to whatever nightmare they got planned for you."

Winston ordered his phone to record the contract. He felt compassion for the young lieutenant, part of a system of unrestrained greed with shakedowns built into every level of the system. "It's all unfolding, and we each have our part to play, lieutenant."

"So, we've got a deal!" the trooper demanded, ignoring the remark while looking at the expensive vehicle and thinking of whether he should keep it, give it to his wife, or sell it.

Winston dictated the contract to his hovering smartphone. "Enjoy your new car, lieutenant," Winston said warmly, ignoring the pain that lingered in his back. "And one more thing."

The lieutenant was only half paying attention as he programmed the incarceration device to sedate for ten hours. "What might that be?" he replied.

"It gets better," Winston promised, with an ease that surprised him. "A lot better. Real soon."

"Not for you, loser!" the lieutenant laughed. He touched his finger to his control device. The needle pressed into Winston's neck, and he was unconscious before the drone could lift him off the ground.

Chapter 20: General Baron

Friday May 5, 2034
11:00 a.m. Mountain Time
Homeland Security Detention Center
Colorado Springs, Colorado
Trump's United Enterprises of America

Winston's eyes would not open; he could not move. And yet he was aware of the sounds around him, as though he were hearing with a third ear, an ear floating in the energy field above his senseless body.

The first sounds he heard were the movements of people arranging things in the room around him. At first, there was little conversation. After some time, a man loudly announced, "The General will arrive in ten minutes!" Then the room got busier, and soon Winston heard murmurs of, "He's here," followed by the sound of a large group of people entering the room at the same time.

A commanding voice Winston recognized from newscasts as that of General Francis Baron began barking questions and orders as he approached Winston's body.

"Is the prisoner conscious yet?" he asked someone near him.

"No, General Baron, sir," came a crisp answer. "It will be another ten or 15 minutes. We are monitoring eight forms of activity, including brain and nanotech sensors in the bloodstream. We will know the moment consciousness returns and inform you at that time."

"Patriot News could accommodate this examination in our fully equipped interrogation chamber, which is where this shit stain works," protested a man near the general. Winston immediately recognized the voice as that of his boss, Roger Rex. "I don't appreciate being summoned all the way from my secure headquarters. I'm a busy man!"

"Mr. Rex," Baron replied evenly, "as you know from my text, this is a subject of national security concern."

Rex rolled his eyes. "This douchebag seems scarcely worth the bother for a man of your rank. Or mine!"

"As commander of our country's Homeland Security Western Division Army, I will decide what is worthy of my rank. We have taken him into custody as per protocol 29-C. You may have five minutes for your final … negotiation in a few minutes, when he awakens from his sweet dreams to the worst nightmare he has ever faced."

Rex chortled, amused.

"While we wait," the general continued, "I have a few questions for you and, if you will, Director Gerbers, as well."

Winston could hear a screen drone hover nearby.

"Smith was returning from a Burning Man rave party in the Golden Gate Canyon Park," Baron explained. "We tolerate these parties as a place where younger Patriots and even children and grandchildren of Super Patriots can blow off a little steam with legal drugs."

"And plenty of profits," Rex grinned.

"That will be the last of your interruptions," General Baron warned ominously.

Winston, through the third ear of his Hive Mind, noticed a severity and high level of stress in the general's voice.

"Would you say," Baron asked evenly, "that Winston Smith is a manly, defiant sort?"

"This candy ass pansy is the last person I would call a man!" Rex bellowed. "He nearly shit his pants a few days ago when I got a little aggressive in a compensation negotiation. The snowflake couldn't stare down a kitten!"

"Something happened at this event," Baron continued. "Something that affected the adrenalin levels in one tenth of the 3,000 people that our men pulled over and tested leaving the event. Last night we took into custody 300 drugged or mind-controlled Coloradans. Using body cams from the arresting cops, our researchers witnessed an inconceivable absence of fear. No fear of the weapons being pointed at their heads, no fear of the possibility that they will soon be tortured and then disappear forever. We are talking about the lowest adrenalin levels we have ever measured."

A third voice, which Winston recognized as belonging to White House Communications Director Joseph Gerbers, spoke in a grave tone. "This is very serious, indeed. Has the Pentagon been notified?"

"Of course they have, Joe," boasted Baron. "I conversed about it with General Trump himself this morning. This is indeed a very big deal. Two dozen specialists from the Division of Biochemical Weaponry are on a plane here as we speak."

"We found in the blood of these 300 a distinct new gene, a gene we have never identified before. We will work to isolate, then replicate this gene and the incredible mind control drug, or brainwashing technique, that mutated it. Imagine: With this drug, our Homeland Security forces, as well as the two million fighters of our international Armed Forces Inc., will no longer fear their own deaths in combat, or the ethical consequences of their violent deeds."

"The perfect soldier!" Gerbers agreed, admiringly.

"Our more immediate need, of course," Baron continued, "is to learn how to destroy this gene in those who have been mutated by it. With the force field of that nation of traitors falling to our Hellfire missile attacks, and with our invasion forces mounted on our western borders ready to reunite our great country, it is only a matter of months before we conquer the treasonous U.P.A. When we do, we will take possession of not only the most profitable technology companies in the world, but 100 million skilled slaves. Fearlessness is not a trait useful in building a docile work force."

"Of course," Gerbers said. "After six years in la-la land, they will need to be taught, once again, how a strong government rules. And what it can do to them."

General Baron continued with the confidence of a scientist carrying out an experiment he had done a hundred times before. "Soon we will see how well this courage-inducing drug, this mutated DNA, holds up against our state-of–the-art interrogation tools. Meanwhile ..."

Winston heard someone pick up something from the floor nearby. "Note the sticker on the guitar case from this photo that Smith took. We suspect it to be a secret code. Have either of you ever seen it before?"

There was a pause. "No," Rex replied.

"I've had researchers on this since 6 a.m. The symbol does not exist in any database," Baron said with annoyance.

Gerbers laughed for a moment. "Before we explore extra-terrestrials, we will find out what Mr. Smith knows about it. Or about her."

The conversation paused. Without seeing, Winston knew they were looking at an image of Dawn from his phone. He was also aware that he felt no blame or discomfort by what he'd done, just a simple surrender to the great unravelling.

"Our biometric files," Baron explained, with agitation, "include every person in the T.U.E.A. and every foreign visitor. No direct matches. She is either a foreigner or, more likely, a terrorist from our traitorous neighbor to the west."

"Shit stain here probably knows," Rex said. "The faggot's parents raised him in California before you sent them to hell. He went to college and journalism school at Berkeley years ago. If that is all you need, I could torture it out of him right now. Probably take less than two minutes with a scalpel on his toenail for me to get this little pussy to ID her and turn her in."

After a short pause, Baron replied, "No, Mr. Rex, the prisoner and the other 300 will be held in this prison for comprehensive study and torture, and then be terminated. We need to learn the cause of this dangerous virus of fearlessness before it can infect others."

"I know my rights, even under protocol 29-C," Rex said, working to control the agitation that Winston detected in his voice. "As his owner, I get a final resource conference with the prisoner."

"You certainly do, Mr. Rex," General Baron replied. "And based on the indicators that my technicians are observing, you will have that opportunity in just a few moments. The prisoner is regaining consciousness. Please be brief; we have important work to do, and time is of the essence."

Winston felt consciousness return to his head as he heard a group of people near him shuffle away, while the heavy, angry breath of his boss seemed to move closer to where he lay. He opened his eyes.

He was in a very large room, surrounded by machines and monitors. Along the periphery of his vision were dozens of white-coated technicians and heavily armed black-uniformed storm troopers. Rex's face and body looked larger than ever as he stood menacingly over Winston's head.

"Good morning, Winston," Rex began. "I trust you have rested well? You seem to have gotten yourself into trouble again. Big trouble this time!"

"Where am I?" Winston asked.

"You are in the Homeland Security special interrogation chamber of General Francis Baron himself, Winston. Do you know what that means?"

Winston stared ahead and shook his head as best he could with dozens of restraints immobilizing him on an operating table. He felt aches from his neck all the way down his spine. Staring intently at his boss, he realized how deeply unhappy Rex was.

Rex answered his own question with a severe tone. "It means, Winston, that at this moment, I am the only person in the world with the power to save you from a slow and very, very painful death."

Rex paused to let his meaning sink in and then continued in a low, ominous voice. "There is a reason they call General Baron the Butcher of the West. I have seen his handwork, and it is remarkable for its ingenuity and barbarity. As your employer, I have some influence with how he dispenses his justice in this case." Rex paused again to make sure his offer was registering. "It is not an easy ask, and one that would involve going upstairs, to the very top, to get special dispensation on your behalf. It may work, and it may even allow you to live. But it will cost you."

"What are you suggesting, Mr. Rex?" Winston asked with calm curiosity.

"Butch, Scribe mode," Rex called his smartphone out to hover nearby, and then dictated the terms. "You transfer to me the remainder of the TV1 payout. Instead of leaving it to your heirs, Patriot News will accelerate the payout and place it into my account immediately upon your death. As well as your $3.2 million retirement account. Do it or die a death more horrifying than you can imagine."

Winston replied calmly, "I would like to ask you one question."

"I am the one asking questions here, Smith!" Rex bellowed.

"Did you find today what you were looking for yesterday?"

"What the fuck do you mean by that, you snide asswipe? You have one minute to answer and complete this transaction, or the Butcher of the West will fry your innards and make you eat them before you die. Do you want a chance to live or don't you?"

"What I mean, Rex, is that your net worth, at this moment, exceeds $20 billion. Isn't this enough? Does your greed have no bounds, sir?"

In a fit of anger, Rex smashed the back of his hand hard against Winston's mouth. He pulled his Glock pistol from his holster, flipped off the fingerprint lock and rammed the barrel hard against the side of Winston's head.

"You will sign our new agreement, or I am going to get great pleasure in ending your pathetic little life here and now!"

Winston sputtered blood from his mouth before answering, with kindness. "You would be happier helping people rather than hurting them. Somewhere deep inside you know this."

"Somewhere deep inside I am going to get immense satisfaction blowing your fucking brains out. You have till the count of four to call my scribe to you and sign. One … two …"

"Mr. Rex!" bellowed General Baron's booming voice as he moved close, his own sidearm pointed directly at Roger Rex's face. "On behalf of the Department of Homeland Security, you will stand down now and release this prisoner into my custody."

A squadron of 20 black-uniformed troopers formed a line between Rex and his half-dozen bodyguards, pointing their assault rifles at their heads.

"Put down that gun and order your men to stand down, Mr. Rex," Baron said in a menacing monotone.

Rex looked around, then slowly lowered his gun to his side. His men raised empty hands in the air to surrender.

"I own this scumbag, and I can kill him if I choose!" Rex complained.

"You make me repeat myself, Mr. Rex," the general replied, the laser of his huge sidearm still targeting the center of Rex's fleshy forehead. "Protocol 29-C grants me the authority to deal with your employee as I choose. It also grants me the authority to terminate anyone, including Super Patriots, who interferes with my actions in any way. You can be sure Trump Family Enterprises would have no regret about taking possession of Patriot News if I pull this trigger."

Rex began sweating and panting. He dropped his Glock to the ground, and it fell with a thud. He stepped backwards, his open hands outstretched. "Please, General Baron ... please ... forgive me. I have no intention of challenging your legal authority here ... I ... I apologize. I was just so surprised that this pussy suddenly grew a set of balls. Something changed him. Suddenly he has no fear of me ... of us ..." Rex looked totally perplexed.

"I understand your surprise, Mr. Rex," Baron said, holstering his sidearm. "We are all surprised by what we are seeing and monitoring, even in the face of what the prisoner knows is about to happen."

Baron pointed to the exit. "Leave now and take your men with you. Know that this conversation, and this prisoner, are top secret. That includes not just the prisoner's family, but even the most senior members of your staff."

"Certainly, General Baron," Rex said, still sweating. The gravity of his offense hit him hard as he backed out toward the exit. "For all that we have accomplished together, in my long and loyal past, might I ask, sir, that you and Mr. Gerbers keep what happened here today ... private, as well?"

Baron paused knowingly, enjoying his power as he savored Rex's groveling and considered his request.

It was the first time Winston had seen the famed general up close. Major General Francis Baron did not resemble the ruthless military man that Winston had long imagined. Despite being a few years older than Winston at 53, he had the face and build of an iron-man triathlete half his age. His salt-and-pepper buzz cut along the sides was interrupted by a stylish, gelled wave of hair in the center. His black Homeland Security storm trooper uniform sported both general bars and the fearsome skull and crossbones insignia of the dreaded Homeland Security Secret Police. Yet he wore the narrow smile of a self-important, confident young man who thoroughly enjoyed his work. Only his cold, pale blue eyes, which glistened with threat, bore evidence of his legendary cruelty.

General Baron looked over at Joseph Gerbers. "Let me ask Communications Director Gerbers what he thinks."

Gerbers, his face sallow and grave, nodded judiciously as he moved closer to study the monitors surrounding Winston's table. "If these indicators are indeed consistent with the other prisoners, I think we have enough of a dilemma to resolve for the president without bringing the actions of my hot-headed friend here to his attention."

"Thank you, Joe, thank you so very much, my friend," Rex said obsequiously, as he collected his guards and made his way out through the high steel doors of the cavernous torture chamber.

As the doors slammed shut, Baron signaled a team of technicians standing around him and held out his hand for a control device. "Now, Mr. Smith, it is just you and me and this convenient tool I have in my hands. I am very proud of this device, which I perfected and have patented for sale to America's loyal allies in our heroic battle against terrorism. It controls laser diodes placed at two dozen nerve clusters throughout your pathetic little body. I call it the Painquilizer."

A smug smile tweaked across the general's lips as he proudly held the device up to Joseph Gerbers to admire. "We will start," Baron continued, "with one simple ground rule. Hesitate to answer my question or try to deceive me, and this will happen."

Baron touched the device in his hand. Pain unlike anything Winston had ever experienced coursed like molten steel dripping through two dozen holes in his body and head. He convulsed uncontrollably as tears poured out of his eyes.

"A taste of the fun ahead," Baron threatened. He held a finger up over the device, pausing sadistically as he watched Winston wince.

Through his tears, Winston saw Baron look at a hovering monitor and exchange a concerned look with Gerbers.

"The resistance is incredible," Gerbers observed.

"Off the charts," Baron replied quietly. "Time will tell how long it holds out."

Baron noticed Winston looking at him. "What are you staring at, you little worm! I could pull your eyeballs out, with my bare hands!"

Baron stuck a menacing finger close to Winston's eye, then stepped back slightly, regaining his composure.

"But we have business to attend to, don't we, Mr. Smith?" Baron pressed the pause switch on the Painquilizer. The consuming pain, which had rendered Winston unable to speak, dissipated. An aide to the general appeared from the shadows and poured a few gulps of water into Winston's parched mouth so he could talk.

"Let's get started, shall we?" Baron said plainly. "A drug was administered in a drink last night to at least 300 of you. Our chemists have found only high potency herbs in your blood samples. What else was in it that beverage?"

"Medicinal herbs; I don't know their names."

"Why did you drink it?" Baron asked with a demeaning snort.

"I was told it would be helpful."

General Baron raised an eyebrow and continued his questioning. "How did they get those birds to attack and destroy more than 800 of our drones? We killed a few and found them to be flesh and blood, not bionic. How did they do it?"

"They … we … asked them to be our allies, and they showed up," Winston replied. The monitor hovering near Baron's face flashed the word TRUE across its screen. "The living spirit within all beings is collaborating to help us. Soon you will be part of our glorious collaboration, as well. And this brutal reality will be transformed. You will know that you are forgiven, that you are loved, that you are one with …"

"Don't lecture me, dead man!" Baron screamed. "Do you know who I am? Do you know what I have done? Do you know what I am going to do to you?"

The general dialed up the pain. A tidal wave of agony again swept through Winston's body. He realized that the marijuana and elixir the previous night somehow made the challenge more bearable, allowing him to step outside his body and witness the pain instead of identifying with the experience of it. He found himself taking refuge in Oneness, in the larger Self that was part of all living things, even those torturing him.

Through involuntary tears, Winston looked deeply at his tormentor. He felt the enormous suffering of his heart, the consuming anger of his soul, stripped of its humanity like an emotional skeleton. Winston felt no fear, just compassion.

This only served to incense Baron more. He glanced at a monitor and said tauntingly, "I am the Commander of the Western Forces who ordered the patriotic fire bomb cleansing of South Lake Tahoe. I understand that your mother and father were among the traitorous scum who received justice on that fine Friday evening. I received a medal and a bonus for that proud event. Think about it, worm. I killed them, and now, at a moment of my choosing, after torturing you for days and nights, I am going to kill you."

Winston digested this news. *So, this was the man who killed my parents,* he thought. Yet somehow, he did not feel hatred or a need for retribution. The victory, he realized, lay not in winning the war against the enemy, but in winning over the enemy to end the enmity.

General Baron glanced at the monitor and shook his head in disbelief. "Still not afraid, dead man!" he screeched, increasing the pain level until Winston lost consciousness.

Winston's third ear, floating above the room, listened as General Baron and Director Gerbers fretted over the reports on their monitors. He found his memory in a dialog with the hive mind, processing what he knew and what was happening. He realized that nanotech robots had been injected in his bloodstream, and the bloodstream of all Americans, as part of the mandatory weekly vaccine "updates." Winston had long considered the endless injections to be part of the corrupt big pharma profit mill, but he now understood that they served an even more sinister purpose: to record adrenalin levels, DNA, perhaps even thoughts themselves and make them accessible to the police state.

Winston awoke to a splash of ice water, followed by a loud slap across the face from General Baron's black-gloved hand.

"Wakey wake, little worm," Baron taunted. "We're ba...ack!"

Baron swiped his smartphone to tilt a hovering monitor over Winston's head. It displayed a close up of the sticker of a radiant human being with tree-like roots on Dawn's guitar case. "What is the meaning of this symbol?" Baron demanded.

Winston was aware of a drug-induced compulsion to answer whatever question was asked of him. "It is a symbol for the destiny of humanity," he explained. "It portends the change that is coming. For all of us."

General Baron rolled his eyes. He shifted the image to a still shot of Dawn as a blue angel, taken from the foreground of Winston's short video. "Who is this cunt?"

Winston was now aware of a different feeling—how strongly he *did not* want to respond. He struggled to resist.

"Adrenalin levels up 300%!" a technician yelled triumphantly.

"TELL US!" Baron shrieked. Tired of waiting for the answer, he tapped his finger on the Painquilizer to send a surge of pain through Winston's body. "Blink twice through your faggot tears when you're ready to tell me her name."

In spite of the paralyzing, searing pain, a voice registered in Winston's head. *Surrender,* it suggested. *Cooperate.*

Winston blinked twice.

Baron released the Painquilizer and beckoned for an assistant to give Winston a few sips of water.

"Her name is Dawn," Winston offered. "I never knew her last name."

"Was this the first time you met her?" the general asked.

"She has been appearing in my visions this past week." Winston noticed that Baron exchanged a concerned look with Gerbers.

"You mean your dreams."

"They were conscious visions," Winston said carefully.

"What else do you know about her?"

"She was in a band."

"WHAT was the name of her band?" Gerbers demanded.

Winston could not prevent his mind from reaching into his memory and bringing the band's name forward. With all his might, he resisted saying the words that surfaced in his conscious mind. Instead, he repeated the question: "The name of what band?"

"Don't play with me, worm!" Baron yelled menacingly, switching the pain back on to an even higher level.

Winston's body quivered in pain. He felt life slowly slipping from him. *Cooperate,* the voice in his head said soothingly. He blinked twice.

Winston tried to gasp out the name, but he was unable to speak. The assistant brought a straw to his arid mouth, and Winston sipped from the cup of water. Finally, in a hoarse, meek voice he scarcely recognized, he offered, "Utopia Rising."

"Utopia Rising," Baron repeated, looking at the word TRUE on the screen overhead, and then at a team of researchers standing at keyboard terminals nearby.

"Found her!" a voice yelled. "Dawn Souljah is her name."

Dawn's biographical data and photos of her as a young woman raced across dozens of screens. "One of two spiritual leaders who founded the United Peoples of America!" Baron yelled gleefully. "Mr. Gerbers, do you realize what this means?!"

"Fantastic!" Gerbers agreed.

"We've got our terrorist ringleader," Baron said. "So, Smith, your betrayal has earned you a very long rest!" The general laughed jubilantly as he dialed the pain so high that Winston was only aware of it for a few seconds until, with relief, he again lost consciousness.

Baron glanced at a hovering screen. "He will sleep for a long time. Segregate him from the other prisoners and monitor all of them."

Like an audio track in another room, Winston's third ear continued to listen.

General Baron was barking orders to many others who now assembled around him.

"Tighten the noose! Cancel all leave. Double security at all airports, bus and rail stations in Colorado and on every road out of state. Add roadblocks in and out of Denver, Boulder, and Colorado Springs. Stop and search all cars; drug test and iris scan ID protocols for every person, driver or passenger, buses included. Notify restaurants of a new public health ban on all beverages that are not in sealed bottles. Terror text alert every citizen with the cunt's photo and news of a $10 million reward. But I want her alive for leverage against her nation of traitors. After defiling her angelic beauty, we will leave it to the President to decide how best to use her. This is a very big opportunity!"

"A very big opportunity," Director Gerbers agreed, exuberantly.

"Smith's inability to protect this cunt's identity from our truth serum was the only thing that caused the little worm to fear us," General Baron observed. "When Smith sees what becomes of her and her pathetic little insurrection, as well as the terrorist state of California which spawned him, he will understand, more than ever, what it means to feel fear."

Chapter 21: Abraham and Sarah

Saturday May 5,2034
08:00 a.m. Mountain Time
Denver Botanic Gardens
Denver, Colorado
Trump's United Enterprises of America

Colonel Jim Morgan of the Western District Homeland Security Army first noticed the crows when he was preparing to address the advance deployment of troopers assembled along the edge of Chessman Park. There seemed to be thousands of them, blackening the trees that ringed the large public meadow where the afternoon's laser combat event would be taking place.

At 40, Morgan was old enough to have been a Boy Scout before the group was disbanded for being both insufficiently patriotic and overly reliant on gatherings in the toxic outdoors. Even during his camping days, Morgan could not recall ever seeing crows assembled in such high numbers. The fact that he was standing in the center of Denver made this even more unusual. He considered shooting them out of the trees, but then, he thought, who would clean up the mess?

Morgan had been briefed on the importance of putting a pristine face on Denver to the outside world. It was the first time the largest western city of Trump's United Enterprises of America was hosting the annual championship of the International Society of Laser Combat Knights, and hundreds of foreign journalists and visitors would be in attendance. All activity at coal and mining and chemical plants had been halted for an entire week to clean the air. The sky looked bluer than it had in years. The massive main lawn of the park had been watered and greened to accommodate 40,000 attendees.

No, Colonel Morgan concluded, the guts and cadavers of thousands of large birds would not be a welcome sight.

Morgan thought of calling his commanding general and asking for advice. But then he realized this was exactly the sort of thing he could be ridiculed about forever. He resolved to ignore the birds.

Morgan gave orders to the 200 troopers assembled under his command to create rooftop monitors, as well as security checkpoints in streets surrounding the large park, around the field, near the stage and in the V.I.P. seating section. He had been advised of Code Red-level potential threats of terrorist disruptions, protests or druggings at public events.

Morgan had received this advisory as part of a classified memo about Thursday's incursion of terrorists from the United Peoples of America. The Homeland Security Army was taking no chances. In addition to more than 200,000 soldiers garrisoned at dozens of points across the border, nearly a thousand more troopers, as well as hundreds of Denver city cops, would join the security effort at Chessman Park.

Colonel Morgan was glad that the 2 p.m. event was not another dull patriot rally with endless speeches requiring applause every 30 seconds. Like most Americans, Morgan had become a big fan of laser combat, the nation's most popular sport. He was looking forward to the exciting open melee battle, pitting the half-dozen tween and teen champions against a half-dozen past champions over 20 who were returning for the special event. His wife and 8-year-old son had gotten their tickets months ago.

Morgan had assigned himself the task of stage security. From that vantage point, he told his son over breakfast that morning, he wouldn't miss a moment of the action.

*

At 8:15 a.m., Abraham Smith's mother dropped him off at the participant meeting point in the parking lot of the Denver Botanic Gardens. Abe carried his laser sword in one hand while using the other hand to balance the huge duffel bag of gear and clothing on his shoulder. He was a little short for his age, but after six years training as a laser knight, he was stronger than many adults and carried his burden with ease.

A small group of other champions and some of their parents had joined the International Laser Combat Society's CEO, Vincent Wellworth, and his staff to help set up a state-of-the-art portable battle arena in the center of nearby Chessman Park. The big awards brunch at 11 o'clock in the serene amphitheater of the Botanic Gardens was being handled by the event's sponsor, Laser Combat Armor, Inc. But preparing the combat field for a massive melee event needed to be done right, so Abraham had volunteered to help.

Abe grabbed a fruit smoothie and joined the cluster of volunteers to receive their instructions. He tried not to feel intimidated by the size of the military officers who would be among the former champions challenging the tournament winners. Their imposing uniforms and huge handguns gave him pause, but their camaraderie and congratulations as they introduced themselves to Abe made them a lot less intimidating. Two of them even texted him their contact information details, should he want to talk to them about following their career and education track to high-ranking military positions.

Abe was glad to see his friend Gen, a 16-year-old Japanese boy whose extraordinary martial arts skills, combined with powerful swordsmanship, had won him the world championship in the 15- to 16-year-old class. He dropped his gear on the ground next to Gen and practiced the Japanese greeting bow he'd been taught. Then they sipped their breakfast drinks while listening to Vince Wellworth instruct them on where to leave their gear and which volunteer tasks he'd assigned them for the setup.

As Abe and Gen carried their gear to their dressing trailer near the stage in Chessman Park, they talked about the differences between their countries. Abraham had never been abroad, but he loved hearing about the shocking amount of freedom that people had in Japan. It sounded like his parents reminiscing on what life had been like in his own country before he was born, before the war on terror began.

The boys followed the others to the massive stage and combat court area and secured their gear in assigned lockers within the well-appointed event trailers. Then they went to their assigned section and helped supervise the workers laying padding and assembling scaffolding sections for side ramps. It was easy work and went quickly. By 9:30, Abe had finished his segment and was ready for a bathroom break before suiting up for the brunch ceremony.

Like most kids, Abe hated portable potties, so he picked up his gear, bypassed the battery of plastic outhouses set out for the big event, and walked ten minutes to the nice permanent restrooms by the popular outdoor cafe in the middle of the Denver Botanic Gardens.

As he left the bathroom, Abe noticed an unusual sight along the walkway. In one of the Garden's dozens of horticulture alcoves, beneath an etched wooden overhang inscribed with the words "Sacred Earth," two girls his age were sparring with light sabers.

Their moves were deft and deliberate, and although they made less contact than Abe was accustomed to, they mixed expert Aikido moves into their practice. Abe stood in the pathway next to other onlookers.

Abe noticed a few women playing and singing on a small bench behind the small clearing; a tall, scrawny man with unusually long bright red hair flowing out of his helmet joined them. They had parked their bicycles nearby and were dressed in cyclist clothes, protective helmets and wide sunglasses. They seemed to be serenading the sparring girls, lending a peaceful rhythm to their morning practice. Abe heard the word "gratitude" repeated many times and noticed that the cyclists turned to face each direction as they sang and took deep breaths between each verse.

Abe was impressed, especially with the darker-skinned, black-haired girl, whose body was covered with an old first-generation laser combat suit colored like an ocelot. Abraham had never seen a girl, or even a grown woman, handle a sword like the lithe ocelot. Competitive laser combat had always been the exclusive domain of boys and men. He wondered whether the ocelot may have come from another country to watch the competition, or whether there were other girls who could fight like her, secretly sparring in their basements and in public parks.

As though she had heard his thoughts, the girl stopped sparring, looked straight at Abe with the darkest eyes he had ever seen and said, "My name is Sarah. We have been waiting for you, Abraham."

"Waiting?" he asked. "And how do you know my name?"

She smiled a friendly, knowing smile, and as an answer, pointed to a paper laying on the ground near her feet.

The blank white side of the paper was facing up. Abraham stepped closer to Sarah, picked it up and turned it over. He expected it to be a request for his autograph from a laser combat fan. Instead, he saw a symbol of a radiant human being with tree-like roots filling the page. He did not know its significance, yet it felt immediately familiar. He stared intently at it, mesmerized, as he recognized it from a hundred dreams from as far back as he could remember.

As he stood there, fascinated by the image in his hands, Sarah and her sparring partner joined the three cyclists in singing beautiful harmonies to the end of the gratitude song, followed by chants of "With all as One" over and over a dozen times, each with increasing passion. The song suddenly slowed down, and the five singers held their arms wide open, thrusting their chests forward as the guitar stopped for the chanting of the final note. The word One resounded like a long Om as the red-haired cyclist rang a pair of ornate bells together. The sweet vibration sailed out over everyone who could hear it.

Abraham felt an energetic wave emanating from the hearts of the five singers whose chests were thrust forward. The wave pulsed through his body, and he felt a shift within, as though it had triggered the awakening of something sleeping deep within him.

Abe could sense that he was being presented with an important decision: to allow this glorious seed within to sprout into the mystic rose of his destiny, or to turn away and suppress its awakening.

From inside his heart, Abraham felt his soul answer more clearly than any choice he had ever made. He said YES! to his Activation.

Immediately, the world around Abe faded from his awareness. He found himself in a realm he had only sensed during some of his more intense visionary dreams. It felt different than the out-of-body journeys and visions he had experienced in the past. Instead of witnessing future events and the often tragic fate of other people, Abe witnessed his own past, through the eyes of an all-loving, all-accepting angel hovering above his body.

This angel exalted Abraham's finest attributes, the essence of the Godly that lay deep beneath the noise and stories, identifications and habits of egoistic life. The angel flew with him through time, to the emotional pains that the 12 years of his life had burned into his soul.

The feeling that recurred most often in Abe's journey through the past, the feeling that seared and shamed his psyche, was that of hopelessness and despair. As a capable, mystical powerful empath in a society that, since his birth, had penalized and crushed the humanistic values of compassion and caring, Abraham had suffered deeply.

Abraham's mystical capacity to foretell the future made this helplessness worse. He relived his pain during kindergarten, when he dreamed of the sudden death of a classmate and her entire family, massacred by the omnipresent Homeland Security troopers during the pre-dawn home invasion sweeps conducted during what became known as the Raids Against Terror. He had known it would happen the previous day, and when he sat in class and saw the girl's empty desk, he realized, with heartache, that it had come true.

His grandparents' fiery death appeared vividly in Abraham's dreams the night before the firebombing of South Lake Tahoe on January 14, 2028. He was only 6 years old at the time, and he did not feel old enough to Skype his beloved grandparents to warn them to leave town before the missiles hit. He had begged his father and mother to make the call for him, but they didn't trust what he knew. He recalled, with tears streaming over his face, the screaming fit he threw, desperate to have his voice, his vision heard. Although it was the first time his brother defied his parents to stand up for him, both boys were ignored.

His parents just scolded them, then dropped Abe and Robert off at school while they went to their busy jobs.

A soothing presence floated over Abe's shame of powerlessness, whispering his attributes of compassion, caring, vision, diligence and courage. These words washed over his wounds, healing the shame he had felt for so long, his powerlessness to impact the misery of thousands of oppressed souls around him, suffering so deeply felt that some days his spirit seemed trapped in a world of infinite darkness.

Sarah stood near him and touched his hand lightly. He looked into the deepest, most understanding eyes he had ever seen and heard her soft voice in his head. *I, too, was born in the caul. On the same day as you. I share the visioning and understand how challenging it must have felt for you to know, yet to remain silent. You were born to protect, born to lead, born to be part of this change. We are joined as one, together as New Evolutionary Warriors, N.E.W. Knights, fighting to create a future in which all living beings thrive.*

"N.E.W. Knights," Abe repeated, savoring the words. "N.E.W. Knights, yes." Breathing deeply, he closed his eyes and saw the symbol that he had seen earlier, the icon that had appeared in his dreams for as long as he could remember. It would be the insignia of their new order.

A message from the hive mind appeared in his mind, not in Sarah's voice, but in his own inner voice. *Our sacred work begins now,* it said.

Abraham began processing what he needed to do. To his delight, the thought was not happening in his own mind, but in a collaborative mind, shared with the small group of Activated, interconnected wonderful people standing next to him: the two girls his age, the cyclists and the small cluster of people who had been watching the song. *Bring the officials to hear our song,* he heard.

Abe headed to the setup area for the brunch event in the Botanic Garden amphitheater, just two minutes away. His friend Gen and many of the volunteers were back, horsing around on the lawn as workers prepared brunch for the 400 attendees who would join the celebration. Laser Combat Society Director Wellworth was talking to the event organizer, as well as the chief executive of Laser Armor, Inc. and a cluster of officials and young military officers.

Abe had never been entirely comfortable around adults, but he now felt a new capacity to connect with anyone. He walked easily into their circle, where he received pats on the back and congratulations on his championship.

"Oh look," he said, pointing to a small group of singers and musicians who had started a song on the edge of the walkway near the amphitheater. "I saw that small choir earlier."

Wellworth and his entourage looked up. Three cyclists, one playing a guitar, along with a half-dozen others, including a girl in an ocelot body armor suit, were chanting, "With all as One." As they sang, they held their arms wide open. A man with long red hair was ringing a pair of ornate bells together.

"I don't think they have a permit to play music in the park," Wellworth said with a frown. "I think I will have security remove ..."

Wellworth stopped in mid-sentence. The 50 early arrivals and dozens of catering workers suddenly fell silent. Abe closed his eyes and felt the warm, bright sun basking everyone around him in the state of connected bliss he'd been feeling since his own Activation. He felt himself one with the hundreds of witnessing, all-loving, all-accepting angels flying in the air above. He heard nearly a hundred newly awakened souls proclaim their choice, their YES, to the Oneness that was their true interconnected nature.

Less than ten minutes later, the hive mind Abe was tuned into had expanded to include his friend Gen, the organizers running the Laser Combat Society, and all the people working on the event. Half of the group headed into the nearby gardens to harvest herbs and prepare elixirs from hundreds of new plants that were overflowing plant beds as far as Abe could see.

Abe stuck around with the rest of the group, learning to sing the sacred Activation song on the event stage. The first round of early guests for the brunch arrived and heard the new choir's song and bell vibration.

When the 400 brunch attendees sat down to eat at 11 o'clock, Laser Combat CEO Vincent Wellworth welcomed them, and then invited a special One True Church choir to sing an opening hymn.

The group, led by a woman in a bicycle helmet and playing the guitar, took the stage. By 11:30, with the exception of a couple of men who had collapsed in their seats, every person in the amphitheater had been Activated.

The planned luncheon was served, accompanied by a special mineral-rich beverage designed to counteract toxins in the bloodstream. By noon, the 400 attendees were volunteering in the facility's kitchen to process herbs into drinks for the millions of people they planned to Activate during the next few days.

Crows patrolled the air around them, clawing to the ground the Homeland Security drones. The insurrection had begun.

Chapter 22: The Final Negotiation

Saturday May 5,2034
11:00 a.m. Mountain Time
Homeland Security Central Prison
Denver, Colorado
Trump's United Enterprises of America

After the longest sleep he could remember, Winston woke to a man's desperate screams for mercy. The door of his tiny solitary cell was solid steel, but a thick wire mesh at the top allowed sound to travel through.

The most horrifying sounds Winston had ever heard lasted for what seemed like hours. At first, he could make out words between the shrieks of agony: a man pleading to let him die, mixed with screams of "NO!" These were followed by cruel taunts, mixed with powerful blows. After a long while, the words disappeared, replaced by screams, then moans, then silence.

Winston took refuge in his breath as he tapped into the Oneness that was his essence. He couldn't believe this practice was only a day old for him; it felt as natural as breathing. The soothing voices of angels sharing his cold, tiny cell heartened him as they whispered his attributes: *You are loving, you are compassionate, you are strong, you are courageous, you are We and We are you and We are eternal.*

Winston opened his awareness to the group mind of the 300 other Activated prisoners captured after the rave party, also being held somewhere in the sprawling underground prison. In his mind, he heard: *Stay alive. You are needed. We have work to do.*

Winston drank water from the small sink attached to the wall next to a seatless toilet hole. He stretched his body, feeling the aches. He continued exercising, then meditating, calming his mind and finding comfort in his inner world, in his shared sense of peace.

After some time, Winston's cell door opened.

"Step away from the door, faggot. Time to suit up," announced one of two prison guards looming menacingly in the doorway.

Winston stepped back. A hovering drone dropped a detention suit down the back of his neck, as a long steel cable covered his spine and clasped his wrists to his side.

"The general wants to see you, queerbait," the other guard said. "Follow me."

Winston shuffled behind the lead guard as best he could in the restricting detention suit. Pain shot through his body with every step. The second guard followed a few paces behind, holding on to the controller to Winston's detention suit.

They passed a dozen small cells on either side, each with a numbered steel door. As they continued down the hall, Winston heard savage sounds, like war cries, emanating from the cells.

Up ahead, he saw a banner hanging down from a wide opening enclosed by thick steel bars—a large Nazi flag with the letters **America First** emblazoned along the top.

The guard in front of Winston stopped. Behind the banner, Winston could make out a filthy, boisterous dormitory the size of a basketball court, where 30 men, dressed and undressed, stood among scattered beds and lockers, tables and free weights. Another banner, with coarse red letters written in blood, hung from the rafters proclaiming: "WE EAT TERRISTS!"

"Take a look at what's on the menu, faggot," the lead guard said, pointing to the middle of the hall, where a few tattered picnic tables surrounded a large propane barbeque. A putrid smoke spilled into the prison hallway from a bloody slab of human body that cooked over the fire. Winston retched uncontrollably, vomiting up water and what little food remained in his belly.

Three white men, shirtless with Nazi tattoos across their massive bodies, poked their beefy arms out through the bars and beckoned to Winston to come closer. One man rubbed his engorged crotch and yelled, "Hey, pussy bait, when do we get a taste of you? GET THE FUCK OVER HERE NOW, BITCH!"

Winston recovered from his nausea and looked ahead. He managed to remain out of reach, struggling to ignore the prisoners' taunts and curses and the two guards' laughter.

After a few minutes, the lead guard pushed Winston to continue their march through the labyrinth of hallways, gates and buildings. Eventually they entered an enormous modern headquarters complex. They brought Winston through a pair of black-uniformed sentries into a suite of secure offices, then locked his detention suit to a standing post across from an oversized desk covered with an array of screens and devices.

"Attention!" ordered an officer from an inner room. The guards hopped to an erect salute as General Baron entered the room.

"Wait outside," Baron ordered the guards, sitting in an executive chair across the desk from where Winston was standing. "Close the door behind you."

"Yes, sir, General Baron, sir," the guards said, saluting again before they left.

The general scrolled his finger across a few screens, studied the data, and pulled a bowl of walnuts from a drawer. He crushed two together and glanced up.

"The fearless Winston Smith," he began, nibbling on the nuts. He opened a can of soda and took a few gulps. "I believe you have had a good look at the rumpus room of your neighbors, this facility's permanent residents. In the event you failed to make sense of their morning symphony, let me explain. First, they gang rape you, in ways few can fully imagine. Next, they toy with your body, while you are still alive, taking tastes along the way, until, finally, in blessed relief, you succumb from your many wounds and amputations and die. That's when your body becomes the meat for their barbeque."

General Baron paused, hooked Winston's eyes with his pale blue stare and continued. "Not very elegant, I acknowledge. But as you might imagine, extremely effective in advancing the sort of negotiation that you and I are going to have right now.

"Simply put, Smith, after we have completed our research on you, by later this week, your usefulness to our understanding of this new terrorist mind-control weapon will be finished, and so will your life." Baron's voice was both somber and ominous as he added, "In cases like yours, I provide Super Patriots, the lucky 1%-ers, with the choice of how you die. Pay me what I ask, and you get this …"

Baron touched a controller that softly pressed the tip of a hypodermic needle against Winston's jugular vein. "This swift lethal injection provides a painless sleep from which you will simply not awaken. Your relatives receive your body back, relatively intact, for a family funeral and the legal right to bury you in any cemetery. If you are unwilling to strike a deal, then the state uses your body like any other terrorist—as meat to pay for your incarceration. In such cases, there are no remains, no family notice, no mercy. You are, if you will, your own last meal."

Baron laughed maniacally at his favorite joke. He cracked more walnuts together in his powerful hands, dropping the shells onto the desk. "Would you like one, Smith? And some water? I know you must be thirsty." Baron stood up and handed Winston a few nuts and a pint container of water.

Winston's hands had been released with sufficient range to reach his mouth. He guzzled the water, stopping only to nibble hungrily on a few walnuts.

General Baron noticed something on one of his screens. Euphoric, he blurted out, "We found her; oh, YES!" Baron smiled and slid his fingers to flip a hovering screen sideways so Winston could also see it. The screen flashed a zoomed-in, candid photo of Dawn, with map coordinates showing the Denver Botanic Gardens and the words, "Reward claim" and a number across the bottom.

Baron jumped up behind the desk, touched one of his screens a few times, and then barked orders to the Homeland Security's ranking officer in the area: "Colonel Morgan," he commanded. "Tighten the noose! Arrest anyone leaving the park. This is warfare. Code Red. The terrorists, no doubt, are at the laser combat event you are guarding that starts in 40 minutes. They will likely try to spread their mind-control drugs in beverages, but we cannot rule out chemical gas, so implement detection testing immediately and have gas masks at the ready."

"Move your riot control tanks into position in the event they have commandeered the main stage audio-video systems. Use whatever force necessary, but no opening fire on the main crowd. Triple the drone deployment to 3,000 for comprehensive biometric scans; I want a list of everyone within the security perimeter. Have the drones identify and detain; if necessary kill anyone not in the national or visa database."

"Apprehend the California cunt if you can, but do not kill her. Update me immediately when you have more info. I will arrive with reinforcements at 1400 hours."

General Baron, animated and powerful, was in his element. He touched the screen and barely stopped to catch his breath before starting on his next set of orders. "General Hax, we have a Code Red terrorist incursion in Chessman Park. Deploy Garrison Units 3 to 6 to the site immediately, and prepare the prison and interrogation halls for as many as 1,000 new arrivals. I will travel with the Alpha Force in two squadrons of assault helicopters. Have the escort join me in my warden suite at 1345 hours for deployment at 1350 hours."

"Yes, sir, General Baron, sir, right away, sir," Winston heard a deep voice respond."

General Baron looked at another monitor, smiled triumphantly and sat down at the desk. He turned his attention to Winston. "It seems that the imminent capture of your precious leader is causing you some discomfort, Smith. Maybe the terrorist cunt has left you wondering why people like me do the unpopular work we do? It would be so much easier to be like you, to coast along as a nice guy, to take the easy road and mind my own business."

"But that's not how we built the greatest country on Earth, and that's not how we protect it! While libtards like you called the

Iraq War 'unwinnable,' I joined my brothers in arms and enlisted, to kill the Islamist cocksuckers there before they had a chance to kill us here. I knew that with George Bush at the helm, we had a government that would stand for a Christian America. In 2008, after five bloody years, I was promoted to major, just in time for the election of Barack Fucken Hussein Obama. For eight years I cried myself to sleep because our country was no longer allowed to be the greatest country on Earth, and instead was run by a Kenyan hell-bent on bringing America to its knees to his Muslim terrorist God."

Baron looked defiantly at Winston, who returned his gaze with curiosity and a sense of compassion.

"My prayers," the general continued, "and the prayers of every God-fearing American Firster got answered by the miraculous 2016 election, in which We, the People, threw out the bloodsuckers and the witches and the Jews and the niggers and the wetbacks and elected President Donald Jesus Trump to make America Great again! By any fucking means necessary!"

"So here we are, on your last weekend on Earth. The true Master Race is ascendant. President Trump, along with allies like President Putin, has shown the world that the days of weak government and mediocrity are gone forever. Lesser nations will yield, or they will perish by fire. Traitors will receive their just rewards, as our iron fist smashes your shit stain of a rebellion into the cold black earth and regains the seditious western states."

With a look of smug satisfaction, Baron continued. "But how can a treasonous worm like you understand the greatness of our military might, of our nation, of our race! Worms like you can only yield to our irresistible power. Yet, even that is a choice. At every juncture in our lives, we make choices. To master other men, or to be mastered by them. To eat, or to be on the menu.

In my house," he laughed, gesturing to the walls around him, "we mean this literally."

The general bit his lower lip and grinned maliciously, pleased with his own cleverness. "Which brings us to the final choice you get to make in this life of yours." Baron opened a drawer and put a clipboard holding an official-looking paper onto his desk and positioned a scribe drone to record the signing. "This is a contract designating me as your sole heir upon your death, to receive all assets in your estate, as well as the 12 remaining years of payments due to you from Patriot News. You will not need them where you are going. In return, you are guaranteed a comfortable death by lethal injection and the transport of your intact body to your ex-wife Suzanne's home, with permission to place your body in a normal cemetery of her choice."

Baron looked up at Winston. "Will you sign it?"

Winston breathed deeply, considered the offer, and the alternative. Then he nodded his assent.

The scribe drone brought the clipboard and pen to Winston's hand and then recorded his signature. Baron looked pleased. "A wise decision, Smith. You are fortunate to be wealthy enough to have been given a choice."

He waited for the prisoner to say thank you, but Winston remained silent.

Baron walked over until his face was less than a foot from Winston's. "Before we kill you, I'm going to bring Dawn Souljah in for a special interrogation and deflower her in front of you. How will you feel, Winston Smith, when your Queen is defeated! When all hope is annihilated!"

General Baron's eyes glowered as he stared cruelly at Winston. "You will pay with your lives for your blood treason and betrayal of your race. The West Coast's technology, aerospace, entertainment and agricultural assets will once again be restored to our unified, great nation, along with tens of millions of slaves. A richer, more powerful America will once again lead the nations of the world, this time on behalf of the One True Church, the Master Race and President for Life Donald Jesus Trump!"

Chapter 23: Showdown

Saturday May 5,2034
2:45 p.m. Mountain Time
Chessman Park
Denver, Colorado
Trump's United Enterprises of America

Abraham Smith stood with his arms wide open. He had joined Sarah and her mother, Dawn Souljah, and more than 50 others on the large stage overlooking 40,000 people assembled in the main meadow of Chessman Park. The final chant of the Four Directions song, the words, "With all as One," was shared by hundreds of others who had been activated earlier in the day. Now, as he looked out over the blissful beings, he marveled at the extraordinary silence.

Every listener, Abe knew, was experiencing the awakening that he'd felt only hours earlier. They were all making their choice to proceed into an interconnected future as they said yes to turning on a genetic switch that opened their hearts to their true nature. Each person was facing his or her shadows, blessing emotional scars of their past with cleansing tears.

Abraham watched in awe as tears soaked every face in the audience. Hundreds of black-uniformed Homeland Security troopers near the stage and along the aisles had removed their ominous helmets, face shields, and black leather gloves and were now wiping their wet faces with bare hands. Even the high-ranking politicos and billionaires in the V.I.P. section were transformed. The experience of Oneness was irresistible.

The fingertips of Abraham's outstretched hand connected to Sarah's. They had reprogrammed their laser armor to proclaim their collective destiny. On the front of their mid-section: the symbol of a radiant human being with tree-like roots that he had seen on the paper that morning.

It's your time, Abraham heard Sarah's voice speaking in his mind. As he walked to the center of the stage, people parted and Dawn adjusted the microphone stand for him. Abe had never spoken in public before, yet somehow, he realized, he was not the slightest bit nervous. He knew the words would come to him.

And they did.

"The peaceful utopia of the United Peoples of America is expanding. It is something that I, like many of us, have prayed for our entire lives," Abe said. "Imagine not being afraid. Imagine being connected. This is our true state, this is who we really are. Now is the time to stand for what is right: for one another and for this sacred Earth."

"I call on all the young people listening to this, boys and girls, rich and poor, whatever your color, whoever your parents are to join us in our loving community, our Oneness. "

"Some of you know me as the Tiger, a warrior champion of the International Society of Laser Combat Knights. I have been that, but today I am more than that. I am reborn as a boy without fear, able to live my dreams and able, for the first time, to work to change things for other people and for this planet that we all share.:

"I am still the Tiger, but I invite you to join me in turning our great game of skill to a heroic calling, a calling to protect others. I invite you to join us as New Evolutionary Warriors, N.E.W. Knights, using what power we have to protect the spiritual warriors stepping forward in the challenging work of transforming our brutal, merciless society into the harmonious culture of the Wetopia we have long dreamed of."

*

As General Francis J. Baron quickly leapt out of his armored black SUV, he almost knocked the elite Alpha Force trooper opening the door for him on the ground. His face was beet red; as he barked orders, white spittle flew in all directions. His bodyguards had never seen him so angry.

Baron was a man accustomed to having his orders fulfilled with military precision. After leaving the Homeland Security Prison, he had been successfully escorted by his elite Alpha Force troopers into one of eight awaiting assault helicopters, their engines purring. He'd ordered a roadway alongside Chessman Park—just a five-minute flight from the Homeland Security Western Division military base and prison complex—cordoned off to serve as their landing strip. His team strapped themselves in, the doors were closed, and the chopper began its ascent at 13:46, exactly on schedule.

But at that moment, everything started to go wrong. Air traffic control radioed in a peculiar sighting of a dark-haired woman in a long white tunic hovering like a ghost at the edge of the runway, with arms extended into the air. Before Baron had time to order her shot, out of nowhere, a hurricane wind swept across the airbase. The wind effortlessly sent the eight helicopters trying to lift off smashing back onto the tarmac while also sweeping three dozen other aircraft and assorted support vehicles into a scrap heap along the high security fence. Emergency vehicles had to be brought from the far end of the sprawling base to rescue scores of injured troopers and pilots.

The hurricane wind disappeared almost as quickly as it had arrived. General Baron escaped with minor injuries and punched to the ground the emergency medical technician who tried to insist that he get checked out at the nearby hospital. He ordered an immediate pickup by his fleet of armored SUVs for him and his top officers and bodyguards, to be followed by a convoy of trucks to transport 12 platoons of Alpha Force troopers.

Because their helicopters had been downed, the General's forces had been unable to get to Chessman Park before the 14:00 event began. At 14:25, while en route to Central Denver, Baron received intelligence from Colonel Morgan, the commanding officer on the ground, that drove home the cost of allowing their enemy to hijack the event. The colonel reported that Dawn Souljah and her accomplices had been surrounded, but not captured. Satellite surveillance was mysteriously malfunctioning, while every one of the army's 3,000 drones had been destroyed by crows, effectively blinding their eyes in the sky. Why Morgan and his well-armed 1200-man team failed to capture Dawn Souljah and prevent the insurgents from taking the stage, Baron thought vengefully, would be uncovered during the colonel's court martial torture session, before the general killed him.

For a military commander who had never known a setback, much less a defeat, the news got even worse. Morgan texted him a video, taken from a few hundred yards away, of the insurgents on the stage at Chessman Park surrounded by an enormous crowd, and next to them, flying full in the breeze, was the flag of the United Peoples of America.

By the time Baron and his assault teams had driven the 22 miles to arrive at the north edge of Chessman Park, it was 14:40, and he was ready to shoot someone. As he marched past a speedy review of his 3,000 Alpha Force Homeland Security troopers waiting in formation, General Baron's mind raced to size up his enemy.

During their six years of secession, he realized, the nation of traitors along the West Coast had added to their impressive force field technology a mysterious new mind-control drug, one capable of transforming meek men and women into fearless insurgents. Their invasion force had also somehow managed to penetrate the border undetected. And their military had successfully deployed a wind cannon strong enough to wipe out his entire air base, along with an inexplicable technology that weaponized thousands of flesh-and-blood birds so they could destroy drones.

The situation keeps deteriorating, Baron thought angrily. The United Peoples of America had chosen a perfect time and place for their massive mind-control scheme. Although the general longed to firebomb the entire crowd and turn Chessman Park into a giant crematorium, his options were limited. The Laser Combat Knight ceremony had attracted more V.I.P.s and Super Patriots to Denver than any event in decades. Even one of President Trump's grandsons was there. He cursed the cleverness of his enemy.

General Baron ordered his soldiers to attention, patched his smartphone into a waiting speaker system, and, in a jingoistic tone matched only by Trump himself, informed his troops that "America is under attack by the largest, most effective resistance outbreak to strike our nation since 9/11!"

Baron slowed down to let the importance of the words sink in. "We exist to defend this great nation, at all costs. What is the remedy to this cancer in our midst, this insurrection spreading just a half mile from here even as I speak?"

"KILL THEM!" shouted 3,000 troopers in response.

"Exactly," Baron continued. "As you know, my first choice would be a massive fire missile strike similar to the one that punished South Lake Tahoe. What do we do with terrorists who dare to hoist the enemy flag in our proud city?" Baron paused to allow his troopers to express their blood lust.

"KILL THEM ALL, KILL THEM ALL!" they shouted, pounding their boots into the ground.

The general held out his hands to quiet them. "You will have ample opportunity to put down terrorists today," he promised. "As you know, true warriors do NOT show mercy or know mercy. But today's slaughter must be surgical. Alpha Platoon 1 and 2 will join me to rescue Super Patriot, celebrity, military, and media hostages in the V.I.P. and press sections. Platoons 3 and 4 will ring the perimeter around the field and ensure that nobody gets in or out. Scan any person claiming to be a V.I.P.; kill anyone who tries to run.

"Platoons 5 to 12, your job is to capture alive and detain Dawn Souljah, whose picture you now have, while killing everyone who tries to protect her. We don't know how many infiltrators there are, or how many they have drugged to help them, but this operation anticipates no more than one prisoner," Baron paused and gave his bloodthirsty troops a knowing smile, "and no survivors."

General Baron stepped off the makeshift platform to a symphony of "Kill, kill, kill!" and the echo of thousands of boots stomping the ground. He gave orders to move a squadron of eight tanks equipped with powerful sound cannons to surround the main meadow, then marched his perfectly formed assault regiment to the edge of the battlefield.

The Alpha Force platoons took their positions along the long west and east ends of the Chessman Park meadow, forming a menacing row of helmeted black-armored storm troopers on each side.

Dawn was singing on stage with a dozen musicians. The crowd of 40,000 was standing and singing in unison, as though they had rehearsed the song for days.

General Baron flipped the optics over his black helmet and scanned the front of the crowd for the V.I.P. and press sections. He noticed an area toward the front, ringed by a few hundred uniformed troopers. They did not have their guns drawn, nor were they attempting a rescue. Instead, they had removed their helmets and were standing, like everyone else, with their arms open wide, singing.

Baron was infuriated. All troopers had been warned against drinking the Kool Aid. He would never have imagined that such widespread treason among Homeland Security forces was possible. He pictured their court martial and execution, but it did nothing to alleviate his anxiety over the effectiveness of the enemy's power.

Baron considered, for the first time, that the mind-control mechanism might have nothing to do with drugs in beverages. It might be something inexplicable, something far more diabolical and effective.

Always one to seek opportunity in adversity, General Baron countered his growing worry by envisioning Dawn's naked torture, at his skilled hands, and the valuable mind-control technology that he would uncover. He felt excitement stir in his groin.

Meanwhile, the words, "With all as One" resounded again and again from 40,000 voices.

"We will shut you up and shoot you down!" Baron shouted angrily, spraying spittle into his helmet microphone. The sound was amplified from eight enormous speakers mounted on the tanks surrounding the meadow full of singers.

"Dawn Souljah," Baron announced. "I hereby arrest you for the crime of treason. Anyone who does not step away from the prisoner and the stage at the count of four will be shot and killed immediately."

The speakers from the stage cranked up and Dawn's voice responded while the chorus of "With all as One" continued. "We welcome you with this song," she said, her voice courageous and clear.

"Firing positions," Baron commanded his troops through his helmet mike. The troopers formed into three lines, standing, crouching and lying on the ground, aiming rifles at people along the edge of the crowd. "Open fire and commence sound cannon at 130 decibels at the count of four."

"One ..." he began.

At that moment, a half-dozen small explosions, sounding like sonic booms, ripped across the sky a few hundred feet overhead. Baron continued his count.

"Two ... three ... four ..."

The general realized that his helmet microphone had failed. He ripped off his helmet and, at the top of his lungs, yelled, "Four! Open fire! Fire! Fire!" while waving his hand in a downward chopping motion.

Three thousand fingers pulled the triggers of their automatic assault rifles, but nothing happened. The computerized circuitry that controlled the gun sights and fingerprint locks had shut down.

General Baron pulled one of his Glocks from its holster and tried the digital fingerprint lock. It refused to turn on. He checked his smartphone. It would not even light up.

He realized what was happening. "Listen men," Baron screamed. His throat felt parched, and he focused all his might on not sounding desperate. "Officers repeat this message down the line. The enemy has dispatched an overhead Electro Magnetic Pulse that fucks up all electronic devices, including guns and vehicles and lights. Deploy riot batons in manual mode NOW! We have the rare opportunity for hand-to-hand combat against unarmed snowflakes. Strangle these motherfuckers one at a time. Take Dawn alive. Kill anyone near her. Let me hear it!"

Three thousand storm troopers set down their rifles and chanted, "Kill, kill, kill!" drowning out the chorus.

"Attack!" Baron commanded. His orders were echoed up and down the line of soldiers who boxed in the meadow. Six thousand boots marched steadily forward, causing the ground to shake.

General Baron expected the crowd to panic and run, but they stood their ground, repeating the incessant "With all as One" chorus while holding their arms out. But he noticed many other people moving to the edge of the crowd. Hundreds of Homeland Security troopers, Colonel Morgan's advance forces, had donned their helmets and unfurled their own riot batons. And running in front of them, rushing to meet the Alpha Force soldiers and protect the meadow full of singers, were more than five hundred young laser knights in close-fitting Kevlar and titanium body armor.

In less than a minute, the battle was joined. General Baron expected his men to sweep aside the laser knights, some of them not yet teenagers. But their agility was astounding. Baron's men had received some martial arts training, but they were more accustomed to using brute force to decimate panicked civilians. Here, though, they found themselves up against the world champions of laser knight combat from all over the world, as well as former champions well in their 20s who had maintained their skills after joining the military.

The laser knights were outnumbered, but they seemed to be everywhere. They spun, they kicked, they easily parried the shorter telescoping steel batons of the troopers with their longer polycarbonate laser sabers, landing body blows against the troopers' heavier, more cumbersome body armor. The troopers were knocked to the ground again and again. They rose back up, got hit, then kicked, tripped and flipped to the ground again.

Those Alpha Force attackers that managed to rush past the knights found themselves squaring off against a defensive line of heavily armored troopers who surrounded and neutralized them before they could advance into the crowd.

General Baron drew his combat knife. He tried to stab at a kid with tiger stripes on his armor who had rushed directly into his command unit. But the kid was too fast, and he smacked Baron across the back with his sword, then followed it with a wide boot kick to the neck. From the ground, the general looked over the battlefield, gasping for air as he realized, with despair, that his troops were doing no better than he was. The Alpha Forces were trained to use different, more lethal weapons, against terrorized citizens. Now they found themselves battling accomplished martial arts. And they were losing badly.

Meanwhile, the song grew louder. Dawn led a final, slow, "With all as Oooonnnne" into a massive Om of 40,000 voices. The voices were joined by the amplified sound of the crisp ring of a Tibetan bell from the stage.

The sound vibration of the collective Om met the ring of the bell, creating an energetic wave of 40,000 awakened human hearts. The wave surged over General Baron and every one of his Alpha Force troopers, switching on a gene that had been dormant in their DNA since their birth.

All fighting, movement, and sound ended as the soldiers stopped fighting and journeyed deep inside themselves and their pasts with an illuminating new awareness.

Suddenly they were not alone.

Suddenly they were all connected.

Suddenly they were one.

The Great Expansion had begun.

Chapter 24: Rescued

Saturday May 5,2034
5:00 p.m. Mountain Time
Chessman Park
Denver, Colorado
Trump's United Enterprises of America

Only two hours had passed since the Homeland Security assault troops had experienced their Activation, but the landscape of Chessman Park and the Denver Botanic Gardens already had been transformed.

Like bees in their hive, tens of thousands of telepathically interconnected men, women, and children worked quickly and efficiently to prepare every useable area of the park and gardens to serve the hundreds of thousands of poorly nourished, distressed and chemically dependent citizens of the Denver area who would soon need assistance.

Tapping into a connected and supportive Mother Earth, newly planted medicinal herbs and vegetables grew to maturity in hours instead of months, fueled by microorganisms and mycelium brought from the United Peoples of America that spread like wildfire through every available inch of soil. Workers stood by to harvest the continually replenishing plants every few hours. Other volunteers processed the nutritionally rich herbs and green vegetables into millions of portions of restorative beverages for the days of massive transformation ahead.

Dozens of field tents and tarp-covered areas had sprung up for holistic therapies and health care, while workers prepared the main meadow to serve as an outdoor dormitory for refugees who were soon expected be liberated from disease-riddled slave labor camps around the state.

Meanwhile, the number of newly Activated people kept growing. Troopers who had been guarding the security checkpoints in the streets around the park had been relieved of their duty by awakened Alpha Force soldiers who had joined the efforts of the unified hive mind. They were sent to a special briefing and informed that they needed to be on the alert for the song they were about to hear. Then Dawn and her growing chorus sang "The Four Directions" song.

Within minutes, nearly all of the more than 4,000 Homeland Security troopers dispatched to Chessman Park had joined the transformation. A handful of troopers had rejected the Activation process and fallen into a mental shutdown state similar to a coma. General Baron was among them.

The Activation process had nearly killed the general. As he realized his Oneness with all living beings, he was confronted with the suffering that his dark past of torture, rape and murder had brought to thousands of people. He struggled to accept his past, to forgive what he had done, to love who he had become. He fell to the ground and his heart dangerously hastened as a debilitating remembrance of his sadistic deeds and the pain of his victims looped through his mind.

Dawn handed the management of the Activation to teams of others, then watched as a group of psychic trauma healers gathered to assist General Baron. Through the hive mind, the healers called a few hundred Activated helpers to open themselves as mediums to Baron's victims. The volunteers closed their eyes and allowed the spirits of hundreds of people who had been objects of the general's cruel deeds to witness his redemption.

Laying on the ground, General Baron shuddered as he felt the presence of the departed souls inhabit those around him. With tears drenching his face, his inner voice begged them for forgiveness. To his astonishment, he received it, from one victim after another. He felt energy flow from the beings around him. His heartbeat slowed as self-forgiveness, a sense of lovingness, and a new sense of purpose grew within him.

Finally, after a long dark journey, Francis Baron opened his eyes and stood erect and tall. He looked at Dawn standing nearby and said, with the kindest tone he had ever spoken, "Let's do this."

By the time General Baron and Dawn walked out of Chessman Park, more than 50,000 singers formed a huge half-mile diameter circle around the surrounding streets, singing "The Four Directions" with their arms outstretched and their hearts exposed. Uniformed but unarmed troopers helped direct traffic and made clear that everyone was welcome to watch. Every four minutes the song culminated in "With All as Oooonnnne," sung like a pulsating Om, and the clang of Tibetan bells. A five-minute silence followed as thousands of onlookers became epigenetically awakened to their full potential, with the new awareness reconciling them with their past and recent realities. Every ten or 12 minutes, the circle expanded by 30 paces and started again, joined by the thousands of newly Activated beings.

By Dawn's calculation, if the circle continued expanding at the rate it was moving, by midnight it would encompass a sixth of the city of Denver and Activate half a million people. Aided by a few dozen specialists who had joined her caravan from California, she shifted her focus to managing the bold communications and military neutralization efforts needed during the next 24 hours.

Millions of citizens in the United Peoples of America were working remotely to support the occupation plan. Snowden's hijacking of the massive surveillance network of the Trump Regime allowed ten thousand specially trained expansion teams to drive caravans of vans, trucks and cars with carefully forged license plates undetected across the border. By Saturday, all of the teams had reached their destinations in every major town and city in Trump's United Enterprises of America.

Soon after arriving at their appointed destinations, the transformation teams had secretly Activated small clusters of residents by breaking into song in local restaurants or coffee stops. Afterward, they were housed and hidden by their newly interconnected hosts. This provided them with undetectable local bases where they could plan for the big day, Sunday, May 6, when they would erupt in town squares and parks and malls and slave labor camps, replicating the Denver transformative ritual across the country.

The caravans carrying transformation teams brought seeds, soil and supplies, but they also carried 100,000 specially equipped drones. At 12:50 Eastern Daylight Time on May 6, immediately following a hijacked broadcast into every household in Trump's United Enterprises of America, the drones were scheduled to explode electromagnetic pulse bombs over every occupied region of the country.

This long-planned Big Bang would shut down all the electronic and digital circuitry in Trump's United Enterprises of America and neutralize the weapons of the military and police. People would have to function without lights, without phones, without computers, without cars. A direct broadcast to the public was central to informing citizens of what was coming and how to respond to it.

Dawn's prime objective was to make sure that Sunday's mandatory Patriot News broadcast could be replaced with the most important news that Americans had ever heard. For the historic undertaking to work, the plan required Winston Smith's collaboration.

Dawn knew that freeing Winston could serve a second objective: Activating the thousands of troopers garrisoned at the enormous Western Division headquarters of the Homeland Security Army, which ran the prison. This would provide the U.P.A.'s occupation forces with a military command foothold that was responsible for half the states in the country.

Dawn was grateful that once he had emerged from his paralysis, General Baron proved to be an immensely capable ally. He set up a field command center a few blocks away from Chessman Park and ordered his aides to gather still functioning communications equipment from the hundred Homeland Security troopers who had been guarding the checkpoints outside the park. Their equipment had been spared permanent short circuiting by the electromagnetic pulse bombs. Baron's technicians transferred security protocols to the new devices, which Baron and his top officers used to prepare the takeover of the Western Division headquarters.

The most time-consuming task was requisitioning city buses to transport the thousands of troopers and helpers that Baron, Dawn and their top aides, with the help of the hive mind, had determined were necessary to transform the gigantic military base and prison. As commander of the Homeland Security Army, the general had the authority to requisition any public or private resources he demanded.

In a series of secure video calls to Thomas Perkins, director of the city's privatized bus service, Baron gave no hint that his inner being had been altered. "Under the authority vested in me during this time of war as Commander of the Western Division of the Homeland Security Army," he demanded, "I am requisitioning 80 buses to be delivered within the hour to the secured region on East Colfax Street between Downing and Corona."

"That's a tall order," Perkins protested. "It will take hours. We will need to call in extra drivers and empty out buses along some pretty popular routes and—"

"Am I hearing excuses, Perkins? Am I? Do you know who I am? Do you know what the penalty is for disobeying a direct order from me?"

"I'm sorry, General Baron, sir. Of course I will move heaven and earth to make this happen. I will drive a bus there myself, if need be."

"That's what I want to hear, Perkins," Baron said, easing up. "This is a highly classified request. American Bus Service will be reimbursed by Homeland Security for the costs you bear, but nobody is to know the purpose of the emergency requisition."

"What is the purpose of the requisition, sir?" Perkins asked.

"What part of *nobody* do you not understand, Perkins?"

"I understand, sir. You can rely on me, General!"

It took 90 minutes and 20 tow trucks to clear the staging area, but the large city buses arrived on time. Long lines of troopers, officers, Californians and recently recruited singers began filling the buses.

As Dawn and her daughter—along with Ridley, Flynn, and Winston's son Abraham—rode with General Baron and his top officers, they continued their afternoon-long strategic planning session en route.

Under the pretense of a Code Red security response, General Baron ordered all Homeland Security drones across the state to return to their bases for special instructions he would provide later that night. He called his top officers from Homeland Security's half-dozen bases across Colorado and the wardens of all the prisons and slave labor camps to a series of mandatory emergency meetings at his headquarters later in the evening. Top secret plans, he told them, would be forthcoming to respond to the spreading terrorist incursion that they had been warned about the day before.

To the non-Activated Homeland Security troopers on duty at the Western Command headquarters, the only thing unusual about the return of the thousands of Alpha Force soldiers arriving with more than a thousand new prisoners, at gunpoint, was their use of city buses. But with the tarmac still in disarray for the wind storms, General Baron's subordinates knew that this was not a typical day, and they dared not ask too many questions.

Baron's first order was to replace all active prison and guard duty personnel with the newly arrived Alpha Force troopers. The replaced personnel were ordered to meet him in the main secure briefing auditorium of the sprawling military complex. It took a half hour to relieve all the prison guards and sentries and for them to be transported to the underground auditorium.

These 600 men stirred restlessly as a carefully planted rumor bounced around the room: the secessionist leader Dawn Souljah had been captured along with 1,000 of her followers and the insurrection had been crushed.

The whispering ceased as the doors of the briefing room slammed shut and the lights were lowered. General Baron walked up the aisle to the stage, followed by a large solemn procession of soldiers with guns drawn, surrounding Dawn, Ridley, Washington and ten of their fellow Californians.

"Foreign terrorists have tried to infiltrate our great nation," Baron solemnly told the crowd. "These are their ringleaders." He paused for suspense. "Their methods and technologies will surprise you. They start with an organizing song they call 'The Four Directions,' which they are working hard to spread. If you hear any part of it, notify your commander, surround the singers, and arrest them before they have a chance to supply drugged drinks to their audience. This is the song they sing."

He turned to prisoners on stage and, in a cruel voice, commanded, "SING!"

Dawn was handed a guitar; she strummed as she and her colleagues began softly, prayerfully, the song's opening "Gratitude … gratitude … gratitude ... gratitude."

Two minutes later, the dozen singers concluded their song: "With all as Oooonnnne." One singer pulled from his pocket a Tibetan bell and loudly rang it. They held their arms outstretched wide. To the surprise of the prison guards and troopers listening, so did General Baron, as well as the soldiers he had brought on stage and into the room.

Ten minutes later, 500 newly Activated guards and sentries, now tuned into the hive mind, returned to their posts. Another 100 set to work preparing the auditorium for additional security briefing sessions that had been scheduled every 20 minutes. The sessions would last late into the night, as off-duty troopers were brought from their barracks into the auditorium, and later, as military and prison brass arrived from across the state.

Baron's top officers took over management of the briefings, scheduling nonstop briefings through noon the next day for military and law enforcement leaders from six states, dozens of counties, and scores of cities and towns in the region.

The coordination effort was enormous, but Baron's leading command officers were up to the task. Their Activation had heightened their already seasoned logistical-management expertise. With the help of the hive mind of thousands of colleagues who shared their Oneness, they planned the systematic conversion of the Western region's military and police forces from brutal oppressors into peacemakers.

Meanwhile, General Baron led Dawn and her team, along with a dozen of his fittest troopers, on a two-mile sprint from the military headquarters building into the bowels of the large prison at the far end of the complex.

Baron quickened the pace as soon as word reached him that 20 of the prisoners captured after Thursday night's Burning Man event had been moved into the America First hall of notorious killers. He learned that a few hours earlier, the prison warden had decided to use the group, selected because they did not have sufficient funds to bid on the means of their execution, as an example of what would happen to the other 280 new prisoners if they couldn't convince family members to pay for a more merciful death.

The warden had placed wireless speakers in the cold pens that held the other prisoners while they awaited their torture and execution. But like Winston, whose cell was only a few hundred feet from the America First pen, they heard and felt the suffering and deaths of the other Activated beings not through the intercom system, but through their hive mind and interconnected souls.

Not since his parents died six years ago had Winston felt such deep despair. While he did not regret the emotional Oneness he felt with those suffering near him, it was hard to bear, especially the horrible pain that his fellow prisoners experienced at the brutal hands of their tormentors.

Winston joined with the hundreds of other Activated prisoners locked in large cells far from his as they breathed in deeply and collectively breathed out healing vibrations to soothe those trapped in the sadist dormitory. They shared visions of the reincarnation and immortality of the soul, the Oneness that survived all pain, suffering and even death.

The victims faced their assailants with less fear than the many who had come before them. While they could speak, a few repeated the same words to their tormentors, with compassion: "I feel your pain, I forgive you, we are One."

Conscious of their hopeless reality, the souls of the tormented prisoners left their bodies quickly. By the time General Baron, Dawn and the others arrived, breathless, to rescue them, they were all dead.

At first Winston was so distracted by his grief that he barely noticed the click of the electronic lock outside the thick steel door of his cell. His eyes widened as the door opened and his heartbeat raced when his senses revealed who was arriving to rescue him.

His son Abraham clad in tiger-striped knight armor rushed into the cell.

Abe pounced into his father's waiting arms. Tears filled his eyes, as he yelled joyfully, "A new day ... a new day at last!"

Chapter 25: The Battle for Patriot News

Saturday May 6, 2034
11:20 a.m. Mountain Time
Patriot News Headquarters
Colorado Springs, Colorado
Trump's United Enterprises of America

Dawn sat in the leather massage chair and cried.

She'd been wanting to sit down for a long cry for six hours, since arriving too late to help the 20 dead prisoners at the Homeland Security penitentiary. But as a leader of her country she had, by necessity, gotten swept up in the doing, with no time to be with her feelings until now. She rested, safe in the comfortable green room of the Patriot News broadcast studio, awaiting a strategic meeting scheduled for midnight.

Dawn connected with her sorrow over the suffering of the murdered prisoners, as well as the many hundreds of others who had died since then in the unexpectedly bloody battle for Patriot News' headquarters. The sadness swept over her like a cloud. She allowed the tears to flow and her voice to sob and whine and whimper so loudly that had she not set her phone to automatically connect all calls from her wife, she might have missed the call.

Dawn's phone hovered a few feet from her face and projected a holographic image of Maria's luminous presence.

"My love ..." Maria began, then, observing her partner's tears, stopped talking.

Maria held out her hands, breathed deeply, focused her being on healing love and exhaled a long, calming breath. As she repeated this, 11 times, she shared the sadness that Dawn was experiencing, and tears streamed down her own face.

Dawn felt her sadness received and supported by her greatest ally. She closed her eyes and sensed Maria's spirit holding her close, as soothing vibrations flowed from her wife's warm body and bathed her in love.

"How are you?" Maria asked softly.

"Better now that you called," Dawn replied, sniffling and wiping her face. "But needing you beside me. I'm falling apart. All the death, all the suffering, despite our years of planning."

"I am so sorry; I wish I were there with you," Maria affirmed, listening.

"It's just so hard," Dawn continued. "So unimaginably hard, on my own, without you. When do you arrive?"

"Two more hours. We crossed over the California border undetected an hour ago, leading a fleet of 20 planeloads of helpers. The cavalry is on the way, darling girl! The Denver Airport, thanks to your advance team's work on the ground, was secured a few hours ago. We can now send out red-eye flights filled with newly Activated beings to dozens of cities. At least that part is going according to plan."

"Yes," Dawn said. "At least that part is."

"Do you want to talk about what happened or wait till the leadership council meeting in a half hour? Selena and Jeff and I will participate remotely, and we'll be patching in Snowden."

"I can talk for a few minutes now, thanks to you." Dawn followed her words with air kisses to the hologram. "So …

soooo," Dawn sighed, then continued, "we had all hoped that the Activation and conversion process, which had worked so peacefully and effectively in Chessman Park and at the Homeland Security base, could be repeated at the Patriot News corporate headquarters.

"Step one went fine. General Baron and a dozen of his awakened officers pulled the guard team at the Patriot News security gate into a special advisory briefing, called us in, as prisoners, to demonstrate the song they needed to watch out for, and by the time we got to the main entrance, the perimeter guard team had all been Activated. As planned, Baron's Activated Homeland Security force of 3,000 troopers arrived a half hour later, at about 9 o'clock, after we had called our top-secret security briefing in the main auditorium of the ground floor. General Baron used his emergency powers to summon all active Patriot News guards, soldiers, and personnel to the briefing."

"Did he order Roger Rex to the meeting?"

"He tried, but that was the problem. Baron was told that Rex, as well as the commanders of his private army, were predisposed and would get caught up later. Rex hates General Baron, and he especially hates it when Homeland Security tries to pull rank on him."

"The old Gotta Be the Boss syndrome," Maria added.

"So true," Dawn said. "And with tragic consequences.
Although Baron's soldiers secured the building entrances, surveillance system, lobby auditorium, and meeting rooms— even the gigantic mezzanine broadcast facilities above the ground floor—this insane corporate fortress runs 20 stories underground."

"I know we can't fly a large electromagnetic pulse to explode above the building because we need the broadcast facilities for tomorrow's big event," Maria said, "but haven't they been able to use the smaller EMP bombs you brought in? We planned to set them off on each floor, snuffing out all electrical devices and then holding the Patriot News soldiers back. It will be dark, so we will be performing the Activation by candle lantern."

"Of course Baron's troops have been trying that everywhere they can," Dawn explained. "But they don't work on the floors that have lead-reinforced security entranceways. Which is most of them. Rex has designed his headquarters to withstand almost any attack, including ours."

"Oh shit," Maria said.

"I know. Below the first few floors of research and accounting offices, that were mostly empty, there are 17 floors that house the top executives, soldier garrisons, core functions, torture chambers, weapon depots, supply rooms, and Goddess knows what else. Every closed door blocked our EMP. Activated troopers thought the EMP would work and did not even bring their stun guns. They went in with batons, only to find themselves facing off against Patriot News soldiers with high caliber machine guns and lasers able to penetrate body armor. They were sitting ducks."

"How bad are the casualties?"

"There are at least 1,100 dead, more than 1,000 wounded, and barely enough of the Alpha Force remaining to help the Activated guards secure the broadcast facility, ground floor and the first few floors below ground—the easy ones. Meanwhile, our small medic unit is overwhelmed, and everyone is waiting for the healers and surgeons in your fleet to arrive. We have called off the unsuccessful floor-by-floor assaults and are now treating the wounded while waiting for reinforcements."

"They are with us on this and the first few planes," Maria assured her. "We touch down in an hour and have a fleet of ambulances waiting on the tarmac for the hour drive south."

Maria paused to collect her thoughts. She sighed and added solemnly, "Those poor men. And their families." Maria closed her eyes and visualized the light that the dead passed into. "Is Sarah safe?" she asked Dawn. "Where is she?"

"Right up here on the secure mezzanine floor in a meeting room off the broadcast facility with a hundred of her fellow New Evolutionary Warriors. She's joined forces with the laser combat knights, and they are coordinating the Sunday morning Activation strategy."

"That's good," Maria said. Her mood lightened thinking about her daughter helping lead the N.E.W. Knights as she had dreamed of for years. "No matter how good she is with martial arts and her sword, she cannot face down trained killers if their guns are still working."

"I know," Dawn concurred. "How is Estrella?"

"She's sleeping, thankfully. I wish I could. So worried about you."

"Thank you. I'm worried about me too, about all of us."

"This is what we came here to do," Maria assured her.

"Ahh," said Dawn, holding out a hand and rubbing her fingers together, taking a mock deep breath with a smirk on her face. "Ahbsolutely purrfect ... NOT!"

The two shared welcome laughter and their moods lightened.

"Is that a massage chair I see you sitting on?" Maria asked.

"Yes; I just happened to find it here in the lux green room for celebrities and special guests."

"You've got 15 minutes before I call back for our crisis management meeting. Can you do me a favor and take a massage?"

"It's a piss poor substitute for your magical hands, but I'll give it a whirl."

"Ah, the things we do for love," Maria said, laughing, throwing her a kiss.

"I love you, sweetheart," Dawn said. "Please get some rest yourself."

The call ended. Dawn programmed a neck, head, shoulder, and foot massage. Despite the comforting call, she felt tremendous pressure in her head from the continuing strife on the floors below her, and a premonition that the worst was yet to come.

*

Fifteen minutes later, Dawn and Winston took a seat next to one another at a meeting table in the massive broadcast studio and greeted General Baron, Colonel Morgan, and two other Activated Homeland Security officers. The holograms of Maria, Selena Jackson and Edward Snowden appeared across the table from them. A dozen heavily armed Activated Homeland Security troopers, their weapons drawn and ready, stood guard nearby, and dozens of others guarded the stairways and elevators leading to the mezzanine.

Because the crisis meeting of the leadership council required her full presence, Dawn found herself consciously removing herself from the hive mind of the troopers—which was involved in coordinating the treatment and transport of the hundreds of wounded on the ground floor, while comforting friends of the recently deceased and listening to the sentries monitoring the elevators and stairwells.

"They can do that without you," Colonel Morgan said with kindness. "This ... this wondrous collaboration is new to us military men. We need your guidance *here*."

General Baron nodded in agreement. "Reinforcements will be here within the hour. But we do not know what to do next. Where do we go from here?"

The table fell silent as the participants shared their vulnerability and fears with one another telepathically. Then Maria's hologram expressed what had been shared. "There is a growing concern among the military leaders," she said, "that the challenges we face are insurmountable in the short timeframe we require if we need to occupy the entire headquarters."

General Baron nodded appreciatively. "A prolonged siege with repeated applications of focused explosives in the entry corridors is the only way we could guarantee success. But we are talking weeks, not days."

General Serena Jackson's hologram raised a finger to speak next. "Are you fully secure on the studio and mezzanine levels? Could we broadcast tomorrow without securing the rest of the building?"

"Probably," Baron answered. "We have 400 men securing the building from below and the outside, where we have stationed a dozen tanks. Reinforcements are coming. But the underground fortress is riddled with secret passages known only to Roger Rex."

"This remains a dangerous location," Colonel Morgan said, responding to concerns he received from the hive mind of the leadership council. "It is not a place for top level officials like Dawn and Maria—or for your daughters."

"Thank you for your concern," Dawn replied, warmly. "Maria and I share it, but we are striving to balance safety with our sacred duty. Tomorrow's broadcast is the linchpin of the entire expansion effort. Without it ..."

A feeling of despair flowed all around the table. Maria pivoted from it. "Before we consider retreat and postponement and the potential consequences of such action, before we abandon the mandatory broadcast objective, let's see how we might work with what we have already achieved. Can we locate and convert one of the other three people needed to approve tomorrow's mandatory national broadcast?"

"Roger Rex and his deputy Scoop live in the bowels of this fortress," General Baron said. "They are below us, somewhere, heavily guarded and almost impossible to access in the time we would need."

"That leaves Joseph Gerbers," Maria said, hope registering in her voice for the first time since the meeting began. "I understand that he lives in one of the residences surrounding the headquarters. Have we located him?"

Colonel Morgan shook his head. "As soon as we made it through the main gate at 21:00 hours, I was tasked with locating and Activating Gerbers for that very reason. But he had already left. He somehow got word that the insurgency had succeeded in Chessman Park and at the Western Command headquarters. He also realized that his communications to the White House had been compromised."

"He became concerned," Edward Snowden's hologram added, "that his updates to Trump's top aides and to the Homeland Security Army National Command were not receiving a response. Of course, our N.S.A. operation, with the support of our home team, has been intercepting all such warning calls and digital communications, routing them into duplicate dummy voicemail systems."

"Gerbers figured it out and got in his car with a security escort," Morgan added. "He headed south and west to avoid capture. We are tracking him and believe he is driving 500 miles to an Air Force base near Wichita, where he plans to catch a flight to D.C. to warn the White House in person."

"Can your men intercept him?" General Jackson asked.

"A missile or drone attack would be easy," Morgan said. "But we are doing everything possible to avoid killing, and besides, that would not get him back here to authorize the broadcast. We are trying to organize a roadblock, but he has a three-hour head start, and we have not yet Activated Homeland Security units west of here."

The mood around the table grew even more sober.

"There is one other possibility," Dawn said, looking protectively at Winston. "When I first met Winston on Maui back in 2022, I knew in some way he was important to our collective destiny. I followed him on a sacred journey he was taking, and after his soul had opened to Mother Ayahuasca,

Winston and I shared a Oneness ceremony, in which I planted a seed deep in his sliver of our collective universal consciousness."

Winston nodded attentively as the others observed him closely.

"The seed was to build a backdoor override into the TV1 security system that he was considering selling to Patriot News. It is a repressed memory that he has helped me try to extract this evening, on our way here, but to no avail."

Winston chimed in, sheepishly. "Since my Activation Thursday night, I have been able to vividly recall Dawn's presence that special night ten years ago. I even recall her suggestion, the seed that she mentioned. But I cannot, no matter how deeply I focus, remember whether or not I ever acted on it. Much less what the workaround might have been. Which makes me think that I never created one, I am so sorry to say."

"I have an intuition," Maria said slowly, her holographic form standing in a long white tunic, swaying, her eyes nearly shut in a deep, trancelike state. "Something unexpected will happen soon to shift things, possibly in a way that overcomes the impasse we are struggling with; possibly not. I am trying … trying to move this premonition to clarity, but it remains unformed, murky, and … dark. I see light swirling around it, but in the darkness, a terrible pain … an unbearable cost!"

In their 17 years together, Dawn had never seen her wife look so distressed.

Dawn joined Maria in her visioning and in seconds jumped up from the table and screamed, "We should leave this place NOW!"

The people seated around the table started to stand when suddenly a wall on the side of the room 100 feet away from them slid open. A battalion of Patriot News soldiers burst into the room, firing their heavy assault weapons in every direction as they poured through a secret passageway.

In their midst, Roger Rex, clad in heavy body armor, trained the laser sights of a sniper rifle on Dawn's face and fired. The hollow point bullet hit her between the eyes and then exploded in her brain, killing her instantly.

Sorrow and panic paralyzed Winston as General Baron, in one swift motion, threw him to the floor and turned the conference table on its side to shield them from the onslaught of bullets. He unholstered two 9-millimeter pistols and opened fire on the attackers.

Winston struggled to breathe. Then, with great effort, he managed to look around. The huge broadcast studio had been transformed into a bloody battleground. The noise of the constant gunfire seemed impossibly loud. Scores of Activated troopers had been shot dead or pinned down as they tried to advance from the stairwells in all four corners of the cavernous studio. Colonel Morgan and another officer from the meeting lay dying beside Dawn's body.

Meanwhile, hundreds of soldiers from Roger Rex's private army immediately set up a square of bulletproof barricades with gun ports around them and started to advance, even as hundreds more heavily armed men continued to pour out of the passageway.

Winston heard General Baron's voice telepathically in his head. "We gotta move back. Zig zag your way into the room 60 steps behind us to the left. Our men will cover you. Now!"

Baron and the remaining Alpha Force troopers in the area telepathically coordinated a small counterattack. All at once, they stood up and coordinated their fire at the soldiers facing in their direction.

Winston looked behind him and could see a half-dozen troopers erect a small wall of shields to protect him once he made it near the room on his left. He moved nimbly, tucking his head low and pivoting from side to side as Baron's troopers drew most of the fire. He gave thanks for the body armor he had been ordered to wear as a bullet stung the side of his body but failed to penetrate the armor.

Halfway to the shields, Winston heard Rex shriek, "Stop him! Kill him and they lose!" The red dots of laser sights appeared around him. A bullet grazed his ear; another struck his foot. Winston was just a few strides away from the shield wall when a bullet from Rex's rifle tore through his unprotected neck.

Winston fell to the ground and noticed the blood pooling around his face. Then the sound of gunfire stopped. The anguish of the lives lost around him stopped. The searing pain in his neck stopped, and the world turned black.

Chapter 26: Informing to Empower

Sunday May 6,2034
8:00 a.m. Mountain Time
Patriot News Headquarters
Colorado Springs, Colorado
Trump's United Enterprises of America

Winston moved slowly toward the light.

His legs, he realized, were not moving. Indeed, he could not feel his body at all.

All he could sense was his being-ness, his essence, a form that was him, floating toward the shimmering warm radiance in the distance.

He was chanting a sweet song. "Gratitude ... gratitude ... gratitude ... gratitude," again and again, like a mantra. He found it comforting.

Winston had no thoughts, no worries, only awareness of what he was experiencing. It was a full blissful awareness, like the Oneness he had felt since his Activation, except now there seemed to be no body to experience it, no agenda or doing to be concerned with. He was beyond that now.

As he drew closer to the magnificent warm light, Winston discerned a small cluster of radiant forms waiting for him, smiling their welcome. His father was there, his mother was beside him, and her mother, his doting grandmother, her arms outstretched, the same way she opened them to call him to her hugs when he was a child.

He felt a soothing breeze sweep over him and with it, delightful memories of times he had been loved by the very people who now waited to be reunited with him. As he sensed how much he missed them, his heart glowed.

This is not a dream, Winston realized. *This is where the dreaming ends. This is my death.*

Just then, Winston heard, to his right, a woman's voice. An angelic, familiar voice, sang a verse of an uplifting song that he had liked as a younger man.

"Remember why you came here, remember, your life is sacred, Remember why you came here, remember, this life is sacred."

Winston turned to face the singer.

It was Dawn, smiling lovingly. Her clear blue eyes glistened like stars, growing larger and larger, until he felt himself subsumed by them.

"Remember," Dawn whispered, as though the word were a prayer. "Remember."

Winston felt himself floating through time. He was a witnessing consciousness, hovering near the ceiling of his old Boulder, Colorado office, watching his exhausted body sleep on a camping pad near his desk.

He recalled those months of late-nighters and all-nighters, organizing technology and documentation for the biggest business deal of his life, the Patriot News acquisition of TV1.com. Working to close the complex deal and its even more complex technology transfer, he spent entire weeks without a night in his own bed. He had never been so sleep deprived.

To his surprise, he watched as his younger self, still asleep, eyes barely open, stood up and turned on his computer. No bed partner had ever mentioned that he sleepwalked, he thought, but there he was, as though driven by a subconscious dream, scrolling though the folder from his trip to Maui in 2022 and opening the picture he took of the frame that hung on the wall of the ritual hut, an image of a radiant human being with tree-like roots. He watched his younger self copy the image into a secret folder in TV1.com.

The screen filled Winston's witnessing vision, as his younger self began reprogramming the security protocols for TV1. He began creating an exception to the requirement that a second person, Patriot News CEO Roger Rex, validate a broadcast transmission. Young Winston coded one exception: If the image of the Utopia Rising insignia followed his personal validated iris scan, a second authorization would not be necessary. He saved his work, closed down his computer, laid back down and resumed his sleep.

The memory dissolved.

Winston heard Dawn's whisper again, fainter and weaker than before. "Remember why you came here!" she pleaded.

Winston Smith opened his eyes.

The first thing he saw was his son Abraham's tear-filled face at the foot of the bed he lay in. Abe was standing, holding hands with others, in a deep meditative trance.

A nearby electronic monitor pinged loudly and Abe's eyes opened to meet his. An expression of shock followed by sheer delight transformed his face.

"He's ALIVE!" Abe screamed. He rushed to the opposite end of the bed, hugged the pillow that held his father's head and showered Winston's face with kisses.

His older son, Robert, wiping back tears, joined him. "Dad," he said joyfully. "You did it! You came back. We thought you were dead."

Winston smiled gratefully. His love for Abraham and Robert warmed his heart, which rekindled an awareness of his body.

He felt numbness around his heavily bandaged neck, shoulders, and foot, as well as a discomforting pain in his head. He noticed a tube and some wires leading to a bank of monitors nearby.

His bed was surrounded by beds and chairs and tables, all filled with other heavily wounded people. They were in the ground-floor corporate cafeteria of Patriot News, which had been converted to a field hospital. Doctors and body workers, uniformed troopers and family members wove in and out through the packed room.

Winston became aware that the hive mind around him was buzzing, but he did not have the energy to tune in. He then noticed Maria's radiant eyes beaming at him as she stood, her hands open in prayer. She chanted *With all as One* repeatedly, alongside her daughter Sarah and a Tibetan girl, whom he telepathically knew was the reincarnated Dalai Lama. His old friend Professor Flynn Washington, Director of Public Interest Communications for the United Peoples of America, was also present.

He tried to express his thanks but his voice was too weak. Robert brought a straw to his mouth, and he drew a small amount of water. Winston had not realized how terribly parched his throat was. Or how painful it was to swallow. It was a relief to hydrate. He slowly took a few more sips.

"Thank you," he said, in a weak, hoarse voice, looking at Maria and the girls. "Thank you for calling me back."

"You called yourself back," Maria replied, modestly.

"Dawn was there," Winston offered.

"We know," Maria said, with bittersweet resignation. "We have been with her through the night on her journey beyond, blessing her way. We will miss her terribly. But she will always be with us, supporting, whispering, loving."

"She ... she led me to the backdoor. The workaround I could not recall. I was sleep walking. I ..." The words stopped flowing.

"Take your time, Winston," Maria said, soothingly. She exchanged a meaningful look of gratitude with Flynn Washington. "This news is such a relief."

"We can override if we need to," Winston offered softly. "Unless you have Gerbers or Scoop to help?"

Flynn shook his head and smiled appreciatively. "We've got only you, my man, but it sounds as though that's all we're going to need."

"Hallelujah!" Sarah proclaimed, filled with joy.

"They never caught Gerbers," Flynn explained. "But General Baron blew up the passageway to the mezzanine floor, trapping Rex and his men there. The battle lasted for hours. After reinforcements arrived and hundreds more were killed, our troopers surrounded Roger Rex and a few dozen of his remaining bodyguards and soldiers. Baron begged him to surrender. Instead, Rex shot Scoop in the head to make sure we could not use him to authorize the broadcast. Then he took his own life."

"The fighting is over," Maria announced, relief resonating in her voice. "But at great cost." She exchanged a tearful look with Sarah and added, "At great but necessary cost. Without this broadcast, people will not hear the possibility of change. They will remain paralyzed in their fear, in their sense of hopelessness. They will not venture out into the parks, where they can be awakened to being the change that is our Oneness. If that happens, this moment could be lost, the Activations suppressed, the missile breaches escalated and this opportunity, as well as our entire nation, crushed."

For a few seconds, a sense of gloom chilled those around Winston's bedside as they considered the stakes. "But with your recovered vision," Maria's uplifting voice continued, "thanks to the sacrifice of so many, we can proceed with the transmission, as planned, at 10 o'clock this morning. I leave you now to work with our team; we will wheel you to the studio in an hour. Would you like Ed Snowden's team to help you with the workaround?

"It's simple," Winston replied. "Just follow my iris scan with an image of the insignia of your band."

"The prophecy," Tenzin added. "Our collective destiny." She touched her phone and a 3-D hologram of the radiant human being with tree-like roots appeared over Winston's bed.

"As long as I can remember, that image has appeared in my dreams," Abe said.

"Mine, too," Sarah said.

"And mine," Tenzin added, laughing. "There's a reason we're all here today. And Abe, tell your father what you did this morning."

"What *we* did," Abe said. "I mean, the New Evolutionary Warriors was Sarah's idea. She and her knight friends in the U.P.A. have been scheming about this for years." He looked at Sarah with gratitude.

Sarah held out a deferential hand. "You tell, Abe. You rocked it this morning!"

"Okay," Abe said. "At 06:00 our time, 08:00 on the East Coast, the International Society of Laser Combat Knights held their annual meeting for all members of all 500 chapters across Trump's United Enterprises of America. They do this every year, right after the championship event. They update everyone on contest winners and new rules and, of course, new equipment available from their sponsors."

"This year, the meeting was a little different, 'cause we'd Activated all the top officials of the league, and all of the contenders and champions, who flew home as N.E.W. Knights last night to make sure they could attend the 200 largest meetings and bring the video of my speech from Chessman Park. When 50,000 laser combat students showed up in every big city in the country, they learned a new song."

"Guess what song it was, Dad?" Robert interjected.

"Fo-ur Di-rections!" Abe followed, not missing a beat. "So today, after the mandatory noon broadcast, and after the Big Bang hits right afterward, all those N.E.W. Knights connected to us and each other are putting on their Kevlar suits and grabbing their sabers and heading out to the main parks in their towns, prepared to defend the Activation teams against attacks by police."

"Whose weapons won't be working; that's an important part," Robert added.

"Basically," Abe explained, "they're gonna do what we did yesterday in Denver. And they're gonna stay out in the parks and in the streets, until we are one connected people, and one country again. More awesome than ever."

"Ta da," Robert announced triumphantly. "We are One, in case you missed the telepathic memo." He was enjoying the Oneness he had been experiencing since the Chessman Park Activation. At 15, he thought the world seemed even funnier and weirder than it did before.

"My ass kicking broski," Robert said proudly, exchanging a secret handshake with Abe. "Our N.E.W. Knight heroes did a lot today, but they don't get credit for the storms. I did that."

"Storms?" Winton asked.

"Actually, I think my mom Maria and a circle of mystics out west, and my mom Dawn, from the other side, and Gaia herself had a lot more to do with it than boastful bobo here," Sarah replied. "A few hours ago, crazy strong wind storms swept across the country, starting slowly and building velocity. After emergency landings, every airport was shut down, and every murderous drone was grounded."

"We don't want any plane crashes after the EMP bursts explode across the sky," Tenzin elaborated.

Winston nodded his approval. The tiny movement hurt like crazy and he squinted his eyes in pain.

"I can't believe you didn't know about the cool wind storm plan, Dad," Robert joked, trying to lighten his sadness at seeing his father in pain. "It was all over the hive mind channel, if you just tuned to Master Plan. Even Activated, you're still clueless, Dad!"

Everyone laughed. They needed the relief. Flynn Washington, looking as though he had not slept in days, moved closer to Winston.

"Hey, don't beat up on your old man before he's done his part to save the world," Flynn joked to the others. "On a more serious note, the challenges are just beginning. In less than three hours, 10 minutes after Maria's national emergency advisory, the wind storms will suddenly die down. Before the Trump Regime's military, air force or drone fleets can respond, 100,000 drones we have stationed at locations throughout the country will release electromagnetic pulses high in the air to fry just about every electronic circuit in the T.U.E.A. It will set this country's communications network back to the 18th century. We will then be empowered to collaborate with our newly Activated neighbors on rebuilding, repairing, restoring and healing a land devastated by boundless greed."

"We've got former Amazonian Jeff Bezos to manage the logistics and the systems of rebuilding and coordinating healing modalities, food and water. But the media buck stops at my desk. Our reunited country is going to need a way to share and model new ways to do things: to collaborate, coordinate, govern, provide for so many in need and empower one another to fill those needs. I'm gonna need a partner. What do you say?"

"Professor Washington," Winston said weakly, but with enthusiasm, "are you giving me a second chance to remedy the shitty choice I made when I didn't join Informing to Empower 20 years ago?"

"That's exactly what I'm doing, young man!"

"I am so in!" Winston replied. He paused and felt healing warmth spread across his body. "I guess this is what evolution feels like."

Flynn smiled assuredly. "That's the name of the game, my brother."

*

An hour and a half later, at exactly noon Eastern Time, millions of citizens of Trump's United Enterprises of America sat with their families in front of interactive video screens to watch Sunday's mandatory viewing of Patriot News.

They expected to hear about terrorists and the latest vaccine they would be required to purchase that week. They braced themselves to participate in the carefully monitored Sunday Hate, and perhaps listen to the president rant about enemies or brag about ways in which God almighty had blessed America to be great for the wealthiest family that had ever lived.

Instead, at a podium in front of a flag depicting the planet Earth surrounded by a circle of hands, they saw the caramel-skinned face of a beautiful woman with luminous jet black hair. Maria's kind eyes filled their screens.

Viewers had never seen a face like that speak on Patriot News, much less on a mandatory broadcast. Their attention perked up as they watched in a state of near disbelief.

"My name is Maria Sanchez, and I am the spiritual head of the United Peoples of America, the utopian nation to your west."

"Our states of California, Oregon and Washington declared our independence because the government of the United States of America had been replaced by a brutal tyranny whose foundation was voter disenfranchisement, deceit, ecological devastation, corruption, greed and terror."

"Forget what you have heard here on Patriot News about our country; we are thriving as the second largest economy in the world, after China. More importantly, we live in happiness and peace. Every person has rights. Every person has work and a comfortable wage. Every person has enough pesticide-free food to eat, a home with their family, holistic medical care, lifetime free education, pure water to drink, and clean air to breathe. Our government exists solely to serve the public interest. There is no crime. There are no prisons and no guns."

"We call our harmonious society a Wetopia. It is not a dream or an aspiration. It is the reality that 100 million people—people who once were your fellow countrymen and women—have experienced for the past six years."

"I am here today to say that we are toppling the murderous kleptocracy that calls itself Trump's United Enterprises of America. On behalf of international law and the human species, I hereby declare illegal and disbanded the conspiracy of oligarchs led by Donald J. Trump."

"The power of Trump's evil regime to terrorize you, to poison your body and our sacred Earth is over."

"A new day begins today, and each of us is part of it. The Second American Revolution has arrived. It is a peaceful evolution to a government that exists to serve the common good. We the people deserve nothing less."

"Fifteen minutes from now, a massive wave of electromagnetic pulses will cause the largest blackout in history. It will shut down your lights, your laptops, your phones, your appliances, your cars, even your flashlights. It will also shut down the weapons of Trump's police state, its guns, its drones, its cameras, including the one spying on you from this monitor."

"We ask that you head outdoors with every member of your family and go to the biggest park in the nearest large town or city. Walk there, even if the distance seems far. When you arrive, look for a crowd singing a song together. Millions of us will be there to help you, to protect you, to provide healing and shelter and free food and drink for all."

"Step out of the darkness into the light of community. Join us."

The camera zoomed out as Maria joined hands with her daughters Estrella and Sarah, with Flynn Washington, with General Baron and General Jackson in uniform, Abraham in his tiger armor, Winston Smith in a wheelchair, and dozens of others.

The broadcast closed by zooming back in on Maria's assuring, loving face.

"Wetopia begins with We," she said with confidence, then paused. "This means you. And me. Every one of us."

As 50 million people watched in wonder, a new hope rising in their souls, Maria opened her arms wide.

"With all as One," she prayed. "With all as One."